DEATH AT KNYTTE

Nobody believes Lord Pickhurst's new young wife is as demure and devoted as she seems, but where in the West Country would she find a suitable paramour? When there is a spate of jewel robberies and a brutal murder Sergeant Beddowes must solve the riddle of how elderly Lord Pickhurst died, or an innocent man will go to the gallows, while the guilty get away scot free.

DEATH AT KNYTTE

DEATH AT KNYTTE

by

Jean Rowden

Magna Large Print Books
Long Preston, North Yorkshire,
BD23 4ND, England.

British Library Cataloguing in Publication Data.

Rowden, Jean
    Death at Knytte.

A catalogue record of this book is
available from the British Library.

ISBN   978-0-7505-3860-2

First published in Great Britain in 2013 by Robert Hale Limited

Copyright © Jean Rowden, 2013

Cover illustration © Roy Bishop by arrangement with
Arcangel Images

The right of Jean Rowden to be identified as the author of this
work has been asserted by her in accordance with the
Copyright, Designs and Patents Act, 1988

Published in Large Print 2014 by arrangement with
Robert Hale Ltd.

Magna Large Print is an imprint of Library Magna Books Ltd.

Printed and bound in Great Britain by
T.J. (International) Ltd., Cornwall, PL28 8RW

Chapter One

It was time. The huge house was silent, wrapped in that deep somnolence that came when the doors were locked and the last footman had been dismissed. Even the lowly scullery maid had crept wearily to her blanket, to snatch a few hours of precious sleep; only his lordship's gamekeepers would be awake at such an hour, and they would be far away, stalking the coverts to protect the estate's game.

Lucille, Lady Pickhurst, slid from her bed and tiptoed into the dressing room which separated her bed chamber from her husband's room. Bending to the keyhole, she listened for a moment to the loud rhythmic snores from beyond the door, while her lips curved into a smile. His lordship had been disappointed when his two guests, pleading exhaustion after their journey, had withdrawn early after dinner, so it had seemed a natural enough gesture to appease him by sitting on his lap to ply him with brandy as soon as they were alone. He had been so distracted by her attentions that he failed to notice how many times she refilled his glass.

Lucille straightened, laughing softly, her

eyes sparkling. She had learnt a great deal in the few short months of her marriage; it was unwise to show any interest in other men, particularly if they were young. On this occasion she had kept her attention fixed on her meal. Laidlaw, who had sparse hair and watery eyes, had presented no temptation; he talked exclusively to her husband, and spoke of nothing but architecture. As for Mortleigh, who looked elegant as always with his carefully tended moustache, and dark good looks, she'd been piqued by his lack of interest. He had kept his taciturn gaze upon the portraits which adorned the wall of the dining hall whenever he lifted it from his meal; their eyes had met only once, when Lord Pickhurst had asked his guests their opinion of summer houses and gothic follies.

Mortleigh had raised his eyebrows, but before he could speak, Laidlaw was in full flow, averring that the old monastery which stood at one side of Knytte was surely more romantic than any folly.

'I have no great fondness for follies, but a summer house enhances any garden,' Mortleigh had said quietly, addressing his hostess as the other two men continued their conversation. 'And such places have a charm of their own by moonlight, when the rest of the world is asleep. Don't you agree, Lady Pickhurst?' Something in his eyes had made her flush a little, and she had given the briefest nod, before dropping her gaze and returning her attention to the roast duck on her plate.

Satisfied that her husband was soundly asleep, Lucille grasped the key. It turned smoothly and silently. She smiled, admiring her forethought. When the key to the old library had proved difficult to turn she had requested that a locksmith be sent for; every lock in the house was oiled and in perfect working order. Although his lordship's planned renovations to the library had been abandoned at her suggestion, he hadn't commented upon her interest in that particular room; as far as he was concerned she could do no wrong.

Flushed with his success in winning such a prize as Miss Lucille Gayne in the face of competition from many younger opponents, Lord Pickhurst hadn't noticed how, little by little, she was wresting the control of the household from his grasp. For her part, from the moment of their engagement she had acted the model of modesty and devotion; like many foolish old men before him, he had come to trust his beautiful young wife.

Lucille knew she must give her husband no cause for jealousy if she wanted to enjoy some occasional freedoms. Being a devious person herself, she suspected that his invitation to Laidlaw and Mortleigh was intended to test her affections; Laidlaw's youthful intensity, and Mortleigh's slightly rakish good looks, might tempt any young wife who was tiring of an elderly spouse. As she trod quietly down the corridor, a light robe over her nightdress, Lucille was well satisfied with herself; she had acted her part to perfection, expressing delight when their guests retired so early, and flouting convention by perching provocatively upon his lordship's lap before the last of the servants had been dismissed.

By any measure Knytte was large. It had been a monastery, until Henry VIII drove out the monks and gave the estate to one of his favourites; there were still hundreds of acres attached, with farms, mills and villages providing for its owners. Each generation had made alterations, and now the rambling mansion was like a rabbit warren, with many unexpected passageways and staircases. The creaking timbers and moving shadows stirred by her lantern held no fears for its new chatelaine; she was a creature of the flesh, not the spirit; she didn't believe in ghosts.

Padding quietly past the nursery, Lucille checked her pace. She dragged her finger-nails softly across one of the doors. A slow catlike smile lifted the corners of her mouth, and a low throaty chuckle escaped her, quite unlike her usual coquettish laugh. A slight sound, a whimper or a hushed moan, came from within the room, and she darted away, a hand pressed over her lips in case amusement got the better of her.

She entered the long gallery. The light from her lamp shone briefly on portraits of her husband's ancestors. Lucille stuck out her tongue at one particularly repulsive old man who reminded her of her spouse. A large French clock, gleaming faintly as she passed showed that it was ten minutes past midnight. She had the first chill frisson of doubt. This rendezvous was not like all the others. Was she being unwise? Shaking the thought away, she increased her pace a little.

A flight of stairs at the far end of the room took her into the oldest surviving part of the house; she was beyond any possibility of discovery. At the bottom of the stairs she turned right, passing the old library. Behind its locked door the ancient books lay collecting dust; Lord Pickhurst had planned to turn the library into a ballroom, a luxury few local houses could boast. To Lucille this intended gift spoke not of his love, but of his sense of acquisition; she was a chattel of great value and beauty, and her husband had intended to use the new room to exhibit her to his friends. However, he'd allowed her to veto the suggestion; that was when she realized the potential power of her position.

At the end of the corridor was a heavy oak door, scarred and black with age. It gave entry to the monk's refectory, the most complete surviving part of the monastery. This must have been a grand apartment in its day, with its wide vaulted ceiling and huge fireplace. Another door, just as ancient, led her to the cloisters, ruined now and lit only by the stars; she left her lantern hidden inside the first carrel, where a monk had once sat labouring over his manuscripts. During the day Jonah Jackman would be at work here, for Lord Pickhurst didn't find the ruins sufficiently romantic, and the stonemason was charged with making what was left of the monastery more appealing to the eye.

Lucille suppressed a shiver, far more in excitement than fear. Warm anticipation began to spread from within her, a wicked glow growing below her belly as if that part of her had an independent life of its own; she licked her lips as her breath came fast and shallow. Once through the cloisters and the ruins beyond she would skirt the lawn to reach the summer house. Her night-time ventures had become almost commonplace, the escape from Knytte too easily accomplished, but tonight would be different. No clumsy rustic lover awaited her this time. Unless she had grossly misread him, *he* would be there.

Hearing something scrape across the nursery door, Phoebe Drake sat straight in her chair and stared at the handle, waiting for it to turn and wishing the door had a key. Her heart began to beat uncomfortably fast, but then the boy in the bed stirred and whimpered in his sleep. Dismissing her own fears the young woman rose and hurried to his side, laying a gentle hand on his shoulder and murmuring a quiet reassurance. Her words drowned out the low laugh and the sound of retreating footsteps.

Rodney Pengoar turned over and settled back into sleep. Phoebe smiled down at him. She had been governess to the Pengoar children for only four months, but she had soon grown attached to the little boy; at ten years old he was already aware of his dignity as the heir to the Pickhurst estate, but the knowledge gave him an old-fashioned generosity, and he was not in the least bit spoilt. It was just as well he expected little, for his uncle paid him scant attention, being wholly concerned with his new wife. Phoebe didn't care for gossip, but the nursery maid chattered artlessly about the days before the new mistress arrived. It seemed Lord Pickhurst had once taken great pleasure in the child's company, even going so far as to allow the boy to join him for dinner once a week.

Sighing, Phoebe went through to the room where Eliza slept. Three years younger than her brother, she was a bright and cheerful child, easy to love, and not given to her sibling's night-time fears. She lay with her arms flung wide, her chubby cheeks flushed. Eliza at least was untroubled by her uncle's neglect, and unaware of her aunt's dislike.

Concerned for Rodney's health, a few days earlier Phoebe had overcome her natural timidity and approached his previous governess when she happened to see her at Trembury market. Miss Hissop was over fifty, and wore a permanently sour expression, but once Phoebe explained her errand she had been pleasant enough. 'The cause isn't far to seek,' the older woman said, 'but it's not my place, nor yours, to speak of it. If Master Rodney's nightmares are troublesome, Miss Drake, why not move into his room?'

'Lady Pickhurst refused to allow it,' Phoebe replied. 'She says it's wrong to cosset him.'

'Does Miss Eliza hear these noises in the night?'

'I think not. She sleeps more soundly. On the occasions when I've found her quiet and pensive, she tells me it's because she misses you.' Phoebe had dropped her gaze at this point. 'She doesn't blame me for the change,' she added, after a moment's thought. 'I hope you are as fair.'

She had been rewarded by a smile that transformed the thin lined face. 'We are all of us helpless before a more powerful influence, Miss Drake. The whims of a lady far outweigh the happiness of children and mere servants. I trust you may find a way to comfort the boy.' With another shrewd look she went on. 'The armchair in Master Rodney's room is not particularly uncomfortable.'

Miss Hissop's comment about the chair had been ironical, but with an added cushion or two it was bearable, and Phoebe was about to return to it when some whim made her walk on into her own room instead. The bed, untouched since it was made that morning, looked inviting. She halted by the window and pulled aside the heavy curtain. The dim glow from the nightlight cast a faint reflection and she looked briefly at the slender figure in its sensible nightgown, with its concealing folds, and buttons high to the neck. A thick plait hung over one shoulder; her hair was her only vanity and she was reluctant to have it cut, although it was difficult to keep up and out of sight during the day.

Phoebe pulled a wry face. It was best for a governess to be plain. Suddenly feeling heated, she rested her cheek against the cool glass. She was grateful to be at Knytte; she'd taken the post to escape from a dangerous situation in her previous employment. She was glad that his lordship was old, and totally engrossed in his young wife. Lady Pickhurst was arrogant and ill-mannered towards those she considered inferior, but that wasn't much out of the common way. A governess had a difficult part to play, being neither fish nor

15

fowl; aloof from the servants, she was far below the notice of her betters. For the present the isolation suited Phoebe; she was content to feel safe. That thought was enough to put a smile on her face. Looking inward and not out upon the garden, she didn't see the dark shape that followed the shadows beneath the yew hedge.

Some distance from Knytte's eastern boundary, in wild moorland where only those who knew it well dared venture at night, a desolate crossroads was marked by a tall wooden stake. There had been a gibbet on this post; in the rough grass to one side of the northern road, the bones of the last man left hanging from it lay half buried and forgotten in their rusty metal cage.

The moon escaped from the clutches of a cloud to shed light upon the crooked figure leaning his back against the ancient post. Flinching as if the light was too bright for his eyes, the man ducked his head further between shoulders that were hunched to the point of deformity. He hardly looked like a member of the human race. The clothes he wore would disgrace a scarecrow, and the hair and beard which haloed his head were as wild and tangled as a crow's nest. It was not his back alone that declared him to be a cripple; both legs were bent at awkward angles, as if the joints were incapable of

16

straightening, and the single hand that was visible outside his tatters clung to the front of his rags, crooked into a claw. Odd boots adorned the man's feet, one almost decent in thick brown leather, the other made of dry scuffed scraps flapping apart, sole and uppers bound in place by threadbare strips of sacking.

The crossroads had an evil reputation. Propped against the stained wooden stake, the vagrant might have been no more than somebody's idea of a joke, a dummy left to frighten passers-by of a nervous disposition, if it hadn't been for the occasional flicker as he blinked, and moonlight reflected from his eyes. In the distance a church clock struck one. He had stood immobile in that exact spot for over two hours, and still he didn't move.

As the last stroke faded to silence, another noise sounded on the breeze. There was a horse on the road. Turning his head an inch or two, the ragged figure seemed to be stretching his ears to catch the sound. The horse was not coming from the west, along the main road, but from the south. It was being ridden fast. Despite the giveaway clink of steel on stone that warned of its approach, the rider appeared suddenly, a shadow against the sky.

The horse shied violently at the gibbet post, but the rider mastered it, pulling up at the side of the road, where an ancient attempt to tame the moor had left a low bank and a remnant of ditch. He dismounted, a slight figure who seemed oblivious of the man standing so still and silent below the gibbet. When he spoke, he addressed the straggle of thorn bushes that topped the dyke. 'Sir Martin? Are you there, sir?'

A man emerged from the shadows behind the ancient barrier of earth, a short rather plump figure with a pistol in one hand. 'Docket? What the devil are you doing here? You'll have been heard all the way to Trembury. You're lucky nobody took a shot at you.'

'I'm sorry, sir, but I thought you should be told. Major Digby is about to leave his post. He says he'll wait until the clock strikes the half, then he's going home to bed.'

'You were there to keep him up to scratch, Docket. If you were seen or heard the rogues won't come near us now.'

'There was nobody on the road, sir, if our villain is coming he's going to be late, so there's a chance I won't have warned him off. I'm afraid Major Digby wouldn't listen to me, but I thought you might want to ride back and speak to him yourself.'

Leaning against his gruesome support, the scarecrow made no move. Docket's gaze travelled briefly over the ludicrous figure, before moving on to scan the farthest reaches of the straggling hedge, as if he expected to see something of more interest, but there was only his employer. Sir Martin Haylmer was Lord Lieutenant of the county, and also its chief magistrate, though nobody would have guessed it tonight, for like his young secretary, he was dressed in plain discreet black.

Sir Martin harrumphed. 'I suppose I'd better. Damn the man, it's all very well for him, he's not the one whose name's being bandied about as a joke in every blasted drawing room in the county.' He stepped down onto the road to take the reins. 'Give me a leg up.'

Obediently Docket linked his hands and placed them beneath the older man's proffered boot to hoist him into his saddle.

'You're in charge here, Docket. I shan't attempt to come back and risk scaring our villain off, that's if he's not already taken fright and ridden halfway to Hagstock by now.'

'I'll stay till first light, sir,' Docket replied.

Sir Martin nodded. 'You'd better take this.' He thrust the pistol into the young man's reluctant hand. 'I'll be at The Chequers.'

He turned the horse and was gone, riding fast. Docket took another quick glance at the tramp before stepping up onto the bank and down the other side, where his head and shoulders remained visible in the faint starlight. From somewhere close by a disembodied voice spoke. 'Might've known the

19

Major would be needed at home, with that pretty young wife waiting for him.'

'Aye, perhaps 'tis catchin',' somebody else put in. 'I 'ear his lordship at Knytte's got the same trouble.'

'So that's why you was up before his lordship with a skinful the other day, Jeb. Hopin' to catch it, eh?'

There was a gust of laughter.

'That's enough,' Docket said shortly. 'Woodham, see your men mind their manners.' He ducked down and vanished from sight.

Below the ancient wooden stake, the shabby tramp shifted his pose, just a little, then with a barely audible sigh, he seemed to shrink against the wood at his back until he too was all but invisible.

Lucille's footsteps faltered. A shape loomed ahead of her. It was a man, standing directly in her path. She wished for a second that she'd brought the lantern; she never carried it beyond the cloisters, for fear of its light being seen from the house. The figure didn't move, and gradually her heartbeat slowed. There was something strange about the shape of his head. She crept closer and a tremulous laugh escaped her lips as she recognized the finely sculpted hair adorned with an olive wreath. The man who had given her such a fright was Zeus, one of several statues that had lined the yew walk, until time and lichen had blurred their features. Jonah Jackman, the mason, had been given permission to set up a temporary workshop here among the ruins while he returned them to their former glory. Obviously this one had been moved since she passed this way.

The thought of Jonah made her bite swiftly at her lip, and for a fleeting second she pictured his hulking shape, almost as impressive as the statue that stood before her. The impulse was quickly stifled; Lucille squeezed past the god's cold unfeeling touch and hurried to the archway leading into the gardens.

She was completely unprepared when a large shape detached itself from the dark shadow beneath the stone arch. A hand was clamped over her mouth and something was thrown over her head and pulled tight about her face; mouth, eyes, ears, all were muffled in thick cloth. Lucille was lifted from her feet, helpless as a new born child in a pair of strong arms. Her scream silenced before it left her throat, she was whisked into darkness.

Chapter Two

Phoebe Drake returned to the chair; her two charges were both asleep and had no need of her for the moment, but try as she might she couldn't settle. She rose impatiently and returned to the window. As she looked out into the darkness she heard a faint sound; the cry of some small bird or animal perhaps, caught in a trap?

Biting her lip, the governess stared out into the night. The last time she'd heard those soft footsteps passing the nursery after midnight she had thought she'd seen something out there in the garden, though she hardly knew what.

The moon was partly veiled by cloud. Nothing stirred by the summerhouse. At first she thought she must be imagining the shadow crossing the grass beyond the lake but then the dark shape passed in front of a white-blossomed shrub and she knew it to be real. Whatever might be happening out there it was no business of hers, yet she felt reluctant to let the matter lie. A sudden thought occurring to her, she went through to the furthest room of the nursery wing, unused because the walls were damp. Here a window looked out onto the old monastery. With a sudden indrawn breath, Phoebe saw the faint flicker of light within the cloisters. She watched for a long time, but the light neither grew nor diminished.

Phoebe's thoughts turned to her cousin. She knew there were rumours about Jonah, and she'd seen for herself how he'd changed since he came to work here. Surely he couldn't be out there in the garden tonight? Would he really be such a fool?

Another sound came to her, maybe the distant bark of a fox. All was still beneath the uncertain moonlight. Waiting, thinking, Phoebe didn't notice that she'd grown cold. Eventually, shivering, she returned to her own room and wrapped herself in a shawl. She heard the boy mutter something in his sleep, and she hurried to his side, glad to have something to distract her from her thoughts.

Draped across a man's shoulders, his bones grinding uncomfortably against hers as he walked, Lucille was completely helpless. She had been only yards from the summer house, but her captor had carried her much further than that. It was impossible to move her arms. Her ankles were held by strong hands; never in her eighteen short years had she been so brutally mishandled. Despite her terror she could still think. Was Mortleigh abducting her?

She'd been a fool to trust a man she hardly knew. A year ago he'd lusted for her, just one of the young men who constantly surrounded her, hoping for a kind word. Despite her automatic rejection of one so lacking in either money or position, when he failed to appear at a ball or a soirée she would feel strangely disappointed.

Exerting power over her suitors had been her greatest pleasure, but Victor Mortleigh was different; he'd never attempted to bid for her hand in marriage. He knew she would marry for money and a title. No matter if his dark good looks attracted her, or that her legs turned to water whenever their eyes met. Lucille stifled a sob as she recalled the exchange in the dining room, that brief meeting of hands as they passed in the hallway and the two whispered words she had barely heard; she'd thought they were born of a hunger that matched her own, but this was where they led. Had he harboured a jealous hatred of her all through this past year? Was he seeking vengeance for her rejection, even though he'd never attempted to approach her?

Another thought swam through the panic that filled her. It might not be Mortleigh who bore her away. But she knew it wasn't Jonah. The stonemason was a gentle lover, with manners far better than would be expected from one of his lowly birth. He would never treat her this way. A shiver ran through Lucille's body. Perhaps her husband had discovered her betrayal. Perhaps she had made the journey through the cloisters too many times.

The best a disgraced wife could hope for was banishment to a religious house or a private asylum. She imagined herself at the beck and call of stony-faced nuns, or dragging out a miserable existence among the insane, subject to the whims of sadistic wardresses. At worst, her very life might be forfeit, for Lord Pickhurst was not a forgiving man; he took enormous pride in his title and his position. Being exposed to scandal, to ridicule, would be anathema to him, and he would wreak a terrible vengeance upon anyone who humiliated him.

Despite the old name she brought to their marriage, she had few influential friends; a man like Lord Pickhurst could have a disloyal wife disposed of in a dozen different ways, and tell the world what story he pleased. Perhaps she was to die this very night.

Lucille strained to hear something beyond the frantic beating of her heart, but she couldn't even make out the footfalls of her captor. If he was carrying out the orders of her vengeful husband, who knew what fate awaited her. Given a chance, she would beg forgiveness, repent, and swear undying loyalty. Let her only try the strength of her charms one last time.

They must be far from the cloisters and the summer house by now. There could be yet another answer. Lord Pickhurst might be sleeping soundly in his bed, unaware that his wife was being abducted and Mortleigh's few words might have been a joke, her own wishes making more of them than he intended.

It was surely unlikely, and yet – half-heard tales, whispered only behind closed doors, raced through her head. Fearful and scandalized, but enjoying the sensation their stories aroused, acquaintances whispered of white women sold into slavery. Fair hair and fair skin, youth and beauty, it was said that no girl was safe if once she was seen and lusted after. The victims of the trade were forced into harems against their will, to perform acts of the basest kind for brutal masters. In the past Lucille had dismissed such stories as fantasy, but tonight, helpless and alone, she was no longer sure.

They came to a halt. Tears pricked Lucille's eyes. A wordless supplication moved her lips; let her only escape unharmed, and she would become a faithful wife. Only give her a chance to beg his forgiveness, and she would be true, no matter how his lordship's dry skin and withered flesh disgusted her.

Lucille was put down. She shivered, although the summer night was warm. The surface beneath her felt soft and yielding, and the cloth that swathed her was being pulled free, yet she was still blind; wherever she had been brought to, the place was in total darkness. Drawing in a breath, she found the pleasant scent of herbs replacing the clogging unpleasantness of wool that had grown damp from her breath. A warning hand was upon her lips, but it was hardly necessary; at that moment she was thinking only of clean air.

'Hush.' The whisper was urgent. Lucille nodded, in fear of her life.

'Promise you won't scream?' he murmured, the pressure on her mouth intensifying. Again she nodded.

The hand was removed. There were slight rustling sounds; Lucille turned her head from one side to the other, trying to work out what they were, but before she could make any sense of them, they ceased, and the man's hands felt for her in the darkness, working their way to the belt of her robe, and fumbling with the knot which secured it. She gave a little gasp; his face was so close to hers that she could feel his breath, hot on her cheek.

'Undo it,' he whispered.

Trembling, Lucille obeyed. Once the knot was released he slipped the garment off her shoulders. Her flesh shrinking, her breath so quick and shallow that she was sure she would faint at any second, she remained immobile as the man pulled her nightdress up and over her head.

There was a low laugh and a sound of movement. Her abductor had taken a step away from her. Lucille heard a scraping sound, and the chink of metal on glass. The flare of light as he lit the lamp was so sudden that she was still momentarily blind.

When sight began to return, she saw the man standing with his back to her as he tended the light. He was naked. Her eyes widened; both Jonah and her husband were modest in her presence, taking refuge in darkness or the enveloping covers of a bed.

Shock and fury overcame her. She knew his identity at one glance, despite his nakedness. Forgetting both her fear and her promise to be silent, Lucille launched herself from her couch, intent on raking his bare flesh with her fingernails. A wordless screech of anger issued from her parched lips.

Mortleigh grinned savagely, capturing her flailing hands before they reached him. 'Such unladylike behaviour must be punished. I've tamed wilder things than you, my sweet.' He pulled her against his chest, stifling her cry by pressing his lips hard against hers. Breathless, realizing she was still helpless and a captive, she yielded under his touch. Against her will, she felt excitement spreading through her body. His skin was soft and warm against hers and he smelt of some musky perfume. She could feel his arousal, and couldn't help but respond to it.

Despite his immense stature, Jonah had never been a masterful lover, and while their encounters had been more satisfying than nights spent with her husband, Lucille had always wished for something more. Nonetheless, she was Lady Pickhurst, and Mortleigh was treating her like some common whore.

His mouth was open upon hers. With careful deliberation she bit hard on his lower lip. Instead of pulling back as she expected, Mortleigh dragged her closer against him, thrusting his tongue into her mouth. He pushed a knee between her legs, turning and tossing her down. She tasted his blood, hot and metallic, then all thought was extinguished as his weight landed full upon her body, squeezing the air from her lungs.

Struggling for breath, she tried to call out, Mortleigh shook his head. Still keeping a tight hold on her hands, he put his mouth to her ear and nipped it gently with his teeth. 'You promised, remember. We're well hidden here, my lady, but will you chance being within earshot of your husband's household? How do you think he'd like to discover us together?'

In answer she tried to butt his face with her head. Dragging one of her hands up to his face, he bit hard at the fleshy base of her thumb. An involuntary squeal of pain forced its way past her clenched teeth.

'Shriek if you must,' he said. 'Anyone who hears will think it's the yowling of a cat. Perhaps they wouldn't be far wrong. Do you still wish to play rough, sweet lady? Don't pretend innocence. I read the message in your eyes as clear as day, despite the way you sat at table like some modest little milk and water miss, intent only on warming the bed of that vile old man. You'll find me far better company.'

'There was no need to lay hands on me! You're vile. I hate you.' Lucille attempted to pull free, but his grip was too tight. 'Let me go! My husband will have you whipped.'

'You think so?' he said, his mouth twisting in a smile. 'How will your ladyship explain your wanderings about the grounds at night? Perhaps you had a sudden whim, to smell the roses by moonlight? Or does Lord Pickhurst know that you leave his bed to grunt and roll and sweat in the arms of a peasant.'

At this Lucille ceased struggling, staring up at him with wide frightened eyes. 'What do you mean?'

He forced her hands apart, gently kissing the palm of each. 'Come now, I'm no fool.

Forget the tumbles you've enjoyed with your rustic lover. I'm here, as you wished. For tonight you shall have different fare. I, at least, am a gentleman.'

'How can you give yourself that title,' she said, trying not to acknowledge how her traitorous body responded to the caress of his lips, which were now moving enticingly up her arm. 'Your behaviour was that of a vile ruffian.'

'You think so? But literature tells us that men have claimed their women by force for hundreds of years. If you've changed your mind you may leave, I shan't stop you.' He had reached her shoulder. Lucille could not prevent the response that shivered through her body; there was an ache in her loins, an involuntary lifting of her breasts towards his roving mouth.

'You see, you can't deny me my prize.' He released her hands. She made no further attempt to stop him. His fingers were gentle now, and his touch was soft and sure. Mortleigh was nothing like the other two men she'd lain with. She didn't resist as he caressed her aching breasts, and she gave a tiny moan of protest when he lifted away from her again.

Mortleigh knelt at her side. 'Patience,' he said. As if intent on familiarizing himself with every inch of her body, his fingers roved together over the arch of each foot, around slim ankles and up her calves to her knees, his lips following where his hands led. He explored every curve of her limbs by inexorable and tantalizing inches, fingertips meandering lightly across her tingling flesh, until they were trespassing on forbidden territory. Lucille's breathing was fast and ragged; no-one had ever given her such pleasure, or such an aching hunger. She should be angry with this man brute, but he understood her needs far better than she could have dreamt. After her bucolic beau's tentative fumbling, and her husband's breathless efforts, she revelled in the attentions of a lover who was truly accomplished at his art.

As he stretched his hands around her hips, speaking no word, lingering now and then to kiss and lick her tingling flesh, Lucille cried aloud with delight. She felt his lips lift in a smile against her skin.

Unable to contain herself any longer, she flung her arms around him, her fingers clutching; the nails she had longed to rake down his face scored deep scratches down his back instead. In response Mortleigh bit down hard upon the curve where her neck met her shoulder, one sinewy hand taking a hold on her throat so she couldn't counter his attack.

For a fleeting second Lucille's fear resurfaced. He was strong. If he chose, he could snuff out her life with no more effort than it took to swat a fly, and perhaps with no more compunction. Aroused, furious and enamoured all at once, she clawed more deeply at his naked flesh with her fingernails. Mortleigh gasped and pushed himself away from her. 'I've captured a wildcat.' He smiled, and there was something akin to evil shining from his eyes dark in the lamplight.

Silent, meeting his eyes, Lucille wasn't afraid. They were well matched. She pulled him back down to her. Finding his exposed neck with her mouth, she bit him in her turn, before curling her legs around his body in open invitation. Their passion rose together; Lucille felt she might die in his embrace without regret.

When it was over they lay moulded together, her hands gentle now upon his back, as she ran her fingers over the bloody scratches her nails had left there.

'A cat, or a vixen,' he said drowsily, 'as yet I'm not sure which.'

'It's no more than you deserve,' she replied, shifting a little so she could see his face.

'At least I didn't squeal like a marauding tomcat and risk waking the household.'

'Where are we?' she glanced at the rough wooden walls and thatched roof above their heads, so out of keeping with the sumptuous couch, and the gilt side table which bore nothing but a dusty wine bottle.

'Don't you even know your own domain? We're in the garden house, at the eastern end of the lake. I discovered it when his lordship showed us the grounds. It's lucky my arrival wasn't too late to allow us to take the tour. This is so much more civilized than the summer house.'

'Lucky? I've been abducted and assaulted, and I shall have to invent some story to account for the bruises you've inflicted.'

He smiled, his fingers tracing lazy patterns across the skin of her upper arm. 'Tell me you wish this past half hour had never happened, and I'll know you're lying. Of course, you have a talent that way; most men would have thought you a devoted wife, despite being married to a man who resembles an ancient tortoise.'

'I'm not the only dissembler,' she replied tartly. 'I might have been forty years old and as dried up as a prune for all the interest you showed me at dinner.'

Mortleigh shook his head and sat up. 'My dear Lady Pickhurst, I never take wrinkled old women to my bed. His lordship might be blind, but I assure you my eyesight and my instincts are excellent. You can't deny me the title of gentleman, for I acted in the very spirit of the knight errant. I answered the plea of a damsel in distress, and so very promptly.'

She laughed quietly and reached for him.

'Then answer it again, if you are able.'

'I wish I could, but alas, I fear I have another engagement tonight.'

'Oh no,' she said, rising to her feet even as he did and encircling him with her arms. 'You won't escape so easily. You owe me more than a mere hour, after giving me such a fright. I might have died of it. What possessed you to seize me and wrap me up that way? I could scarcely breathe.'

He released himself from her hold, before taking hold of her chin and tilting her face so he could kiss her lips. When he withdrew he was smiling. 'Believe me, I leave with some reluctance. As for scaring you, I merely added a little spice to your adventure.'

Lucille pouted, taking a step back, but he twisted a finger in a lock of her hair, and used it to pull her close once more. 'I know women, Lady Pickhurst. I understand you far better than that empty husk you married, or the yokel you've been bedding. Don't worry, I shall be back by morning, long before any of the household know I was gone. And if your doting fool of a husband can be persuaded to extend his invitation for a few more days, perhaps you may have your wish and spend a little more time with me.'

'You can hardly plead weariness and retire early every night,' she replied, stung that he could read her so easily, 'perhaps his lordship will find himself awake enough to claim his rights tomorrow.'

'Perhaps,' he said, moving away and picking up his clothes. 'But in my luggage there's a little bottle. The drug it contains is harmless, and quite undetectable. It is easy to administer, and I find it guarantees even the most suspicious husband a sound night's sleep.'

Chapter Three

The ragged man leaning against the old gibbet stirred, his head lifting as the distant clock struck three. It wasn't the bell that roused him; somebody was coming. The scarecrow figure gazed along the road towards the west, giving a faint nod once he could make out the two riders. They were muffled from head to foot as if against the cold although, even at this hour, the summer night was mild.

Eyes narrowed, the watcher didn't move again, his gaze fixed on the newcomers. There seemed little to distinguish between them in build, or in the way they leapt from their saddles: young men, both of them, and in a hurry. They strode towards the foot of the wooden stake where the vagabond stood waiting.

As they drew near, the leader's horse baulked, rearing in alarm, just as Docket's mount had done two hours earlier; possibly animals sensed an ancient evil lingering in this desolate spot. Even men, insensitive creatures as they were, usually chose to avoid the place at night. The beast's rider cursed softly, trying to subdue the terrified animal, but it refused to approach any closer. After a moment the man flung the reins to his companion and went on to meet the tramp alone.

'All quiet?' the man demanded, a hand shooting out with incredible speed to grasp the rags at the vagrant's neck and pulling them tight until the ragged cloth began to tear. His tone was low, barely above a whisper, but the way he spoke marked him a gentleman.

'Ain't seen a soul,' his captive rasped in reply. 'Been 'ere since eleven,' he added, with a hint of reproach. 'I hopes it's you what's got summat for me.'

'A knife in the ribs, or a bullet in the head, if you double-cross us,' the gentleman replied. Almost lazily, he moved his grip to the tramp's throat.

The second rider dismounted, dragging the two nervous horses with him so he could approach the other men. 'No need for that,' he murmured. 'He knows what his life's worth if he betrays us, don't you, Cobb?'

The man addressed as Cobb nodded, as far as the grip on his neck would allow. 'I keeps me mouth shut an' I takes me pay. You got me word.' His voice faded to a throaty whine. 'I needs to breathe. Please to let me go, y'r lordship.'

His captor laughed, but he released his hold. 'I'm not a lord just yet.' He glanced back at his companion. 'Give us time, eh? A few more months and who knows, we could both be dining at the palace.' From inside his coat he pulled something wrapped in thin leather and tied with string. 'So, this once we're dealing with the organ grinder instead of one of his monkeys. I was wondering if we'd ever meet you again. You know what to do with this stuff, and you'll bring our share back here. I've a good idea of value, if you try taking more than your cut I'll know, so keep your thieving hands off.'

The strange tramp who had waited so patiently at the crossroads shook his head indignantly. 'Fetch'n'carry Cobb, tha's me. You dealt wi' me before, an' if that ain't enough then you ask them as knows. I'm good at me trade, an' I ain't never pinched nothin'.' He held out a hand to take the package.

'Come on,' the man with the horses urged, as the other hesitated, 'the longer we're away, the more chance there is of something going wrong. As it is, your games tonight might have cost us dearly. You and your whoring– It'll be light before we get back to...'

His words were cut off with a hiss as his fellow conspirator swung round to strike him a stinging blow across the face. 'No names, you fool! All right, Cobb, I suppose you're as honest as any of your kind, though that's not saying much.' Still with some show of reluctance he surrendered the package to Cobb, and it vanished swiftly inside the ragged shirt.

'Faugh,' the gentleman said, taking a step backwards. 'I'm surprised you can live with your own foul stink! Take good care of our property, or you'll live to regret it.'

The man at his side laughed, rubbing at his face. 'But not for long!' he breathed. 'Double-cross my friend, Cobb, and your miserable existence will come to a messy end.' He turned suddenly to look behind him, his hands fumbling on the bunched reins, separating his mount's from the other. 'Did you hear something? You never should have risked starting so late, you and your damned appetite for petticoats. Hurry up and give him the directions, and let's go.'

'There's nothing there. You'd jump at your own shadow.' His companion dismissed his concerns with a shrug, closing in on Cobb, his fingers reaching for the man's throat again. 'We need to arrange our next meeting. I hope you know the moors as well as you know London, Cobb. There's a foul little gin house called the Crooked Man, twenty miles east of here. It's about a mile north of the London road, not far from a village called Kerwannick.'

'Wha's wrong wi' the gibbet?' Cobb grumbled, twisting to look up at the blackened wood above his head. 'Ain't this quiet enough for yer?' He made a strange strangled noise as the gentleman's fingers tightened.

'I never use the same place twice, Cobb. The Crooked Man,' he repeated, a little louder than before. 'It's owned by a villain called Slaney, speak to him and nobody else; tell him you're looking for Mr Pike, and he'll send you to me. Speak to Slaney, ask for Mr Pike. Got that, Cobb? Exactly four weeks from tonight, and make sure you're there.'

'Crooked Man, name of Slaney. Ask for Pike. Four weeks.' Cobb repeated hoarsely, one clawed hand scratching feebly at the fingers squeezing his windpipe. 'Lemme breathe, y'r honour, for Gawd's sake.'

'A moment more, I want to be sure I have your attention. Nobody double crosses me.' He glanced round to see his friend mounting his horse, still peering warily into the darkness, and he gave a faint scornful laugh. 'It seems we're in a hurry. Are you listening, man?'

Cobb's mouth worked but no sound emerged. He nodded his head.

'Right. While you're in London I want you to find a good market for a pair of...'

This time there could be no denying the noise that broke the surrounding silence, or that it came from somewhere close by; it was a cough, and unmistakably human.

'What was that?' The rider circled, staring wildly across the ragged thorn bushes topping the nearby bank.

Abandoning his hold on Cobb, the other man thrust a hand inside his coat and drew out a long-barrelled pistol. 'Who's there?' He cocked the weapon. 'Answer me or I fire.'

A light flared into existence not fifty yards away; somebody had struck a match and thrown it into the hedge where the dry wood caught instantly, and the flames spread, lighting up the crossroads more brightly than any moonlight.

'By God, the bastard's betrayed us!' The man with the pistol leapt for his horse, tearing the reins from his friend's grasp.

Cobb half fell back against the gibbet post and clung there, gasping for breath and looking wildly around him. His tormentor, mounted now, swung the weapon towards the tramp, but before he could take aim a voice barked from the darkness. 'Stay where you are, you rogues! Stand or we shoot!'

The rider hesitated for a second. Cobb didn't waste his one chance, and dropped sideways to the ground. A bullet narrowly missed his head, the sound of that first shot lost in a ragged volley; a row of men had leapt belatedly to their feet, showing now above the low rampart.

'Aim for the horses, bring 'em down!' A rougher voice this, coming from the far end of the earth bank, but the shout came too late, for the two fugitives were already spurring away.

Cobb stayed flat, a wise move, for the shooting was wild, and several shots passed close above his head. For a full minute all around him was a chaos of tramping feet, shouts, and the deafening crackle of gunfire. The roar of the dry thorn bushes crumbling to ash grew louder; the flames leapt to eat greedily at the grass surrounding the gibbet post, parched after a dry spell.

'Hold your fire!' Cobb shouted, in a voice that would have brought a squad of army recruits to a quivering halt. Despite coming from such an unlikely source, the order was instantly obeyed. Choking, he came to his knees, squinting into the distance; the two riders were out of range and galloping free, evidently unharmed.

Docket came to stand over the tramp. 'I'll thank you not to give orders to Sir Martin's men, Sergeant Beddowes,' he said mildly.

'Somebody needed to,' the man who had called himself Cobb replied shortly, rising to his feet and straightening his back with evident relief. He was almost a foot taller than he'd appeared while hunched against the gibbet post. 'The rogues are well away and there's no point wasting ammunition. I suppose there's no chance that Sir Martin will have persuaded Major Digby to remain at his post?' The question was civil enough, but there was something in its tone that sug-

43

gested censure.

'I doubt it; he was always a reluctant recruit to our cause. I'm sorry, it looks as if we've lost them.'

'Reckon I may 'ave winged one of they rogues, Mr Docket, sir,' a man called. 'I reckon I 'eard 'im yell.'

'There's a chance then,' Docket said.

The tramp shook his head. 'If he couldn't hit a target as big as two horses, I've not too much hope he'll have nicked one of the men.' He shielded his eyes against the ever growing light from the flames. 'If we don't put out that fire we'll have the moor alight from here to the coast.'

Several minutes of furious activity saw the worst of the fire out. Leaving the other men to finish the job, Docket drew Beddowes to one side. 'At least we have one piece of good news for Sir Martin. What did that man give you? I assume we've recovered a little of what has been stolen.'

'I'd rather have taken the man than the goods,' the sergeant said sourly. 'That's what I was sent here to do. Given another minute that poxy rogue might have told me something useful. He was asking about a market for something special.' He reached within his rags and pulled out the package he'd been given, untying the string that secured the contents, and unfolding a piece of soft leather to reveal a black velvet bag.

Gesturing to Docket to hold out his hands, the sergeant carefully poured the contents into them.

The last flickering light from the fire sent bright shards of colour cascading from the stones that dropped into the young man's palms. Docket gasped. His hands were almost overflowing with rich red rubies, white glittering diamonds and a scatter of blue and green, from sapphires and emeralds. A murmur arose from the men who'd abandoned their task to edge closer, fascinated by the sight of a fortune in precious gems.

Beddowes jerked his head and the two men moved further away before returning the loot to the bag. 'Here, pretend to put it out of sight, then pass it back to me,' Beddowes muttered, thrusting the packet at Docket.

'Don't you trust me, Sergeant?' Looking annoyed, Docket did as he was asked, delivering the package back to Beddowes once he was sure the manoeuvre couldn't be seen. 'I'd assumed we'd go to Clowmoor House together at first light.'

'I'm not going to Sir Martin. Don't you see? If we return these jewels to their owners then we'll lose any hope of catching the thieves. Of course, if his lordship decides that's what he wants then I'll obey his wishes. I can't say I'd be sorry to lose these rags and get a decent meal inside me, but I've no wish to let the beggars go free.'

'I don't understand.'

'This little debacle will have put our villains on their guard. There's just a chance, if I return their loot to them, that they might be persuaded to trust me again. That's if I can find them, because you can be sure they won't turn up at the rendezvous we arranged.'

'No, they'll be sure you betrayed them. Sergeant, you can't seriously intend to try and keep up the pretence? Not after tonight? They're sure to blame you for what happened, what other possible explanation could there be for their walking into a trap?'

'I'll need to come up with something, and fast,' Beddowes conceded, scratching his head unthinkingly, before looking with disgust at his filthy broken fingernails. 'Who coughed? Another minute and I'd have downed our man, and by now we'd all be on our way back to our beds.'

'I set his lordship's chief gamekeeper to find out,' Docket replied. 'Woodham, come over here and tell us who ruined our night's work for us.'

Woodham was a short square man; as they set up the trap he'd treated Beddowes with a lack of respect that bordered on contempt, but Sir Martin's head gamekeeper was meek and obedient now, standing before his master's secretary with a look of unease on his blunt features.

'Well, it's like this, sir,' he began, twirling his cap nervously between his fingers. 'We was a bit short of men, what with Abe Lidden and his bad back, and Tom Pencarne's boy going off to join the navy so sudden. I asked around at the market in Trembury, and this chap was eager for a night's work. Said his name was Bragg, and he'd worked for Mr Detreath at Clow Head, until the mine closed. He looked to be down on his luck, but he seemed a reliable sort, so I agreed to take him on. I told him I'd see how it went, and maybe put in a word with his lordship about taking him on proper like. Fact is though, he seems to have run off in all the kerfuffle. Nobody's seen hide nor hair of him since them shots were fired.'

'You knew this operation was to be kept secret, yet you engaged a man you'd never even seen before?' Docket shook his head in disgust. 'It's a wonder the rogues came at all. He could have tipped them off before they came within miles of us!'

'He had no chance to tip anyone the wink, sir,' Woodham said. 'I made sure of that. He was pretty much under my eye all day.'

'That didn't stop him giving those villains a warning, did it?' Docket cast an apologetic glance at Beddowes. 'I'll speak to Sir Martin about this, Woodham, I'd have thought you'd have more sense. Anything else you want to ask this fool in the meantime, Sergeant?'

'There is something I'd like to know, Woodham,' Beddowes said. 'Could you and the rest of the men hear what was being said between me and those two rogues?'

'I only heard one thing,' Woodham said, sounding sulky at being forced to speak directly to the man from London, whom he clearly despised. 'And that was when the gentleman mentioned the Crooked Man. I was a lot closer than Bragg, but there's a chance he heard it too. I was thinking maybe the cough was an accident. Perhaps he got something caught in his throat, like, and couldn't help himself.'

'Then why would he run off?' Docket said.

'Well, he'd know he was in trouble, with the game flushed and nothing in the bag,' Woodham replied.

'How old was this man Bragg? Was there anything of note in his appearance that would help to find him again?' Beddowes asked.

'Aye, he had a scar across the side of his chin,' Woodham replied, drawing a finger along his jaw. 'You could see it through his beard, that being a bit on the thin side. He wasn't a young man, forty maybe.'

'Where does that get us?' Docket asked, turning back to Beddowes.

'I'm not sure,' Beddowes confessed, 'I'll let you know if I find out.'

Docket sighed. 'If you're not coming back

with me, I suppose I'd better go and report to Sir Martin. You're sure you don't want to spend a few hours in a comfortable bed and get a good meal inside you while there's a chance?'

'Best not, sir, thank you,' Beddowes replied stolidly. 'I'll bed down somewhere of my own choosing if you don't mind. No point risking being seen with you. It's bad enough having to trust your men to keep their mouths shut, especially in light of what's just happened.'

'Don't worry about that,' Docket looked grim. 'Sir Martin will put the fear of god into Woodham over this, we'll have no more mistakes.'

'Nevertheless, I'll be better leaving by myself,' Beddowes said. 'I'll be in touch when I have news.' As he turned away he seemed to shrink, and it was an old hunch-backed vagabond who went slinking away into the dark.

'Odd sort of man,' Docket commented, speaking as much to himself as the gamekeeper who stood at his side.

Woodham snorted. 'Can't say I was sorry he decided not to come with us, Mr Docket. I'm no bed of roses, but I've an idea that stench could carry half a mile.'

Chapter Four

After a disturbed night Phoebe made up her mind; she must visit the ruins. If Annie, the nursery maid, wasn't the worst kind of gossip, she might've left the children with her for a while, but Annie was the kind of girl who wouldn't believe there could be such a thing as a perfectly innocent meeting between a governess and a young working man. At least it was a fine day, and that gave her an idea.

'It's time Master Rodney learnt a little more about the history of Knytte,' Phoebe said, as Annie finished fastening Eliza's coat. 'We shall begin with the ruins of the monastery. Not many children are fortunate enough to have so much of the past at their fingertips. Once you have finished your duties here you may come and join us if you wish, Annie, it would be a treat for you. The development of the monasteries is a fascinating subject.' She knew from past experience that the nursery maid hated listening to any sort of lesson.

'Oh, I'm sorry, Miss, but I've orders to help with the downstairs, once the nursery is done.'

Not wishing the girl to guess at her relief,

Phoebe looked disapproving. 'Suppose I should need you?'

'I'm sure one of the gardeners would send a boy with a message, Miss Drake. I don't think Lady Pickhurst would approve of me trailing round with Master Rodney and Miss Eliza half the morning if it's not necessary.'

Pleased with her little subterfuge, Phoebe nodded. 'I expect you're right.' Annie was a lazy girl; she'd have been more than willing to accompany them if they'd been bound for a stroll by the lake, rather than a lecture.

They didn't linger on the lawn for long. The children were eager to run ahead, but Phoebe kept them by her side, knowing they would probably be overlooked from the house until they reached the ruins. She held their hands as they stepped under the ancient archway, where the regular tap of metal on stone told her the stonemason was at work.

'Good morning, Mr Jackman,' Phoebe said, brightly impersonal.

The young craftsman hadn't seen them coming and his thoughts must have been far away. At the sound of her voice he jumped violently. The chisel slipped on the stone and the hammer thudded on his thumb. Eliza giggled, swinging on Phoebe's hand.

'That must have hurt,' Rodney said, abandoning the governess and coming closer with a child's curiosity, perhaps hoping for

51

the sight of blood.

'I've had worse, and thank you for your sympathy, I'm sure.' Jonah Jackman straightened. He towered over Phoebe, six feet ten to her five feet two, a huge handsome giant, despite the covering of stone dust that whitened his fair hair. Phoebe had always been able to read her cousin's expression, even when they were children, but today his face was closed to her; there were secrets behind his wide blue eyes, and the knowledge was weighing heavily on them both.

'We are here to study the monastic system,' Phoebe said. 'Master Rodney is to find all the features in the old buildings I have told him about, while Miss Eliza will see if she can identify any of the herbs they used, for medicines and seasoning. I've noticed several, growing among the old stones, so I shall be disappointed if she doesn't find four at least.' She directed this last comment to the little girl, giving her a serious look.

The child beamed back at her. 'I shall find six,' she declared, freeing her hand from Phoebe's clasp and running off to start her task, followed more sedately by her brother.

'Jonah, I had to speak to you,' Phoebe said, half turning away and fiddling with the buttons on her glove. 'I have never attempted to influence you, how could I, being younger, and a mere female, but I owe you a great deal, and I hate to see you...' she broke off, too embarrassed to go on.

'Don't say any more,' Jonah said, bending to retrieve his chisel, then standing back to check that his error hadn't damaged his work. 'You mustn't listen to gossip. I've never known a place with so many vicious tongues. Knytte's more full of lying rumours than Buckhaven fish market.'

'I just don't want to see you hurt, Jonah. Against my father's wishes I became your friend, and I'd like to think we've stayed friends.'

'And I appreciate that, Phoebe, you know I do. When I was apprenticed I wouldn't have survived without the food you used to bring me. Fact is though, folks don't expect a lady to associate with the likes of me, for all that we're related. Your father being a clergyman and mine a mason, that's reckoned cause enough to keep us apart. I reckon that's where all this chatter started. They're jealous, that's all.'

She turned her back on him completely to face the cloisters. The children were still busy with their tasks, and it was easier to talk to Jonah if she didn't have to face him. 'If the talk was of you and me I shouldn't be concerned. You're as close to me as a brother, and I don't care who knows it. But if talking to me is seen as wrong, what happens when they find out who—'

'That's enough!' he said angrily. 'I'll not

listen to any more of this. Keep your place an' I'll keep mine. You'd better fetch those littl'uns and get out. I've work to do.'

Phoebe blinked back the tears threatening to spill from her eyes, but she stood her ground. 'Somebody from the house was out in the garden last night,' she said abruptly. 'And I know who passes by the nursery at midnight when all decent folks are in their beds. You're right, it's no concern of mine, but I'd hate to see you in trouble, Jonah.' She started towards the children, but a large dusty hand was laid on her arm.

'You've got me wrong.' He swung her round and studied her face. She was alarmed by the fury in his eyes. 'I was in my bed and sleeping sound last night.'

She pulled free and backed away. 'I hope you're telling the truth. I'm not blind, nor deaf, nor stupid, and that goes for others at Knytte. If you've any sense you'll leave, Jonah, before you get yourself into serious trouble.'

Thomas Beddowes had made good time across the moors, despite stopping for a nap in a haystack. He was heading for Trembury. With no obvious way to contact the men he'd so narrowly missed arresting the previous night, he was looking for Bragg instead. Since it had been his warning that allowed the jewel thieves to escape – and he'd then vanished – it was logical to assume he knew them.

A lucky coincidence had led to the arrest of Fetch'n'carry Cobb three months before; he'd been caught in possession of a priceless necklace belonging to the Countess of Bisworth. Questioning the villain with the use of none too subtle threats, Sergeant Beddowes had wheedled a great deal of useful information from him. At his age and with his body already crippled, Cobb wouldn't last long if sentenced to hard labour.

The notorious fence had admitted his part in handling the stolen jewellery. He'd been selling loot from robberies carried out by two audacious thieves who were working their way across south-west England.

Even before Cobb was on his way to prison, Sergeant Beddowes had decided to take on his identity. Armed with the date and time of the next meeting, he would see these men for himself; they'd only met Cobb in person once, a year before, in the murky back room of a London pot-house. Since then all transactions had been through a third party, different each time. Beddowes's confidence in the deception had seemed justified, until Bragg had coughed and ruined things.

Reaching inside his rags and fetching out an unripe apple stolen from a wayside orchard, the sergeant sighed; in turning down the offer of a bed, he'd also forfeited the chance of a decent meal. The previous night there'd been hope that the days of near starvation were coming to an end. Beddowes shook the thought aside; as a soldier he'd been used to short commons. At least here in the English countryside nobody was trying to kill him. The thought brought a smile to his face. That may no longer be the case. If he located the jewel thieves again he'd be hard pressed to persuade him that he hadn't attempted to betray them.

Beddowes, hunched and limping as be-fitted his part, reviewed what he'd learnt about the two men from the previous night's encounter as he plodded towards Trembury. Both were gentlemen, well spoken and well dressed enough to pass in the best company. They were excellent horsemen, aged about thirty at a guess, and the animals they rode had been decent mounts, not nags hired from some roadside livery. The man who'd taken him by the neck had a powerful grip; it had taken all Beddowes's resolve not to betray himself by fighting back.

It was midmorning when Beddowes came to the King's Arms, some five miles from Trembury. The place was busy; a coach had just arrived and the team of horses was being changed. Some passengers had rushed in-side to have a hurried meal, others watched as the fresh horses were put to the shafts. One man was grumbling loudly about the failure of the railway to reach Buckhaven.

Beddowes skulked on the edge of all the activity. He was hungry; the scent of meat and onions wafting from the kitchen made his mouth water, but although he had a couple of coppers hidden among his rags, strange bedfellows for the fortune in jewels tucked alongside, he wouldn't attract attention to himself by paying for a meal. He found a stone to perch on; he'd try begging for a scrap or two once the coach had left.

His eyes upon the bustling ostlers and pot-boys, Beddowes didn't notice he was being watched. By the time he saw the two men approaching him, it was too late to evade them. One, a stocky character with a bulbous nose, had a thin beard which didn't hide the long scar on his chin, and when the other spoke, Beddowes' suspicions were confirmed. 'You sure this is 'im, Bragg?'

'That's the man,' Bragg replied, and before Beddowes could do anything to prevent it, two more men had moved in from behind him and taken a grip on his arms. He was pulled to his feet and dragged out of the yard.

Beddowes could have broken free. Despite odds of four to one he had a good chance of escape; they wouldn't expect resistance from a lame hunchback. He let the opportunity pass. He'd set out to find Bragg, and here he was.

As they hustled him through a narrow

57

doorway behind the stables, one of the men slipped away, reducing the odds even further, but Beddowes had made up his mind to see the encounter through, and he allowed himself to be pushed into a poky little room, lit only by a single small window, and very dim once the door had been pushed shut behind him. Almost at once he began to wonder if it had been a bad decision, as one of the men landed a solid punch on the side of his skull, making his head ring and knocking him to the floor.

Beddowes rolled away from the boot that was aimed at his ribs, curling himself into a corner. 'What you want wi' me?' he whined. 'I ain't done nothin'.' The pouch with its fortune in jewels felt suddenly heavy against his ribs.

The door opened again, and the man who had dodged away entered, followed by another. It seemed this man was in charge, for the rest of them drew back. In the poor light, Beddowes couldn't make out what the newcomer looked like, but he looked to be a little better dressed than his supporters.

Doing his best to look like a penniless vagrant with nothing on his mind but surviving until his next meal, Beddowes crept from his corner, eyeing the opposition and measuring his chances.

Lord Pickhurst had gone to Middlebar, and

would not return until the afternoon. Before he left he had given his wife careful instruction as to the entertainment she must offer their guests.

'Really, my dear,' he said, placing a proprietary hand on her shoulder as she sat at her dressing table, 'you were barely civil at dinner last night. I thought the company of two young men would please you.'

'By now you should know there is only one man whose company I care for,' she replied, rising to give his wrinkled cheek a kiss, 'but I shall spend the morning with Mr Mortleigh and Mr Laidlaw, if you wish it.' Sighing, but with a smile, she made her reluctance plain; it wasn't wholly manufactured, for she considered Laidlaw a boor, and she could think of better ways to spend time with Mortleigh than a stroll in the garden.

'Such a pity Laidlaw is indisposed this morning,' Mortleigh said idly, as they made their way across the terrace. 'He has a great interest in architecture, and he was particularly looking forward to inspecting the ruins of the monastery.'

'There isn't a great deal left to see,' Lucille replied. 'You heard my husband's plans; apart from the tower, what remains is being made into a folly, with archways that lead nowhere, and artful arrangements of fallen masonry where plants may be trailed among the stone.

'I trust Mr Laidlaw is not seriously ill,' she went on. 'It will be a shame to be denied his company at dinner this evening. Perhaps I should send for a physician.'

'No, he's well enough, a day's rest is all he needs. My man Tomms is looking after him. There's no need to show me these ruins if you don't wish it, Lady Pickhurst.' He stopped as if to admire the herbaceous border, which enabled him to face her for a moment. 'Would you prefer to seek some other society?' His eyes danced as they met hers, a dangerous light in their depths.

Lucille did her best to retain her composure, but the previous night was too recent; there was an ache between her thighs which was hard to ignore. Looking away from him, she spoke lightly, as if commenting upon the flowers, but kept her voice low, in case anyone was within earshot.

'Why dissemble, Mr Mortleigh? We can both think of better ways of passing the time, yet we can do nothing but dally in the garden.' Lucille's lips lifted in their smallest catlike smile. 'Perhaps you shouldn't abuse my husband's hospitality too far; he is almost as proud of his folly as he is of his wife. It would be ungrateful in you not to spare a little attention to the one, before you cuckold him again with the other.'

At that he laughed aloud. 'Admirably put.

Show me the wonders he is creating, and tell me of the plans for a ballroom. It is rare for such an old man to have an interest in dancing. But then again, perhaps being married to a young wife can truly bring about a miracle and rejuvenate a man, even if he's old as Methuselah.'

Lucille led him under the arch, where a roof had been fashioned to make a narrow covered entrance some six feet in length. As Mortleigh followed her into the passage he put a hand upon her buttock and squeezed it, hard enough to hurt. She drew in a sharp breath, torn between anger, amusement and lust; much as she wanted him, she wouldn't conduct the affair entirely on his terms. While they were still hidden from view, she swung round and grabbed for the spot where she knew men were at their most vulnerable. Exerting all the strength she could, she was gratified to hear him gasp as she inflicted a little pain on her own account.

'Come, Mr Mortleigh,' she said gaily, walking on. 'Don't dawdle. I shall introduce you to Jonah Jackman. He can explain his work on the folly. If he makes it exactly to his lordship's taste, Jackman will be given the commission to build the ballroom. Since I vetoed his plans to use that horrid old library, we are to add a new wing on the far side of the house.' Ahead of them the air was hazy with dust, and the sound of a hammer

61

on stone was suddenly loud. A huge man of about the same age as Mortleigh, but at least a foot taller, was picking steadily at a block of masonry.

'This is a great honour, Lady Pickhurst.' Jackman put down his tools and turned to greet them.

'I am here at my husband's request, Jackman,' she said coolly. 'This gentleman, Mr Mortleigh, wishes to see the work you have in hand. I thought he should see the view from the old tower.'

'Of course.' Jackman nodded, inviting them to precede him. The tower overtopped the mansion by a few feet, but only because it had been built on elevated ground. 'Some believe this was an ancient burial mound, or it may be the monks themselves built the little hill so the tower would be more impressive,' Jonah said. 'It held a bell to summon the monks to their devotions.'

It was dark and several degrees colder inside the tower; the stone walls sprouted plants and lichen in places, and there was the steady drip of water from somewhere. 'It will be drier once the roof is complete, but we have to make the stairs safe first,' Jackman explained.

'But it is possible to reach the top?' Mortleigh asked. 'I am eager to look at the view. I imagine, Lady Pickhurst, you too would wish to see your magnificent house from such an ideal platform.'

'I'm not so ready to take risks as you suppose, Mr Mortleigh,' Lucille answered coolly, as she followed the mason up the curving stone steps. 'My husband has given orders that nobody should go beyond the second floor until the steps are made safe.'

'But you, Jackman, you must have been up there in the course of your work?'

'Yes, sir, but the stones are very worn, and unstable in places,' Jonah replied, his disapproval plain. 'I wouldn't attempt it, sir.'

Mortleigh laughed as they reached the second floor. 'I doubt if I weigh half what you do, man, and I rarely take advice from anyone, even good advice.' He looked at the dark archway which led further up. 'Fetch me a light. I'll be safe enough as long as I can see where to put my feet.'

When Lucille made no protest Jackman went running back down the stairs. Mortleigh immediately stepped across to her and took her in his arms. He kissed her on the mouth, plunging his tongue urgently between her lips, and pulled her body against his. 'You wear too many damn clothes,' he grumbled, as she broke free. There was time for nothing more, as Jackman could be heard returning. Her cheeks flaming, Lucille went to one of the windows and lent into the embrasure to hide her face from the young mason. She felt as if she'd been struck by lightning; the hunger Mortleigh's touch aroused in her was so unexpected, so extreme, she barely knew how to contain it. The tingles of anticipation were a torment, more pain than pleasure.

Mortleigh had vanished further up the tower. She turned back and found Jackman standing so close she couldn't step away. 'My lady,' he whispered, 'when can I see you?'

'I am here now, am I not, Mr Jackman,' she replied, though the intensity of her emotions made her voice shake.

'I've missed you so much,' Jonah said desperately, putting a tentative hand on her arm, 'you shouldn't make fun of me.'

She couldn't help herself. Her body was aflame, and he was there, towering above her, his touch warm upon her arm. Taking the step that seemed to cancel out the great gulf between them, just as she had a dozen times before, she stepped into his embrace, but this time was different. Every fibre of her being was yearning for what Mortleigh had shown her in the garden house.

Jonah Jackman closed his eyes as his mistress melted into his arms, her lips seeking hungrily for his, with a passion she'd never shown him in all their clandestine meetings. Their bodies couldn't touch, and yet this was a greater intimacy than they'd ever shared. He groaned aloud, barely keeping control of himself.

'When?' he whispered, as the woman suddenly thrust him away. 'You can't leave me without a little hope.'

'I'll send a message when I can,' she replied, smoothing down her dress and turning hurriedly to the stairs. 'It's difficult when we have visitors in the house. If you truly care for me, make my excuses to Mr Mortleigh and keep him occupied for a while. I need time to compose myself.'

Jonah nodded. He would obey, as he always obeyed. Lucille ran back into the sunshine and across the garden. The beginnings of an idea were forming in her head. Since her night with Mortleigh she had no need of Jackman's fumbling attempts as a lover, but she might have another use for him.

Chapter Five

'Who are you? What's your name?'

Beddowes was puzzled; he'd expected to find himself confronting the men he'd met the previous night. This individual's manner suggested a better education and perhaps more intelligence than Bragg, but he was no gentleman.

Busy with his own thoughts, Beddowes didn't answer. One of the yokels grabbed him by the shoulder and pulled him roughly to his feet, while Bragg came forward swiftly and planted a hard blow below their captor's ribs. 'Speak up,' he growled, 'the parson asked you a question.'

His eyes watering with pain, Beddowes eyed his inquisitor. The man was indeed dressed as a clergyman, though apparently a very poor one; a spare figure, no more than five feet tall, he had a high forehead, and a mouth that slid downwards at one side.

'M'name's Cobb,' Beddowes rasped. 'Don't 'it me no more. What you want wi' me? I ain't done nothin'.'

'If that's true you have nothing to fear. Stand back from him, Bragg. Well, Cobb, I ⁀ther you were at the gibbet cross last night.'

Beddowes nodded, thinking fast. This ill-assorted crew seemed unlikely accomplices of the two thieves; the man who had been so guarded with his words last night would never share his secrets, or his profits, with so many.

'Told yer,' Bragg said. 'Come with the feller in black, he did, him what works for Sir Martin, the magistrate. They was talking proper friendly, an' I 'eard mention o' the militia. That's when Sir Martin rid off. I ain't made no mistake, parson, it were a trap.'

'We've already heard your account, Bragg,' the parson said, silencing him with an impatient wave of the hand. 'Let this man have his say. Tell us, Cobb, how did you come to be with Sir Martin Haylmer? You know he's the Lord Lieutenant?'

'I knew 'e was summat, the sort could get me hanged if I dun't do as I were told,' Beddowes mumbled, thinking fast. 'Never met none on 'em till yesterday. That man Docket, it was 'im what took me there, I didn't know the other gents. See, all I ever done was take a message. A piece o' paper, tha's all, what was give me by a cove at the Crooked Man. A shillin' he promised me, if I took it to a man at the old gibbet. "Wait all night if you 'ave to," he said, "but deliver that note an' you'll get paid." Well I ain't,' he added, raising his voice, as if suddenly recovering his wits a little. 'I ain't got paid. Them nobs, Sir Martin whatever it is, an' that Mr Docket, they took it off me.'

'Took it? What, the paper?'

'Aye. Stopped me they did, jus' after I left the Crooked Man, an' threatened to lock me up. I telled 'em what I'm tellin' you, there ain't no 'arm in carryin' a message. Then that Mr Docket, he give me tuppence.' He reached and fumbled for the coins and drew them out to show his inquisitors. 'An' 'e said there'd be more if I did as I were told.' He scowled. 'Didn't get it though, did I. Don't reckon I got no more to say. Wha's in it fer me, eh?'

There was an angry growl from the men around him, and they moved in close, threatening. Beddowes ducked as a fist swung at his head, and he fell to his knees, cowering at the clergyman's feet.

'Don't let 'em hurt me,' he whined, touching the parson's black skirt with a clawed hand. 'I tells ye, I ain't done nothin' wrong. Dun't mean no 'arm to nobody.'

The parson waved his attackers back. 'Listen Cobb, I'm not a man of violence, but if you don't answer my questions I'm afraid I shall be forced to leave you to a swifter form of justice. Nobody is allowed to lay information in these parts. If you've betrayed the brotherhood there is only one penalty.'

'I ain't betrayed nobody,' Beddowes said

quickly. 'I don't know nothin' about no brotherhood, so 'ow can I do it no 'arm? Twasn't my fault they took the paper, couldn' stop 'em, could I?'

'Tell me the rest of the story. You went to the gibbet crossroads with Mr Docket. What happened there?'

'He cleared off, an' the rest of 'em ducked down out o' sight. Waited, di'n't I, like they said. Stood like a bleedin' statue till me legs was numb. An' them riders come. Two of 'em. I didn't 'ave the message no more, but the one you say was Sir Martin 'ad give me another piece of paper, said they was to 'ave that, if they asked.'

'You were talking a long time,' Bragg said. 'Friendly with 'em, like. An' I heard 'em laugh.'

'What was that about?' the parson asked sharply.

'One of 'em was askin' a lot o' questions what I couldn't answer, and then 'e starts squeezin' me throat, fit to do me in. I asked 'im to let me go, real polite, an' I called 'im y'r lordship. Tha's when he laughed. Said 'e weren't no lord yet.'

'This makes no sense.' The parson turned from Beddowes to frown at Bragg. 'You said you'd heard of a trap being set, but there was nobody out last night. Besides that, we've nobody at the Crooked Man, Slaney buys his goods elsewhere.'

'How was I to know that?' Bragg said. 'When I 'eard Sir Martin's gamekeeper was lookin' for help, I reckoned he was workin' with the excise men again, like last time, so I got taken on. An' I busted up the trap right enough,' he went on defensively, 'busted it up so them two riders got clear.'

'That's another thing.' The parson was becoming impatient. 'Riders, and you said they were gentlemen. It doesn't fit with anyone we know. And where was the cargo?'

'Maybe we got competition. There was talk of a boat off East Clow Head three nights ago,' another voice put in.

The parson shook his head. 'Three nights! If somebody ran a few barrels in three nights ago, they'd be long gone.' Once again he turned to Beddowes. 'Do you know what was in the note, Cobb?'

'Nobody told me,' he said, sullenly.

'You can't read?'

A shake of the head answered this. 'Very well. You gave the two men the note, the one Sir Martin had supplied. What happened then?'

'Tha's when some cove coughed, an' afore I knew what was goin' on, it was like the end o' the world was come, wi' flashes an' bangs an' fire. Laid down flat I did, till Mr Docket come an' telled me to get out, or they'd drag me off an' lock me up. Two shillin', tha's what I was promised, an' all I got was tuppence an' the fright o' me life.'

With a sigh, the parson took a coin from his pocket and handed it to one of the yokels. 'Bring him a jar of ale and something to eat. Look Cobb, keep quiet about what happened here, and once you've had a bite you can go. Strangers aren't welcome in these parts. Go back where you came from.'

'You lettin' him go?' Bragg scowled at Beddowes. 'What you reckon was goin' on, then?'

'I don't know, but it's no business of ours. And since it's likely Sir Martin Haylmer will be looking for the man who spoilt his plans, Bragg, not to mention maybe the militia as well, I'd say the advice I've given Cobb holds good for you too. Clear out for a while, and keep your head down.'

'You look pleased with yourself.' Mortleigh was leaning in at the side of the arbour, a lazy smile on his lips. Lucille glanced at him then looked away. She had been alone for almost half an hour after leaving Jackman at the tower and the excitement she had felt as the plan took shape in her mind had subsided now.

'I trust you enjoyed your tour of the ruins,' she said, her tone cool and admirably detached.

He ignored this, staring at her as if studying some interesting specimen. 'The wildcat

71

at peace, with her sharp claws hidden, but woe betide those who are taken in by her air of docility.'

'I cannot imagine what you mean.' She shifted aside an inch or two, so there was room for him to join her, but he made no move.

'You present a picture of total perfection,' he said, 'to make an artist reach for his colour box, or a writer of romance to pick up his pen. There, they imagine, sits a lady thinking of her true love. The question is, which man fills her thoughts? Not the elderly nobleman, surely. Perhaps the rustic Lothario, the artisan; a man built like Hercules and proud of his calloused hands; such a shame he has the heart and mind of a peasant. And don't deny the connection, I'm neither blind nor stupid.'

'You misname poor Jonah,' Lucille answered calmly. 'He's not a peasant, nor is he a promiscuous seducer. He's devoted to me. He'd give his life for me if I asked it.'

'A fool for love, a mere plaything for a bored and loveless lady. Poor Jonah indeed.'

'As if you care,' Lucille said. 'And you're a fine one to speak of play. Are you forgetting how you delighted in acting the pirate?'

He pretended to be hurt by her words as he came to sit at her side. 'Am I so heartless? As to the stonemason, I found him an estimable young man, so very knowledgeable about his trade, so very willing to speak about the joy his work gives him.' Mortleigh feigned a yawn, lifting two elegant fingers to shield it from her. 'He became so animated he might even have been talking of a mistress, rather than blocks of granite. I'm surprised he doesn't bring a chisel to your bed.'

He placed a hand upon her sleeve and ran his fingers down her arm until they reached her bare wrist, where the contact of flesh on flesh awakened her senses; even his lightest touch could rekindle the fire of the night. His eyes widened, as if he felt it too. 'You're no lady,' he whispered, leaning close to speak into her ear, so his breath was hot on her face. 'I swear you're a witch. I have never felt my appetites so far beyond my control, not for the want of any woman.'

'And yet you must have encountered so many,' she replied tautly, moving away from him. 'I don't doubt some pretty dairymaid, or foreign aristocrat's wife must have pleased you more. After all, despite my title, I am a mere provincial nobody, stuck here, far from polite society.'

'Shame,' he mocked, 'did your marriage lose its lustre so soon? And yet you're wed to one of the most powerful and wealthy men in this part of the country, quite a catch for a young woman with little fortune of her own.'

'You know nothing of me or my fortune,' she retorted, stung that he could hit so near the mark. 'Both my father and mother were of noble blood, with connections to half the royal houses of Europe.'

'And yet they were reduced to living on the charity of others, and gambling on the chance of a fine match for their only child.' He reached to touch her again, this time to caress the curve of her neck above her bodice. 'You think I've forgotten all those London soirees? I have ears, my pretty one, and even in the best of houses, gossip is easy to come by.'

'And what of you,' she snapped back. 'You think I haven't met men like you before? You have the manners and accomplishments of a gentleman, and use them to steal crumbs from the tables of your betters.'

'Oh, a little more than crumbs, I think you'll find,' he said, his hand straying now over her breast, 'or did I dream what happened last night? If that's the case perhaps you need reminding what a perfect hussy you made of yourself. Perhaps we should repeat the experiment.'

'Don't be a fool.' In one more moment Lucille was afraid she would melt into his arms, her body becoming a piece with his, so they could never be separated again. 'You think I won my place here so dearly, to risk throwing it away on you?'

'Hazard adds spice to life,' he replied, not relinquishing his hold on her.

She flung him off. 'Somebody is coming. Must I scream rape and bring the servants down on you?'

'It's only Tomms, my man,' Mortleigh said, though he moved away from her. The upright black-clad figure approached slowly and bowed.

'Forgive this intrusion, your ladyship. Mr Mortleigh, I have to report that Mr Laidlaw is becoming agitated. He begs you will come to him.'

'Can I help?' Lucille asked, reluctantly recollecting her duties as a hostess. 'If Mr Laidlaw is ill I am sure my husband would wish a physician to be summoned.'

'That won't be necessary,' Mortleigh dismissed the idea with an airy wave of a hand. 'My friend is very much given to dramatics; he exaggerates. Tomms, tell him I shall be with him very shortly.'

'I shall come with you,' Lucille said. 'There may be something I can do. Cook has an excellent receipt for a posset which would help him to rest if he has a fever. Let me send an order to the kitchen.'

'Thank you, your ladyship, but I beg you will allow me to go alone. Knowing Laidlaw, he will not be suitable company for the gentle sex at the moment.' Mortleigh rose quickly and bowed low over her hand.

'Please, excuse me.'

Lucille watched them go. Tomms was at Mortleigh's elbow, whispering urgently in his ear. She had been striking blindly when she accused Mortleigh of being little better than a beggar, but something in his eyes made her wonder if the barb had struck home. The discovery made no difference to her feelings for him, but it might lend power to her plans; she could make good use of that knowledge in the future. As soon as the two men were out of sight she gathered up her skirts and almost ran to the entrance at the side of the house, where she hurried up the backstairs, cursing a startled maid who got in her way.

Despite the passion they had shared, despite her conviction that no other man would ever satisfy her as Mortleigh did, there was some part of Lucille that resented him. She was accustomed to having men under her control, and she sensed that, while Mortleigh declared himself bewitched, he would always put his own needs before hers. Such freedom couldn't be allowed.

On fleet and silent feet, Lucille raced along the corridor, slipping into an empty bedroom. It was next to a small antechamber, furnished to act as a parlour for the rooms occupied by Mortleigh and the sick man. As she closed the door she heard Mortleigh's voice; he and his servant must have reached the top of the stairs. She clambered onto the bed, pulling aside the silk hanging to reveal the wooden panelling behind its head. Lucille had discovered the peephole within a week of her arrival at Knytte; she had always had an inquisitive nature. Expecting to be spied upon by her aged husband, or maybe the servants who were so sullenly obedient to her orders, it had seemed prudent to familiarize herself with all the secrets of the big old house. Still, she had never imagined herself finding such a use for her knowledge.

The encounter with Jonah had left Phoebe uneasy. He hadn't listened to her. It was strange. The only time she'd been convinced that he was telling her the truth, was when he swore that he hadn't left his bed the previous night. If that were true, what of her other suspicions? She had been certain that the ghostly sounds outside the nursery had been made by Lady Pickhurst.

With only half her mind on the children, she led them to the lake and allowed them to waste time standing in the shade of the willow trees, watching the fish that rose for flies. From this vantage point she'd seen Lady Pickhurst walking through the gardens towards the ruins, in the company of one of his lordship's guests.

'Please may we go through the elm avenue?' She hadn't noticed Rodney Pen-

goar return to her side, leaving
throwing twigs into the water.

'Miss Eliza, stop that if you ple
ladies do not throw sticks It's ti
turned to your studies indoors. M
ney, but we shall go by way of th
and the vegetable garden if you wis
would bring them to a little-used pa
skirted the ruins on the opposite si
might give her a chance to speak t
cousin again, if her ladyship didn't ling
the ruins too long.

In this she was disappointed. As
turned from the lower end of the elm ave
she caught a glimpse of Jonah, carrying
lighted lantern into the tower; evidently h
visitors wished to ascend its heights, whi
meant he would be occupied for some time.
With her attention drifting again, the children had stopped to admire a large fungus on
a beech tree, and rather than admonish
them, she lingered too, feeling a sense of
shame. It was not in her nature to spy, but
she was worried about Jonah.

The glow of light glimpsed through the
narrow windows showed where the explorers
were, its progress slowing as they neared the
top; she knew the steps were old and worn.
Suddenly somebody appeared at the base of
the tower. It was Lady Pickhurst. Her face
was unnaturally flushed, and she almost ran
to the arched passage that would take her

back to the gardens. As she vanished another figure burst from the tower. It was Jonah; even at a distance she could see his expression, and guess his thoughts. Phoebe blushed with embarrassment, both for herself and for her cousin. After a few moments the large man's shoulders drooped and he returned the way he had come.

A light was showing from the highest window in the tower, and very soon after that a head appeared over the parapet. Phoebe recognized the guest who had been escorting Lady Pickhurst. She bit her lip. Jonah and her ladyship had evidently been alone for some time. She knew what the gossips would make of that. If he wasn't careful her cousin's clandestine involvement with Lady Pickhurst could ruin them all.

Chapter Six

'I fear my friend is adamant,' Mortleigh said. As if reluctant to approach her, he stood just within the room, while Lucille kept to her seat by the window, her glance straying now and then to the garden. 'He insists on returning to London this very day. Since I doubt he's well enough to sit a horse all the way to Hagstock, I must ask for another indulgence; I beg you'll order a carriage for us.'

'Us? You go with Mr Laidlaw?' Lucille tried to feign indifference. She didn't want Mortleigh to leave, and the depth of her emotions unsettled her. What she had heard at the peephole was intriguing; it seemed there was some mystery surrounding their visitors, and that made her even more reluctant to let her lover go.

'Only to make sure he gets safely to the train. I've offered to send my man to London with him, and once Laidlaw is home and being cared for, Tomms can return. Since my poor friend refuses the attentions of a local physician, I feel I must do all I can to deliver him safely to town. I have no wish to be a nuisance, Lady Pickhurst, but if you will lend us some small conveyance, that would suit very well. I prefer to drive myself.'

Lucille rose to look out of the window, so he couldn't see her face. 'You, then, are in no such hurry to leave?'

Mortleigh came closer at last, and lowered his voice. 'How can you ask that? Bewitched as I am, every mile I travel away from you will be a torment, and only the knowledge that I shall be returning will make it bearable.' He spoke now in a husky murmur that awoke memories of the brief terror he'd inflicted upon her, and the heights of passion which followed. To hear such words from him was balm to her soul.

'I shall return unencumbered,' he whispered, 'and I shall drive the horses hard, in the hope of joining you for dinner. No doubt Lord Pickhurst will be tired tonight, worn out by his duties as magistrate. If not, there's that little bottle; you only have to say the word.'

She gave him no direct answer, though thoughts of the night made her pulse quicken. 'You wish to leave at once?'

'The sooner I leave, the sooner I'll return.'

With a decisive nod she pulled the bell-rope. Orders were given, and Mortleigh went to help his friend prepare for the journey. Lucille walked about the room, unable to be still, her thoughts in turmoil. Mortleigh had no idea that she'd overheard his conversation with his friend. He'd been lying. Had it been for her sake? Laidlaw had expressed no wish to leave Knytte, although it was true he was very agitated. His concern had been that his illness, whatever it might be, needed immediate attention. It was clear that Mortleigh and his servant, Tomms, had done their best to care for him, but it was Mortleigh who refused to have the local physician summoned, despite acknowledging that Laidlaw's condition was worsening.

Listening at the peephole, Lucille had flushed as Laidlaw laid the blame for his troubles on his companion. 'Your whoring has cost me dear, Mortleigh. Didn't I warn you against it?' This puzzled her; Laidlaw was angry about the time Mortleigh had spent with her, but she couldn't see how it was connected to his illness.

Lucille had been gratified when Mortleigh launched into a furious tirade, accusing Laidlaw of cowardice, of being eager to run away long before there was any scent of danger. 'You call it whoring, but I tell you, Lady Pickhurst is a rare find, and I'm damned if I'll regret a moment I spent in her company.'

'That's easy for you to say,' Laidlaw had replied, 'since you're not the one paying the price. This needs to be tended, and soon.'

The whole argument seemed illogical; neither man was in danger at Knytte, the idea was preposterous, unless the illness was wildly contagious, and threatened the lives of all who lived there. She had waited, breathless, eager to hear Mortleigh's reply to this accusation, but she learnt no more. Mortleigh brought the conversation to an abrupt halt. He had turned away from his friend, stating his intention to ask for a carriage, and Lucille had been forced to race downstairs, so she would be innocently occupied in the morning room when her guest came looking for her.

Gracious to the unwanted Laidlaw, now she was to be rid of him, Lucille went to wish the invalid a comfortable journey as Tomms aided him into the landaulet. The man was pale, and his pace slow, but he didn't look to be at death's door. 'I'm sure you will recover soon enough, once you are home,' Lucille said. 'Lord Pickhurst will be sorry to have lost your company. I hope you will visit us again, once you are well.'

The young man nodded, saying a brief word of thanks, and then they were gone, with Mortleigh at the reins; he hardly gave her a glance as he took his place. Lucille stood upon the steps, watching until they were out of sight. It would be hours before he returned. Only now, when it was too late, did she wish they had made more definite plans for the night.

Her need for him was like a physical sickness; she longed to repeat the intimacies of the previous night, even if it meant creeping to his room once the household was asleep. Having lunched swiftly and without company, Lucille wandered back to the rose garden. She was alone here too, the gardeners discreetly vanishing when she appeared. Her imagination showed her a future she'd never dared hope for, and she paced agitatedly along the narrow paths between the flower-laden bushes.

Thoughts circled through her mind in ceaseless motion. Lord Pickhurst was old. He could die at any time. But she might wait ten or twenty years before she was free of him and by then she herself would be growing old. Her husband was forever boasting that his grandfather had lived to the age of ninety-three, while he was not yet seventy.

When she married she'd been prepared to make the best of her situation, but now there was Mortleigh; his arrival changed everything, or it could, if he was the kind of man she suspected him to be. Why should she not decide her own future? Fate might be kind, or it might be cruel; why should she not take some part in determining which it was to be?

Men had such privileges. The world had grown, so many things were possible, yet still the fair sex had few rights. The freedom that was guaranteed to men made them fickle; they had no fears of being left alone and impoverished once their natural attractions had left them. Mortleigh's affections might soon fade. Lust and her seductive skills couldn't be relied on to hold him forever.

At this point Lucille suddenly halted. There were other inducements. He was certainly a risk taker, and he had few scruples. Lucille rubbed her hands together as if to warm them, although the day wasn't cold. A woman could be mistress of her own property, not necessarily surrendering all her worldly goods to a husband when she married. Unless she had a son, Knytte and most of her husband's estate would be hers when he died. It was surely a tempting prize for any man.

She walked on. Almost feverish with the ideas revolving frantically within her mind, Lucille hardly noticed that she'd wandered into the ruins; she turned a corner and found herself face to face with Jonah Jackman again.

Beddowes stood on a little-used road, trying to decide what he should do. He judged he was several miles to the north-east of the King's Arms, having been thrown roughly from the parson's rickety dog cart by Bragg and another man, with warnings not to return. He had been fed, though poorly, at the parson's command, and there was a crust of bread stowed inside his shirt for his dinner.

Threats or no, the sergeant would have retraced his steps towards Trembury if necessary, but the encounter at the King's Head convinced him it was pointless. Bragg had foiled Sir Martin's ambush because he'd thought they were after smugglers. Aching and disgruntled, Beddowes decided he'd pass on what little information he'd gained as soon as he had a chance. The so-called brotherhood were powerful in this part of the country, and any help he could give would be welcomed by the customs men.

Staring along the road, which wound roughly from north to south, Beddowes couldn't decide what his next move should be. The thieves might be anywhere, even on a train back to London, although if that was their intention, why make him travel so far to collect their booty? They would lie low, surely, for a few days, after so narrow an escape. From their voices and apparel they belonged to the gentry, or were able to ape them sufficiently well to fool those they met; they wouldn't sleep rough. That wasn't much help, for there were a hundred inns where rooms could be hired.

The sergeant often did his best thinking on his feet, but to walk north in search of the London road seemed like an admission of defeat; the crimes he'd been summoned to investigate had all taken place within fifty miles of where he now stood. He wasn't ready to return

Beddowes ma...
Docket, which me...
moor. Sir Martin's secr...
to contact than the Lord...
He would take the next tra...
although he couldn't be too...
would take him; the unmade road...
parts followed devious routes,...
around deep bogs and peat hags.

When he'd been entrusted with the ca...
Beddowes hadn't had much opportunity to
study the notes the local police had made;
perhaps it was time to begin again, and see
if some clue had been missed. Half a dozen
large houses had been robbed; if there was a
pattern, some link between chosen time and
place, perhaps he could hazard a guess at
where and when the thieves might strike
again. Then there was that intriguing reference, so annoyingly interrupted by Bragg. A
pair of something of great value was to be
among the next expected haul. A pair of
candlesticks? Or earrings?

Deep in thought, Beddowes had walked
no more than a mile before he heard the
thud of hoofs and the rattle of a carriage
behind him. The road was bad, and the
carriage would demand the most level way;
mindful of his part as a ragged and crippled
tramp, he slouched to the edge of the ditch
that ran alongside. Here he halted to allow

icle came
ssing give
is balance
almost as
assed him,
sly that the
hafts threw
m squealing
nals' spank-
rantic clatter
l and walked
this act of
wan.... cruelty had anything to do with him,
until the driver threw ... reins to a servant
who had hurriedly dismounted from the rear,
and leapt down from the box.

The road was dusty and the sun bright, which might have excused the wide-brimmed hat drawn down over the man's brow, and the scarf wrapped across the lower part of his face, but the day was warm, and as he approached he pulled the scarf higher. Beddowes felt a prickle of apprehension on his skin, as if some sixth sense was issuing a warning. This encounter was not to be a friendly one.

'You!' the single word confirmed Beddowes' fears. He had seen little of his attacker the night before, but he recognized the voice at once.

With no time to think, the sergeant's hand

[partial vertical text on folded corner:] to Scotland Yard just yet. ... e up his mind to see ... nt heading for Clow- ... tary would be easier ... ieutenant himself. ... ck to the west, ... re where it ... s in these ... inding

went instinctively to his chest; there was no weapon there, but he drew out the package. 'Is that you, y'r lordship? 'ere, I got it safe. I was lookin', but I di'n't know where to find you.'

His fist already drawn back to deliver a blow, the man halted, staring at the package. He snatched it, tearing it open to stare at the contents. Rewrapping them roughly, he strode to the landaulet and tossed the jewels to the man who sat hidden inside. 'Check it's all there.'

Within the shadows under the hood, Beddowes saw no more than an outline of a pale face, with feverishly bright eyes. 'Is it him?' a voice croaked. 'By God, if I didn't feel so damned weak I'd help you give him what he deserves.'

The sergeant recalled that one of Sir Martin's men had claimed to have scored a hit at the crossroads; evidently he'd been right. Cringing back, his eyes once more on the shrouded figure of the man who stood before him, Beddowes assessed his opponent. From his stance the man had studied boxing, and he already knew the strength of his grip. He had only one advantage; this man would expect little resistance from the crippled Fetch'n'carry Cobb. Even now, Beddowes was reluctant to give himself away. If it came to a fight he couldn't be sure of success; there was the servant to contend with, and the injured man, who might be armed. This might be his last chance to keep contact with the thieves; lose them now and there was little chance he'd get close to them again.

'You miserable piece of filth.' He was seized by his ragged collar and shaken. 'We were nearly taken last night. You sold us out.'

'I never,' Beddowes whined. He'd had plenty of time to invent his story, a different one from that he'd told to Bragg and his cronies, but that encounter had given him information which made his tale more credible. 'It weren't my fault. Them gents come by the gibbet soon arter I got there. What was I to do? They 'ad sojers with 'em, I couldn't 'ardly run, could I? They said I'd do 'ard labour for the rest o' me days if I didn't do as I was told. I 'ad no choice, y'r honour. But they weren't arter you, see, so 'tweren't so bad. They was lookin' fer a gang o' rum-runners workin' the coast 'ereabouts, tha's what I 'eard, once all the shootin' an' the shoutin' stopped.'

'How did you get away?' The fingers moved to tighten on his windpipe 'I can't believe they set you free, and never even searched you.'

Beddowes winced; his throat still ached from their previous encounter. 'The fire got out of 'and.' His voice was a barely audible whisper. 'I crep' down a dyke while they was beatin' at it, and jus' kep' goin'. I 'eard 'em chasin' arter me, but I ain't that easy to catch, not me. Listen, y'r lordship, I'll take that package for you, jus' the way you want, I swear.'

The smile that greeted this offer was somehow more frightening than the cold fury that preceded it, and Beddowes realized he hadn't deflected the man's original intent.

'I think not. No, I think Fetch'n'carry has outrun his usefulness.' He beckoned to the servant, who secured the reins before going to the rear of the carriage, where he lifted two wooden bludgeons from the boot. Giving one to his master, the man tossed the second from hand to hand, as if to show off his prowess with the weapon.

They moved so fast that they almost caught Beddowes unawares. He began to dodge, but wasn't in time to escape the first blow completely; the force as it hit his arm was enough to send him reeling. He teetered along the edge of the deep ditch. Unable to regain his balance sufficiently to jump it, he dropped down into the shallow mud and floundered past his two attackers, aiming to reach the horses. The beasts were still unsettled, and they might provide a diversion.

His enemies were too quick for him. Several hard knocks struck him as he clambered out of the mire and back onto the road. The two men were getting in each other's way when either of them alone might have finished him, but even so he was taking too much punishment. Unless he could strike back before long a lucky blow would bring him down, and then the attack could only have one end.

Beddowes flinched as a cudgel whistled past his ear to land squarely on his shoulder; both sound and sensation led him to suspect that a bone was cracked, if not broken. There could be no future for Fetch'n'carry Cobb. If Sergeant Beddowes hoped to survive, it was time to fight for his life.

With the blood-curdling roar that hadn't issued from between his lips since the battle for Kandahar, Beddowes turned, his hands no longer arthritic claws but powerful bunched fists. He dove in under the bludgeon wielded by the servant, whom he judged the physically stronger of his two assailants. A full bodied blow to the belly, followed by a vicious uppercut to the jaw, put the servant out of the fight, although the victory came at the cost of a severe blow on the skull from the man's master. He reeled dizzily, but rallied almost at once.

He hadn't fought in so desperate a cause for many years; the sergeant of old would have trusted in his strength, but that had been many years ago, and he'd been on meagre rations. The chance to gain a weapon was too tempting. Beddowes reached to pick up the heavy wooden stick the groom had dropped; the realization that it was a mistake came too late. It wasn't brawn that mattered here, but brains; he should have attacked the organ grinder, not the monkey. In the time it had taken for him to deal with the servant, his master had moved into the perfect position, and now he swung with all his strength.

The bludgeon crunched against the right side of Beddowes skull, just where the previous blow had landed. The world split apart in jagged lightning strikes. A tiny voice in his head had just time to say *'I'm dead'*, before everything went black.

Chapter Seven

'Lady Pickhurst,' Jonah was all formality. A few feet behind him, a sketch book in one hand and a pencil in the other, stood Miss Drake, the governess. The girl gave as gracious a curtsey as she could manage with her hands full, while her face took on a faint tinge of pink.

'Are you neglecting your duties, Miss Drake?' Lucille was quick to take advantage of the girl's obvious discomfort and she was pleased to see Phoebe Drake's cheeks flush more deeply.

'No, your ladyship. Master Rodney and Miss Eliza are taking their usual afternoon rest, just as Lord Pickhurst ordered. They've not been left unsupervised, Annie is in the nursery, and she knows where to send for me, should I be needed. I am here because Master Rodney has been learning the history of Knytte, and I thought I would spend my free time making drawings of the monastery. They might usefully be compared to the old etchings which were made when it was almost intact.'

'So you are an accomplished artist?' Lucille was amused to see Jonah fidgeting uncomfortably. He was embarrassed to be found with this girl. She knew they were cousins, but that didn't necessarily prohibit another kind of relationship. Miss Drake's attentions would be unwelcome in front of his mistress; while he was so deeply enamoured he wouldn't want to have his name linked romantically with any other woman.

'Hardly that. I can copy, that's all.' Phoebe made to open the book to show her work, but Lucille shook her head dismissively.

'It doesn't matter, I have no interest in seeing your attempts. Pray don't be late in returning to your duties, Miss Drake, I shouldn't like to see you dismissed.' With that she swept back through the archway, sensing rather than seeing Jonah Jackman's disappointment. When she looked back from the shelter of the rose arbour only a minute later, it was to see the young governess hurrying from the ruins, her face set as if she was biting back tears.

Lucille watched the girl hurry to the rear of the house. She believed Jonah when he insisted no other woman had ever taken his eye, that she alone had captured his heart, though a man of twenty five, especially one of his stature and appearance, should have made many conquests. Jonah was tiresomely upright and moral. He spoke of his guilt at their liaison almost as often as he told her of his love.

Bored, annoyed with Mortleigh and illogically irritated by not finding Jonah alone, Lucille returned to the ruins, the steady crack of steel on stone growing louder as she approached. She tiptoed through the arch, and stood watching him at work, slightly stirred by the rippling muscles of his back and shoulders. It had been his physique that had led her to seek out his company a few weeks after her arrival at Knytte; the monotony of married life had already threatened to overcome her, used as she was to a round of balls and parties. Since flirtation with men of her own class was denied her, she'd tried her art with the stone mason, and found a lover who was willing to grant her every wish. Jonah Jackman, she was sure, would die for her, were it asked of him, in the true tradition of romantic chivalry.

'Poor Jonah,' she said softly, 'did I spoil your romantic assignation? It must be hard to find a time to meet your pretty little inamorata.'

Despite her quietness he must have known she was there, for he answered at once, and seemed not to be put out by her accusation. 'Phoebe Drake is my cousin,' he said, 'as you well know. We were brought up almost like brother and sister for some years, and that is how we think of each other.'

'So, you were speaking of family matters when I interrupted you. That hardly seems to account for Miss Drake's pink cheeks, does it?'

A slight frown furrowed his wide forehead. 'She's concerned for me; somehow she's come to suspect our attachment.'

'Poor Jonah,' she said again. 'And now that we have visitors in the house I must be so much more careful. There can be no moonlit meetings for a while. My husband sits later with his guests, and their rooms overlook the grounds. We mustn't risk being seen.'

He turned to her at last, a look of pain crossing his face. 'I don't know how you can bear being tied to that old man, lord or no lord; it was wrong of your parents to make you marry him, but you *are* married, and our brief spells of happiness are equally wicked.'

Lucille nodded gravely; she had invented a miserable childhood, woven around with a web of intrigue, to win this man's sympathy and quiet his conscience. To that she added tales of her husband's cruelty, although he was innocent of any crime except that of being old.

'So must our love be seen as sinful? Can there be no justification for finding a little warmth and affection in our lives? Perhaps you're right. What we can't change, we must endure,' she said, her voice breaking.

'I'll be guided by you,' he said softly. 'Phoebe may be right, my feelings have made a fool of me. The world will never allow us to be together. I ask nothing more than the few snatched hours I've already spent with you. Their memory will keep me warm through the coldest and loneliest nights.'

'Dear Jonah, must we condemn ourselves to being alone? It's so unfair, for you are free and one day you'll leave and find another love. Perhaps this should be our last meeting.' Glancing around to see that they weren't overlooked, she stretched up and pulled his face down to hers, bestowing a lingering kiss upon his lips. 'Don't leave me, dearest love, not yet.' With a sigh she left him, suppressing a laugh as she turned away; the lovesick fool would have a chance to prove his devotion before too long.

The afternoon passed slowly, and after many attempts to occupy herself, Lucille called her maid, and spent an hour deciding what she should wear that evening, berating the woman at every opportunity. Her husband was home by the time she made her final decision; she chose a gown that accentuated both her slim waist, and her pallor.

Mortleigh had not returned, but as Lucille dismissed her maid she looked out of the window to see the landaulet bowling up the drive. Her heart quickening, she hurried to accept her husband's proffered arm as he came to her door. Leaning on him as they descended the stairs, she brought her mouth close to Lord Pickhurst's ear. 'I trust you're not excessively tired, dear husband. You did not visit me last night, and I am pining for want of company. Now that our guests have gone I have you to myself again.'

She had timed it perfectly. A young footman was just bowing Mortleigh into the house, but something was wrong. The servant gave a gasp as he straightened, unable to hide his reaction to the visitor's appearance. Lucille found herself staring too; her new lover was dusty and dishevelled. Blood trickled from a cut upon his forehead, and there was a livid bruise on his cheek. Once she recovered from her shock, she felt a malicious wish to laugh. Had he been a few minutes earlier he might have slipped up to his room without being seen by his host and hostess, and repaired his appearance before the dinner gong sounded.

'What a fortuitous return,' she said haughtily, clinging more tightly to her husband's arm; she wanted Mortleigh, and his dishevelled state merely aroused her lust, but she would be content if neither man knew what she was feeling. It was pleasant to watch her lover humiliated, just a little, as payment for the fear he'd inflicted upon her.

'I apologize, your lordship, Lady Pickhurst,' Mortleigh said, 'for returning so late. I fear I took a tumble from the carriage. The horses took fright at a grouse. I was perhaps unwise to drive back without a groom, but I didn't want my sick friend to travel alone, so I sent Tomms to care for him on the train.'

'We shall delay dinner for a few minutes,' Lord Pickhurst said. Waving away his guest's attempts to protest, or to apologize, he gave the appropriate orders, and had Parkes, his valet, sent to Mr Mortleigh's room.

'I dislike having the servants put about in this way,' Lucille declared, once Mortleigh had gone upstairs. The colour had rushed to her face at the sight of her lover, and she knew her husband would notice; let him interpret her excitement as annoyance. 'I had so hoped we might be alone tonight,' she added in a whisper.

'I am flattered, my dear heart,' Lord Pickhurst said, patting her hand. 'Perhaps our guest will be tired after his ordeal and not wish to sit too long over the brandy. We must be grateful that he's returned safely.'

She gave him her most brilliant smile. 'I shan't pretend to share your interest in the gentleman, but what pleases you can be nothing but agreeable to me.'

During the meal Lucille took little part in the conversation, being civil to Mortleigh, but no more. She rose as soon as it was polite to do so. 'I'll leave you to the decanter and cigars,' she said, darting a meaningful look at her husband. 'Do not hurry. I shall retire early. Goodnight, Mr Mortleigh.'

'Lady Pickhurst.' He bowed low, a sardonic smile on his face. 'Thank you for the loan of your landaulet, I trust I shall find a way to repay your generosity soon, and I assure you my friend Laidlaw will be eternally grateful. I wish you a very good night.'

Beddowes' head was full of cannon fire. He didn't move a muscle, yet pain erupted somewhere behind his eyes, spreading with awakening consciousness down through his neck, shoulders and back until his body was a red hot agony. Except his legs. He couldn't feel his legs. Fear gripped him; had they gone? Had shot or shrapnel left him with nothing but bloody stumps?

He put out a hand and encountered something ice cold. The feel and texture was familiar and he knew it to be dead flesh. Only now did he force his eyelids open, breaking the crust of dried blood that had held them shut. He was lying on the naked body of a dead man. Only inches from Beddowes's eyes there was a mass of blackened bloody flesh; his gorge rose as he realized that what he was looking at had once been a face.

The two of them lay snugly at the bottom of a hole, a narrow space about eight feet long, and almost twice as deep. It appeared to have been dug a long time ago, for the sides had sprouted grass and weeds, while the sky up above was almost obscured by a thick overhang of gorse.

Beddowes had been a soldier too long to let the cadaver bother him, once the initial shock had passed. He returned to the matter in hand, and, teeth gritted against the pain, he curled his body round, searching with his right arm until he located his thigh. He pinched it hard, and a whole new set of fiery needles were thrust into his flesh, all the way down to his foot. Knowing that sensation could lie, he didn't accept this as sure evidence, but continued exploring with eyes and fingers until he had satisfied himself that no vital parts of his body were missing. As to his injuries, his head and his left arm seemed to have taken the worst damage. One side of his skull was matted with the blood which had glued his eyes shut and run into his mouth. His left arm was swollen, and he had no doubt that it was broken.

The barrage of shot had faded into the rhythmic thud of his own pulse, hammering inside his head. A lull in the battle perhaps, or had the sounds existed only in his mind? Beddowes shouted as loud as he could, hoping to summon some other survivor to his aid. His mouth was dry and his voice lacked its usual volume, but he was confident it should be heard above ground. There was no response, however, and after a while he fell silent. He began to think, and his first thoughts were troubling; he couldn't remember where he was. His clearest memory put him at a skirmish not far from Maiwand, yet he was sure he had survived it. Hadn't Colonel Margrave complemented him on his conduct during a parade a few days later? As he pondered, the scene became clearer, and he lifted his right arm, remembering something. He was mildly puzzled to see the filthy tattered sleeve; he wasn't in uniform, but for the moment that was unimportant.

Beddowes gripped the thin cloth in his teeth and tore it away. He stared at the small white scar in astonishment; it was old, barely visible under the layer of dirt that caked his skin. He'd been unlucky enough to take a spent bullet in the arm as they flushed out a nest of rebels from the ruins of the town. In the heat of battle he'd barely noticed, completing his mission before reporting to the surgeon to have the pellet of lead removed. This had been the subject of Colonel Margrave's commendation and, as more slivers of memory returned to him, he recalled that the incident had resulted in some good-natured leg-pulling from his platoon.

Hurt, baffled and exhausted, Beddowes allowed his eyelids to drift shut, and for a while he gave no more thought to his predicament. He awoke in darkness to a new problem; he had a raging thirst. A faint sound from above suggested it might be raining, but only a few stray spots of water made their way through the tangled bushes above, most of them falling on the cold naked flesh of his silent companion. He licked at these damp spots avidly; he knew of men who turned cannibal when it was their only chance of survival, and was grateful that for the present he wasn't bothered by hunger.

To distract himself from thoughts of fresh water, Beddowes investigated his clothes, and found that all of them were as filthy and dilapidated as his shirt, and none bore the faintest resemblance to any kind of uniform, except one of his boots, which might, a very long time ago, have belonged to a soldier, though it had been a man with feet at least one size smaller than his own. He found, to his disgust, that his hair was as long and matted as his beard, and that it was infested with lice, a plague he'd fought successfully during most of his military career. Beddowes had no idea how or when he'd come by a discharge. More importantly perhaps, he couldn't understand how he'd fallen into such abject poverty, to end his days starving and thrown into a pit.

By dawn the rain was falling harder, and showering down upon him; a trickle of water was dripping off the leaves of a plant a few feet above Beddowes' head. He drank thankfully, though his body began to shiver as the wet penetrated his ragged clothes. Hugging his right arm around his chest for warmth, his hand encountered something tucked inside his shirt; it was a lump of bread, hard, but perfectly edible. Soaked in water, this made a welcome breakfast.

Fed and watered, Beddowes looked at the walls of the pit which might well be his grave; with two sound arms it would have been easy enough to heave himself out, but crippled as he was, the process would be difficult, maybe impossible. The rain stopped, quite abruptly, which gave him heart for the task. As he attacked the wet mud with the heel of his one half-decent boot, a flash of memory came to him. He'd returned to England, he was sure of it, and he recalled exchanging his military uniform for another, that of an officer of the law. It was a heartening thought. But what then?

No matter how he racked his brain he had no recollection of the reason for this fall into destitution; all he achieved was an increasingly severe headache. At last he gave up and concentrated on digging his way to freedom.

After some time the sky above him turned to a deep summer blue. The sun crept along the top of the wall of the pit, coming gradually lower until he could feel it warming the top of his head as he worked. With three steps dug into the wall, and some hopes that he might be able to climb out, Beddowes turned to look at the dead man who lay at his feet, illuminated now by sunlight. The cut of his thin hair and the softness of his hands proclaimed the corpse to be that of a gentleman, as did the faint scent of some kind of pomade, now overlaid with a far more pungent and unpleasant odour. Since the man had no features, it was doubtful if anybody would be able to recognize him. He'd been of slender build, and perhaps a little over five and a half feet tall. There was no clue to suggest any link between them.

Since his memory had failed him, Beddowes turned to speculation. It seemed likely the two of them had been attacked at the same time, and the other man robbed of his clothes because they were of some value, whereas even a scarecrow would have provided better garb for a thief than his own poor rags. Was it chance that obliterated the man's features, or had it been a deliberate attempt to make him unrecognizable? His right hand had also suffered a severe blow, perhaps as he tried to protect himself; it was black with blood and grossly swollen.

Beddowes' eye caught something that looked out of place among the dried gore, and he bent to take a closer look. There was a ring upon the man's little finger, only the barest glint of silver giving away its presence; the thieves must have missed it. Beddowes looked about him but there was nothing sharp, not even a stone, which he could use to cut away the dead flesh that surrounded the tiny glimmer of metal. Despite his desperate poverty, he felt a surge of distaste at the thought of stealing from a corpse; if only he could remember something about this man. He might have been a friend, or a deadly enemy. The thought brought another, but common sense assured him that he hadn't killed his silent companion. The absence of the man's clothes, the similarity of the injuries they'd both suffered, not to mention being hidden together from prying eyes, all suggested otherwise.

The removal of the ring with no tools but one bare hand and his teeth was an unpleasant task, but Beddowes managed it eventually. Without stopping to examine his prize he wiped it clean and tied it up in his shirt tail. A few minutes later he climbed into the warming sunlight, aching in every part of his body but very much alive. He found himself in a bleak moorland landscape. A jagged ruin of stone, evidently the remains of a chimney, gave the world a two-fingered salute, only yards from the pit. He had no recollection of ever seeing such a place before.

He felt sure he was in England. A clear

blue sky stretched above him. The plants at his feet suggested late summer, as did the height of the sun. He needed no other compass but the one in his head, although he had no idea which direction he should take. Some instinct, perhaps some shred of recall, turned him to the west. With his back to the fallen chimney, he chose a lone tree and began to struggle towards it through the wilderness of gorse and heather.

Chapter Eight

Lucille tossed and turned in her bed. When Mortleigh returned from his mission of mercy, she'd been shocked by the strength of her feelings for him; she'd never known such a powerful longing, and during that first evening it had been difficult to keep up the pretence of a civil conversation with her husband while her lover sat at the table. Every time she met Mortleigh's eyes she saw the naked hunger in them, and knew her own were answering with equal desperation. All her life she'd been independent, and emotionally cold. To care so much for anyone was deeply disturbing. She was enslaved, in thrall to a man; it dismayed her to acknowledge she was as helpless to escape as the foolish Jackman.

She reminded herself that she was Lady Pickhurst; thanks to her father's careful handling of the marriage settlement she was one of the richest women in the country. It had been her choice to accept the empty attentions of a doting old man in return for a life of wealth and ease. It was too late now to wonder if she'd done the wrong thing.

When Lord Pickhurst came to her bed at

the end of the evening, she welcomed him with warmth. While her thoughts were with her lover, she was able to close her eyes and her mind sufficiently to prevent recoiling at her husband's touch. When he rolled away from her and began to snore, she was free to think of the man who lay sleeping in the guest wing. She edged to the side of her bed, lying wakeful, aching with longing to be in Mortleigh's arms. It was pointless trying to pretend; ever since that first encounter, her body burned for his touch. For a moment she even considered going to him, but she dared not.

Having slept badly, Lucille felt weary and distracted the next morning; Mortleigh knew how it was with her. It was obvious in his secret smile and the kiss he blew off the top of a finger when Lord Pickhurst's back was turned. The day passed in long hours of torment; even to see her lover sent a rush of heat through her body, but it was impossible to avoid him. Now she lay in her bed again, listening to the familiar rhythmic snorts from the next room.

She would be free of her husband's attentions for a few hours; he rarely had the energy to visit her two nights in a row. Tonight, once again, the men hadn't stayed long at the table, but when her husband came upstairs he hadn't come near her door. She heard him grunting peevishly at Parke as the valet

110

helped him into bed.

Mortleigh had hardly spoken to her all day, but as he passed her in the hall before dinner he had whispered a few urgent words in her ear. He intended to give his lordship a sleeping draught; she would be free to come to his room once the household was safely in bed and asleep.

Despite the fever running through her veins Lucille tossed restlessly in her bed as the clock slowly ticked away the hours. Her thoughts were a torment. She'd always considered lust to be a sin which ensnared men, not women. If some particularly fiery sermon briefly pierced her armour of self-esteem, Lucille might acknowledge herself capable of greed, jealousy, even hatred, but to her, the physical cravings of the body had always seemed a particularly masculine sin. Lying in bed for a second lonely night, she knew she was wrong.

She had no faith; the threat of burning in hell held no fears for her, and yet she delayed. Arrogant and worldly as Mortleigh was, she had no wish to add to his hateful self-assurance. She told herself he was no better than a thief and a rapist, stealing her virtue in the night, and yet she couldn't deny him; she'd been his from the moment his hands first touched her flesh.

The clock on the mantel struck one. She shuddered, her whole body aflame with desire. The battle was lost.

Knytte lay silent, only the faint creak of old timbers accompanying her as she crept along the deserted passage. Mortleigh let her in at once when she scratched at the door, reaching to draw her into the room and into his arms, his mouth hungrily upon hers before she had a chance to utter a sound, his free hand groping for her buttocks and pulling her roughly against him, so she could feel his hardness. Something inside Lucille rejoiced in his impatience. His need matched hers.

Mortleigh pushed the robe off her shoulder, nuzzling down her neck. Suddenly Lucille drew back, pushing him away. 'No,' she said.

For a second he was stunned to immobility. A wicked smile curved his lips but didn't light his dark eyes. He took her wrist in a vice-like grip. 'Oh, are we to play games, my pretty little tease?'

'No,' she said more urgently. 'There must be no more marks. It was hard enough to hide the souvenirs you left before; I scratched and scraped at the bite on my neck to disguise it, and made up a story about slipping in my bath. My husband is not a fool.'

'You offer me milk and water when I've already tasted strong wine,' he grumbled, but he relinquished his hold, and his hands were gentle as he stripped the robe from her, smiling when he realized it was all she wore.

'There are many different wines,' she said, stretching her arms above her head and making a slow and sinuous pirouette, 'and each of them has their place upon the table of a discerning man.'

He carried her to the bed, where the light from the lamp was stronger. For a long tense moment he stared down at her naked body. Lucille slowly put her hands to her breasts, cupping them invitingly, and moving a little to the yielding softness of the mattress. Still he only stood and looked. Driven by her mounting need for him, she caressed her own flesh, tracking the lines his fingers had followed upon her body on their previous encounter, as if his touch had left unseen traces.

Mortleigh delayed his response until she was almost ready to scream with frustration. 'I shall do my best to suit my tastes to the occasion,' he said at last, lowering himself on top of her.

Later, as the first light of dawn showed through the heavy hangings at the window, they lay wound together, sated by a night such as Lucille had never experienced. Despite her words of caution, there was a darkening bruise upon her thigh; in response her fingernails had gouged new scratches down his back.

'What do you think of Knytte?' Lucille asked, hoisting herself up so she could study his face, dark upon the pale linen.

'I haven't seen much of it,' he replied, opening his eyes to look into hers. He spoke carelessly, but his expression matched hers; this was no idle talk. 'It appears to be a very rich estate.'

'Oh yes, very rich. And one day it will belong to me.'

Fully awake now, he stared at her, open greed upon the sallow features. 'Surely it's entailed. I heard Lord Pickhurst has an heir, his sister's child. Didn't I see him in the garden?'

'If he lives, the boy gets the title,' Lucille said carelessly, 'and an old manor house across the moor, with a few hundred acres of land. It was the family seat, long ago.' She curled herself against him, catlike, rubbing her face upon his cheek. 'My father is not a man to make mistakes, his lawyer checked the exact wording of every document before the marriage was agreed,' she said softly. 'Women are entitled to own property now, and to keep it. When my husband dies, Knytte will be mine. Of course, his lordship hopes to produce a son, that's why he chose to marry again so late in life.' She laughed. 'He buried two wives without producing so much as a sickly daughter, which suggests the task has always been beyond him.'

'I hate to think of his hands on you,' Mortleigh said, surprisingly vehement.

'Oh, he has the use of a great deal more than his hands,' she teased. 'Considering his age he is reasonably proficient. You must share me for a little while. Nobody knows what the future holds.' Lucille smiled at the shadows above his head. 'Old men die.'

'Yes,' he mused, tracing a finger down her cheek, and not quite repeating her words. 'All men die.'

'You're leaving so soon?' Lucille hissed angrily, watching the door warily as she and Mortleigh stood confronting each other across the salon. It was dangerous to converse openly while her husband was in the house, but since Lord Pickhurst had spent the day at home there had been no opportunity to talk.

'Laidlaw promised to write, as soon as he had seen his doctor,' Mortleigh said. 'It has been two days and I haven't heard from him. There were letters from town this morning, but nothing from my friend. Naturally I'm concerned.'

Lucille pouted. 'Why didn't you instruct your man to stay with him, if you felt it was so important? Anyway, you don't need to travel to London yourself. Send a message. My husband has an agent in Holborn, he could be instructed to call upon Mr Laidlaw on your behalf.'

'But by that time two more days will have

passed.' Mortleigh was calm but implacable; as always when she argued with him, she was losing. 'I must go to London, but I shall return. Don't you know your own power? I can't escape your bewitchment so easily.' He drew closer; they were almost touching. 'What is this hold you have over me? Do you slip some love potion into my wine at the table every night?'

'Don't be a fool,' she snapped crossly, turning her back on him and storming across to the window. 'It's too late to catch a train tonight, it will soon be dark. You must stay until the morning at least.' She dropped her voice to a seductive whisper. 'My husband will be tired, after riding around the park with you for so long, I have no doubt he will sleep soundly. Must I wander the house like a ghost in my shift, looking for company and finding none?'

She watched his reflection in the glass while pretending to look out at the garden; a hint of a smile reached his cold eyes. 'How could any man refuse you? Laidlaw can wait a few more hours, but I shall leave at first light and catch an early train. All being well, I shall return to Knytte on Tuesday.'

'Tuesday?' She rounded on him. 'I thought you expected to find the wretched man better, yet you're staying long enough to bury him.'

He chuckled. 'You have such a charitable

spirit, Lady Pickhurst, I swear you are the most soft hearted woman I ever met. I doubt if Laidlaw will require more than an hour or two of my time, but I have other affairs which cannot be neglected.' He strode across and took her hand. 'I shall not sleep tonight until you come to me,' he said softly, 'no matter how late.' He touched each of her fingers in turn with his lips. 'The days will pass. Only the most spoilt child doesn't learn that waiting for a treat makes it all the better when the desired day arrives. On Tuesday a poor weary traveller will present himself at your husband's door yet again, and a few hours later I shall be with you, while he sleeps with the help of my little bottle.'

'As always it's a woman's part to wait,' Lucille said peevishly, 'and to trust in a man. In case my company is not enough to make you honour your promise, there is something else you might keep in mind. I shouldn't like you to be tempted into the bed of some other rich man's wife.' Lucille stood on tiptoe to whisper in his ear. She spoke only a few brief words, but Mortleigh turned away, his eyes deep unfathomable pools as he stared out on Knytte's lush garden. After a long pause, he lifted her hand again, and bit down hard upon the cushion of flesh below her thumb.

'You wish to tie me tight, your ladyship,' he said lightly, 'like a spider spinning her deadly web.'

'Is my offer not sufficiently generous to tempt you, sir?'

'I have never heard better,' he replied, 'but a man may take a little longer than a woman to agree to sell his soul.'

Beddowes had lost track of time since he climbed out of the pit that was intended to be his grave; it might have been two days ago, or three, he couldn't tell. Spells of delirium overcame him and he wandered aimlessly across the moors, only to turn towards the west whenever his senses returned to him. For a while he was convinced that his old sergeant major, a man who had fought at Balaklava, was marching at his side, barking commands in his ear, or leaning close to share some illogical advice. 'Survival, lad, that's the ticket. Keep your back straight and your rifle clean, and make your poor mother proud. One foot after the other, but make sure it's left, right, not right, left, got that? Be a bloody officer, you will, long as you do what I tell you.'

During his more lucid moments Beddowes knew himself to be hopelessly lost, but since the alternative to struggling onwards was to lie down in the mud and die, he walked on. He'd done his best to tend his broken arm, sacrificing most of his ragged shirt to bind it tightly to a piece of rotting wood he dragged from a bog, and strapping it high across his chest. This at least had returned some feeling to his swollen fingers, and now and then they would strum a beat in time with the thunderous drumbeat that crashed through his aching head.

There was stained brown water to be had occasionally, so he was rarely thirsty, but he had eaten only grass stems, a handful of bilberries and a few clover flowers since he finished the lump of bread. As another day began, and he struggled to his feet yet again, Beddowes felt a weakness in his limbs that warned him he was nearly at the end of his strength. Setting his back to the sun, he started off, only to come to a halt almost at once. A bird was flying low towards him, with something in its claws. The instinct for survival hadn't deserted him; he bent to pick up a stone, and flung it with careful desperation. His shot missed the bird, but sent the raptor spiralling higher in alarm. A small dead rabbit fell almost at Beddowes's feet.

A soldier learns to eat what and when he can. It wasn't the first time the sergeant had eaten raw meat; he tore at the warm carcass with his teeth, sucking every morsel of goodness from the gift fate had sent him. He still had no idea where he was, or how he'd come to be trapped in this godforsaken moorland, but some scraps of memory had returned. Despite the evidence of his tattered clothes and the state of his hair and beard, he believed himself to be Sergeant Thomas Beddowes, a detective in London's police force. That conviction was all he had, and all he needed, to keep him moving.

The old library had provided a great deal of material on Knytte's history, and Phoebe had fetched books and maps for Lord Pickhurst's heir to study. She had also brought up some books with coloured illustrations of flowers to occupy Eliza. Once the children were settled, she picked up the keys she had borrowed; the butler hadn't been too happy at letting them out of his sight, and she must take them back.

'I am going to look at the cloisters again before I return Mr Henson's keys,' she said. 'I shan't be long, and you have plenty to occupy yourselves. Annie, you're to stay with the children while I'm gone. Master Rodney, I shall expect to see those notes complete by the time I return.'

'Yes, Miss Drake,' the child answered, his mind already on the document he was unfolding, his eyes alight with the thrill of discovery. She smiled, pleased with his enthusiasm, took one last look at the little girl to make sure she was equally engaged, then slipped out of the room. She hurried downstairs, along the corridor to the ancient door that led through the monk's refectory and thence to the ruins. Going this way, it was unlikely anybody in the house would see her leave.

Jonah was not alone, there were two other men working with him. Phoebe hid in one of the shadowy carrels lining the cloister and watched anxiously; she mustn't be long, but she was reluctant to leave without having a word with her cousin. Five full minutes passed before her opportunity came; Jonah ordered his assistants to carry one of the new steps up into the tower.

'Jonah.' As soon as he was alone Phoebe called, beckoning him to join her. He came, but there was a frown on his normally open features.

'What are you doing here?'

'I had to speak to you. I know you have feelings for Lady Pickhurst. I'm sorry but you must listen. You know how dangerous it is. Go on as you are and your life will be ruined.'

'You've got no business spying on me, or trying to interfere with my business!' He loomed over her, a fist raised in anger.

Phoebe had never seen her cousin lose his temper before. She took a step away from him, tears brimming in her eyes, but she lifted her chin, refusing to be cowed. There might never be another chance to persuade him to give up his folly.

'If you don't care about yourself, at least

think about her ladyship. If you were discovered together her reputation would be ruined. Who can guess what Lord Pickhurst might do?'

'Are you threatening to tell tales?' His face was contorted. It was like looking at a stranger; the boy she had known and loved all her life had vanished.

Phoebe gasped. 'How can you say such a thing? You're as close to me as a brother, Jonah, and I care about you. I want to help, that's all. Please–'

'Don't say another word. I didn't believe Lucille when she told me you were jealous, but she's right, isn't she? You've set your mind on having me for yourself, because you're afraid you'll never find a man any other way. I suppose even a cousin would be better than nothing, even if he's not a gentleman.'

Shocked to silence, she stared at him. 'I've never...' she began, struggling to find words. He was already turning away.

'Jonah,' she called after him, recovering her voice. 'I've only ever wanted to be your friend, your sister. If you ever need me, I'll be here.' He gave no sign of having heard, vanishing swiftly into the tower.

Chapter Nine

Lucille didn't want to attend the garden party. It was being given by Reverend and Mrs Stoppen to celebrate the nineteenth birthday of their daughter, Agatha. The girl was pretty, in a vacuous kind of way, and she flirted outrageously, keeping a dozen or more suitors constantly at her side. As a married woman Lucille was no longer allowed to encourage the attentions of young men, or not openly at least, and she hated to see single girls like Agatha enjoying themselves.

Having considered inventing some minor malady to keep her at home, Lucille decided against it. Since Lord Pickhurst's greatest wish was for a son, he was tiresomely solicitous whenever she was indisposed, imagining she might be showing early signs of pregnancy and preparing to provide Knytte with an heir.

Putting on a new dress, adorning her hair, neck and arms with some of the jewels he'd bestowed upon her, and her face with a gracious smile, Lucille went downstairs to accompany her husband to their neighbour's house. Lord Pickhurst took her arm and led her to the carriage, looking as if he might burst with pride.

They went in the dress chariot, bought for their wedding. At least Lucille could be confident that nobody would arrive in smarter style. She had mixed feelings about Mortleigh's absence. Since he was her husband's friend she could have danced with him once or twice without arousing suspicion, but then she would also have to watch Agatha and her friends competing for his attention.

Dunsby Court was attractive, though small in comparison with Knytte. The grounds were acknowledged to be very fine, the approach being flanked by a double avenue of beech trees, with woodland to the west to act as a windbreak. Lucille stared unseeingly at the trees. Thinking of Agatha had aroused her suspicions. Perhaps Mortleigh had gone to London to see another woman. If so, would he ever come back? The thought tormented her; he'd promised to return. He must return. And once he did he must be persuaded to accept her scheme, and never leave again.

A small movement caught Lucille's attention. Beyond the avenue, a horseman was picking his way through the wood, only visible for a moment now and then. He was bending low, as if trying not to be seen. It struck her as strange that anyone should choose such an inconvenient approach to the house. She looked away for a second, to see if her husband had noticed the rider, but he was studying the herd of cattle grazing beyond the fence on the other side of the avenue. When Lucille turned back the horseman had vanished.

The chariot bowled on, and very soon Dunsby Court came into sight. Several carriages were drawn up at the entrance, but instead of entering the house, a trickle of guests were strolling towards a large marquee on the lawn, beside which a group of musicians were playing a pastoral melody.

'How pleasant,' Lord Pickhurst said complacently. 'Of course the house has no room to accommodate so many, they have nothing here to rival Knytte, the garden has always been the best feature of Dunsby.'

'I suppose so,' Lucille said absently.

'My dear?' Lord Pickhurst patted her knee. 'Is anything wrong?'

'You will think me petty minded if I tell you,' Lucille replied, wearing her sweetest smile. 'I find Miss Agatha Stoppen a terrible flirt. I hate to see such unbecoming behaviour.'

Returning her smile, her husband nodded. 'She's been over-indulged, but we shan't be obliged to spend much time in her company.'

Lucille sighed. 'You're always so good tempered. To me, garden parties are a trial. The dirt ruins my shoes, and I don't care to prance about doing country dances.'

'Poor Lucille. By next season you shall have a ballroom that is the envy of the county, and if you find the local families tiresome, we'll send to London for better company.'

The event was all Lucille had expected; she found fault with the garden, the heat inside the marquee, the intensity of the sun outside, and almost every person she encountered. Very soon she developed the headache she had considered inventing that morning, and begged her husband to take her into the house, where the light would be less bright.

'Of course, my dear,' Lord Pickhurst took her arm as she rose from her seat. 'That will suit me well. Reverend Stoppen has recently added some new paintings to his collection, and he invited me to inspect them at my leisure.'

With all the guests on the lawns or in the marquee, and the servants tending to their needs, the house was strangely deserted. They saw nobody as they ascended to the third floor, where the gallery filled the west side of the house. Lord Pickhurst instructed his young wife on the merits of half a dozen paintings, and she maintained an air of polite interest, until they came to a semi-circular bay window. A chair was conveniently placed to give Lucille a view of the gardens and with a blind drawn halfway down to shade her from the sun she was content to leave her husband to continue his tour alone.

From this height Lucille found herself looking down on the woodland where she had seen the rider. The trees were sparser near the house, and there was only a narrow belt of them curving around to the north. Even so, it took her several minutes to spot the dark shape that moved a little amongst the greenery. A horse, completely hidden from the revellers in the garden, and almost certainly the one she had seen earlier, was browsing quietly from the tree branch where it was tied.

Lucille was intrigued. She wondered if Miss Stoppen had an unsuitable lover; it seemed likely that some young man had come to the party uninvited. Five minutes elapsed before the horse made a sudden movement; it lifted its head, ears pricked. Lucille looked to see what had caught the animal's interest. A figure, muffled and cloaked in a way that was totally unsuitable for such a fine warm day, came hurrying from the rear of the house. He was visible only for a moment, but he reappeared between the trees and she saw him unhitch the horse and step into the saddle. For a second he glanced towards the house, his head tilted up so the sun caught it.

Lucille drew in a gasp of astonishment.

Unless he had a twin, there could be no mistaking the man she had just seen; it was Mortleigh.

A hand descended on her shoulder, and she jumped violently.

'I'm sorry, my dear, I didn't mean to startle you.' Lord Pickhurst moved around her to sit at her side. 'What are you finding so fascinating out there? Assignations in the shrubbery perhaps?' he added playfully.

'No, nothing like that,' Lucille said, recalling herself to the part of doting wife with some difficulty. 'My thoughts were far away.' In fact they were riding through the belt of woodland. Mortleigh's betrayal beat in her head like the thud of a drum, and it was all she could do to hide her fury from her husband. Why had he told her such a blatant lie? He'd never intended to return to London. It must have been his intention to pay court to Agatha Stoppen all the time.

'Your contemplation seems to have made you unhappy,' Lord Pickhurst commented, and Lucille at once put a hand over her eyes.

'You are so good at seeing such things, my love,' she said. 'I have the most unpleasant headache. Do you think we might go home without giving offence? The pain is making me weary, and the bright sunlight is really more than I can stand.'

All concern, Lord Pickhurst ordered the

128

carriage at once, and they made their fare-wells with indecent haste. Agatha Stoppen was nowhere to be seen, which seemed to Lucille to be of great significance. She sat in silence all the way back to Knytte, hiding behind closed eyes. In the red darkness she imagined Mortleigh standing on the road before them, and pictured the body he'd taught her to worship being trampled into the mud beneath the hoofs of the horses. Her fury was almost too much to bear.

As soon as they were home Lucille retired to her room, getting rid of her husband by declaring herself in need of sleep above all else. She couldn't think clearly. Her mind was filled with images of a dozen acts of vengeance, all of them impossible to carry out. Mortleigh was clever, and physically strong. If she hoped to punish him she needed an ally.

Marching towards the old stairs some min-utes later, too angry to be cautious, she heard sounds from the nursery, but the doors were shut. Nobody saw her as she let herself out into the ruins. She heard the chink of tools. There were men working there, Jonah among them; the slow rhythm of his deep voice was unmistakable. It wasn't necessary to speak to him, or even to see him. They had long since worked out a system of messages; she had only to work her way to the stone carrel where he habitually left the hat and coat he wore on his way to and from his work. She dropped a glove there, a plain cotton thing, but scented with a perfume he would recognize.

Lucille returned to her room on light feet. In time she would find a way to pay Mortleigh for his betrayal. An assignation with another man was merely the start and Jonah's adoration would be balm for her wounded pride. The possibility that her faithless lover wouldn't return to Knytte flickered briefly through her thoughts. She could guess why he'd gone clandestinely to Dunsby Court. Reverend Stoppen was a very wealthy man, and everyone knew he hoped to marry his only daughter into the nobility; a suitor who had no title would be unwelcome. Perhaps, Lucille thought, her fury making her cheeks flame, he planned to carry Agatha off in the middle of the night.

'Docket, there you are.' Sir Martin slammed a hand irritably upon his desk. 'Where have you been? It's almost time to dress for dinner, and you know how her ladyship hates to be kept waiting.'

'I'm sorry,' the young man replied, doing his best to slap the dust from his coat. He'd been riding most of the day, and he was as tired and jaded as his horse. 'I believe I may have some information regarding Sergeant Beddowes. I fear it's not good news.'

'What do you mean? Where is he?'

'As for that, I still don't know. The rumour is several days out of date, and it comes from a source that isn't totally reliable, but it's the best I could do.'

His employer scowled. 'And you call this information? Well, spit it out, man.'

'A derelict answering the sergeant's description was seen at the King's Arms, the day after we left him at the cross-roads. Apparently he was accosted by several men known to be involved in smuggling. My informant tells me he left shortly after with a pair of these rum-runners, one of whom was probably Bragg. If it was Beddowes, I'm afraid he may have received some rough handling, my informant said the tramp didn't go with his captors willingly.' He hesitated, looking at Sir Martin as if to judge his mood. 'I was wondering if you would allow me to offer a small reward for information. The brotherhood is loyal in the main, but somebody may be willing to tell us more, given an incentive.'

'It would be unwise to betray his identity, so how would you explain our interest in a tramp?'

'I thought we might suggest that he's a possible witness,' Docket said. 'There can't be a soul in the county who isn't aware of the jewellery thefts by now, and it's quite feasible that a travelling man might have seen or heard something useful to our enquiries.'

Sir Martin nodded. 'Very well, offer five guineas for information leading to his safe delivery, either here or to my office in Hagstock.' He rose to his feet. 'Now, if there's nothing more...'

He was interrupted by a knock at the door. A message had come from Dunsby Court, and it was marked MOST URGENT. Sir Martin broke the seal and read quickly, his expression darkening. When he had finished he thrust the paper into Docket's hands. 'I want Beddowes found,' he barked. 'Go to the printer at once and get some handbills out. Have him work through the night if necessary.' He strode from the room.

Docket read the message, his eyes widening. 'Another one,' he breathed. 'There'll be sparks flying if you don't turn up soon, Sergeant. Mind you, if I was a betting man, I'm not sure I'd risk a guinea on ever seeing hide or hair of you again.'

Phoebe had trouble persuading Rodney to go to bed, and she sat with him for nearly two hours, reading quietly. At last, when her eyes ached with the strain of making out the letters in the flickering candlelight, the boy's breathing became slow and regular, and with a sigh she straightened her aching limbs and rose, stretching. The boy's nightmares had diminished a little recently, and Phoebe wondered if she might risk leaving him alone, to spend a night in her own bed.

Annie was shirking her duties as nursery maid again; many of the more mundane evening tasks rightly belonged to her, but with a mistress who cared nothing for the children and even less for their governess, there was nobody to whom Phoebe could report her insolence, apart from the house-keeper. She suspected if she did so the servants would close ranks against her, and make life even more intolerable.

She knelt to sweep the grate. The girl had sulked when ordered to bring up coal, retorting that it was too early to have a fire. True, autumn had barely begun, but Rodney found firelight a comfort, so she'd told the girl to light it and stop grumbling, which was probably why she'd neglected her other tasks.

Those who lived below stairs saw the post of governess as a position of privilege, but there were times when Phoebe wished she was a humble maid, for at least then she might have company in the servants' hall. With the fire raked to a dull safe glow she tidied the room and went to close the curtains, another of Annie's jobs.

No lights shone from the house, although it was only a little after ten. A sliver of moon illuminated the gardens, and Phoebe stopped to look out at their ethereal beauty. It was early for the household to have retired to bed, but she had gathered from Annie, before the girl was overtaken by her sullen fit, that Lady Pickhurst had returned from the garden party feeling unwell. With the lady of the house not joining his lordship for dinner, and no other company, the meal would have been short, and everyone released from their duties sooner than was usual.

The loveliness before her eyes seeped into Phoebe's spirit and calmed her; she was fortunate to be able to enjoy such a sight, and there was no point worrying about what might happen in the future. She had reasons enough to be content; Rodney was an apt pupil and they both enjoyed their lessons, while Eliza was a permanently cheerful child. Tending the children was a pleasure, and she could be satisfied with that for the moment. A breeze had sprung up and the tops of the trees were moving against the moon. An owl called, before flitting across the lawn like a ghost, flying from its home in the ruins and heading for the rough grass in the park.

Half smiling, Phoebe began to turn away, her thoughts on sleep, but a sense of some movement among the shrubs at the far side of the lawn made her pause. The branches of a bush were moving where no wind stirred. Phoebe bit her lip, worry flooding back and all her good intentions forgotten in an instant. This had happened before, and she thought she knew who lurked there, where they had no business to be.

Sure enough, the figure of a large man appeared, walking half bent as if that would make him less visible. She saw him for only a second, but there could be no mistake; it was Jonah.

She saw him again, as he crossed an open space and ducked swiftly into the shadow cast by the summerhouse. He didn't re-appear. Phoebe, her hand to her mouth, sank onto a chair. She'd hoped the liaison was over. Suppose she wasn't the only person standing looking out at the moonlit garden?

Sitting in the dark, watching the moon-shadows moving inch by inch across the lawn, Phoebe listened for the slight creak of floorboards. She dreaded to hear the familiar scratch at the door and the mocking laugh which so disturbed Rodney's sleep; it would certainly start his nightmares again. Going out for her clandestine assignations, the woman who made those sounds must have heard him cry out; it seemed she delighted in frightening the boy.

Phoebe was suddenly angry. To Lady Pick-hurst, rich, beautiful and spoilt, the children meant nothing, and nor did Jonah Jackman. He was merely a diversion, a plaything to be tossed aside when she tired of him. He would be badly hurt, but if the affair was discovered he would suffer a great deal worse than a broken heart.

The footsteps came, soft and swift, just audible in the silence of the night. This time there was no scratch at the door, but a line of light moved across the gap at the bottom, before fading away. Phoebe dug her finger-nails into the palms of her hands; if only there was something she could do, some way to cure Jonah of his infatuation. She knew what Lady Pickhurst's true character was, the whole household was aware of her selfishness, the streak of idle malice that made her so hated by those who had to serve her.

With sudden decision, Phoebe rose. She hadn't prepared herself for bed and was still fully dressed. She fetched her dark brown coat and put it on. Opening the door an inch, she peered out and saw a wavering light shining from the stair. With exaggerated care, she stepped out, closed the door behind her, and set off to follow it.

Chapter Ten

Phoebe felt her way cautiously along the corridor and down the stairs, inching each foot forward carefully for fear of falling. A sound told her that Lady Pickhurst, if that was whom she was following, had opened the ancient door. When it closed total blackness descended. It had been foolish to come without a candle, but she'd only thought about remaining unseen.

It took a minute to reach the door, and another to summon up the courage to open it. The wind had strengthened and it was difficult to keep the heavy oak door open while she slipped through; Phoebe almost had it snatched from her fingers as she eased it shut behind her. A glimmer of moonlight lit her way across the old refectory, but the place was cold and full of shadows, while the wind whistled eerily through gaps in the stonework.

Phoebe almost turned to flee. The thought of Jonah stopped her; she wouldn't see him dismissed and disgraced, not if there was any way to prevent it. She ran across the room to escape into the cloisters. Here a light showed dully from within one of the carrels. Shivering with fear and with her heart pounding, she pressed her back to the cold stone wall. There was nothing to hear but the moaning of the wind, nothing to see except the dim steady glow. It took a long time to persuade herself to go on, and when she did she found only a lantern, left unattended on a stone shelf. The mistress of Knytte had gone on, relying on the moon to show her the way.

Gathering her courage, Phoebe ran on silent feet through the ruins, where imagination suggested a dozen kinds of evil lurking unseen among the deep pools of darkness. The night crowded closer, feeding the ancient terror that lies hidden in every human heart. Reaching the archway which led into the garden she stopped, leaning gratefully against the old stones; this was a familiar spot, a refuge from her earlier panic. It took only a moment to regain her breath and her composure. When there was a lull in the moaning of the wind she could hear the hushed sounds of the creatures that took over the garden by night, and once, pitched low, there was the murmur of human voices.

Crouching low to avoid being seen, Phoebe made her way slowly towards the summer house.

'You speak of love, yet you refuse me the one small thing I ask of you.' Lady Pickhurst's voice came to her, quite clear in the silence. It was filled with an overwhelming sadness. If Phoebe hadn't known her, hadn't seen how deceitful the woman could be, she might have believed the emotion to be real.

'You know I'd give my life for you,' Jonah protested. 'I love you, with all my heart.'

'Then hold me,' the woman murmured. 'Show me this love and help me bear this awful burden my life has become.'

Jonah made a sound that was barely human, between a groan and a sigh. 'You make me a sinner in the eyes of God and man. This is so wrong, yet I can't help myself...'

Phoebe turned and stumbled back the way she'd come, too overcome with what she'd heard to fear the darkness awaiting her in the ruins. How could Jonah be so foolish? If they were discovered he would lose every-thing, all for the sake of an hour in that wicked woman's arms.

When she reached the lighted lantern Phoebe paused. At the very least, she would let them know their rendezvous had been discovered. Poor Jonah was blinded by love, but Phoebe didn't believe Lady Pickhurst would jeopardize her position in society, perhaps her very life, for any man, let alone a poor stonemason.

She picked up the lamp and took it with her, back towards the old refectory. Turning the wick down until the flame died, she placed the lantern on the floor in the brightest of the moonlight, where anyone coming that way couldn't help but see it.

Phoebe opened the door and stepped through, but as she turned to close it the rising wind caught the heavy oak planks. The door crashed back into its frame, the noise so loud it hurt her ears. Stunned, she stood in total darkness as the sound echoed around her. It must have awakened half the household. Frantically she groped for the wall; there should be no obstacles to impede her, apart from the doorway of the old library. Here she almost fell, but then her hand smacked into the door and she recovered her balance, to run blindly on in the dark. At the foot of the stairs she stumbled again, landing on her knees.

Sobs rising in her throat, Phoebe scurried up to the first floor. She was at the top of the stairs and halfway to the nursery when she heard a door open. A light appeared from below and a querulous voice called out, it sounded like Mr Henson, the butler.

'Who's there?'

Phoebe ran on, grasping the handle of the nursery door, unbuttoning her dress with urgent fingers as she went through. Only seconds later she was back, wearing a nightgown and with a candlestick in her hand, as if she had come directly from her bed.

Coper, one of the footmen, appeared at the top of the stairs, a light held aloft. 'Miss

Drake, is that you?'

She hushed him with a finger to her lips and pulled the door closed. 'Don't wake the children,' she whispered, hurrying to join him.

'I take it that noise didn't come from the nursery?' Coper said. 'Mr Henson told me to come and check.'

'No, I thought it came from downstairs,' she said softly.

The murmur of voices wafted to them from below. They went down together, to find Mr Henson and half a dozen other servants gathered there.

'It wasn't upstairs, Mr Henson,' Coper said, 'Miss Drake is quite certain.'

'It wasn't from the library either, as far as we can see,' another man reported.

'The door then,' Henson said, striding to the end of the corridor. 'Good heavens, it's unlocked! But I checked it myself, no more than two hours ago.' He lifted the latch and peered into the gloomy refectory. From where Phoebe stood she couldn't see outside, but she feared he must notice the lantern.

'Perhaps it was the burglar,' one of the maids said shrilly. 'He's come to steal her ladyship's jewels. He might be hiding in the house this very minute. We could all be murdered in ours beds!'

'Don't talk such nonsense,' Henson said, closing the door. 'Miss Drake, are you sure nobody went past the nursery?'

'Quite sure. I was awake when I heard the noise, and it only took me a moment to get to the door.'

'And nobody came through into the servants' wing. Coper, Wills, go up to his lordship's study at once, and check that nobody has been in there.'

The girl who had spoken before gave a little scream. 'Perhaps he's already made off with his loot.'

Henson glared at her. 'Be quiet, girl. There's no call for you to start shrieking. If the sound we heard was the thief leaving then we'll soon know.' He sent pairs of servants to search the other main rooms, with particular instructions to be quiet. 'It seems his lordship and Lady Pickhurst have managed to sleep through all this upset. I'll not disturb them unless it's absolutely necessary.'

Phoebe stood in shivering silence, listening to the excited whispers of the remaining servants. If Lady Pickhurst returned to the door before the hunt was over she would be discovered, and who knew what might happen. Biting her lip, Phoebe prayed, though for what she couldn't be sure. By the time the men returned she was cold to the bone, but they brought reassuring news; all was as it should be.

'Well, it seems there's no harm done,' the butler said. 'I don't understand how this door came to be unlocked, but the matter can be looked into tomorrow, once I've spoken to his lordship.' He took a bunch of keys from his pocket and locked the door, then shot the huge bolt at the top, which gave a loud grinding protest as it was pushed home. 'Back to bed, everybody, and no lingering to gossip; I'll have no lateness in the morning.'

Sleep was impossible. Phoebe prowled the nursery, going often to the window and staring out towards the summer house. The night seemed to last forever, and it was a relief when Rodney cried out in alarm at four o'clock, needing her comforting presence. She stayed by his side, at length dozing in the armchair, only to wake cold and cramped an hour later to find that dawn was breaking on a dull and cloudy morning.

It was Sunday, when the usual routine allowed her to leave Annie supervising nursery breakfast before she dressed the children ready for the early morning service. Phoebe ventured down to the servants' hall. She dared ask no questions, but she deduced that Henson had stood by his decision not to wake his lordship, and that Lady Pickhurst's maid had already been summoned by her mistress.

How it had been done Phoebe couldn't imagine, but somehow her ladyship had returned to the house without the alarm being raised. The maids began to gossip about the noise in the night and the mystery of the unlocked door, but they were quickly silenced by Mr Henson.

'You might learn from Miss Drake,' he admonished the youngest of them. 'She comes to her meal on time and in a ladylike fashion, and engages in no senseless tittle-tattle.'

Phoebe blushed and gave the elderly butler a small nod of thanks, taking the earliest opportunity to leave.

It was no great surprise to see Lord Pickhurst set off for church without his wife; she preferred the shorter evening service, and even avoided that when she could. Once his lordship's carriage had drawn away, Phoebe watched the children being helped into the dogcart, and settled herself between them, glad to find that Nunnings, the under coachman, was driving. He was a pleasant young man, always ready to give her a hand into the carriage, but keeping a respectful distance.

'Did you hear the noise in the night, Miss Drake?' he asked. 'I gather it came from somewhere near the nursery.'

'I heard it, but I can tell you nothing about what it was,' she replied, flushing a little at the lie. She couldn't imagine how Lady Pickhurst had re-entered the house, once the door from the refectory had been locked. 'Has Mr Henson discovered the cause?'

'No.' Nunnings chirruped to the horse.

'Nearly everyone seems to think it was young Master Rodney up to some mischief,' he added, giving her a wink as he glanced back at the boy.

'I was sound asleep,' Rodney said indignantly. 'I wish you'd woken me, Miss Drake.'

'If I had you'd be tired and miserable this morning,' she said evenly, 'and none the wiser for it. Sit straight now, you are slouching. Eliza, put your glove back on this instant.'

Lucille lay staring at the lace hangings above her bed. She felt feverish, thoughts racing through her head too fast to make any sense. Thanks to Jonah's insistence on seeing her back to the refectory, her absence hadn't been discovered. Fetching a ladder he'd forced a window open on the second floor and crept silently downstairs, surprisingly quiet and agile for such a large man, to let her in at the refectory door. While Lucille raced up to her room, he'd bolted and relocked the door again, before returning the way he'd come.

The mason's lovemaking had been intolerably clumsy after Mortleigh's expertise. She wanted her new lover, but jealousy ate at her; she was still furious at his deception. What could he want with a silly child like Agatha Stoppen? To be sure, the girl was an heiress, but she had nothing to offer that compared with Knytte!

Jonah swore he'd do anything for her, but he was a pious soul at heart. Committing adultery was preying on his conscience; he would never agree to the greater crime that was so necessary if she was ever to be free. Lucille shifted restlessly as she ran through her plan again. Everything depended on Mortleigh.

The distant clangour of the doorbell broke into her reverie. Lucille half rose from her bed. It was most unusual for anybody to call at this hour on a Sunday. Perhaps it was Mortleigh, pretending to have returned overnight from London. Suddenly calm and ice cold, she reached for the bell rope and pulled it to summon her maid. The girl arrived breathless and pink-cheeked. 'My lady, Sir Martin Haylmer is here, with another gentleman. When they heard that his lordship wasn't home from church, they asked if you'd be kind enough to see them. Mr Henson has shown them into the morning room.'

'Sir Martin?' It was most unusual for the Lord Lieutenant to come visiting, particularly on a Sunday. 'I suppose I shall have to see him. Quickly then, help me to dress.'

The two men were standing by the fireplace, the Lord Lieutenant at his ease, the other shifting awkwardly from one foot to the other, his gaucheness reminding Lucille of Jonah Jackman, ill at ease as he was in the elegant room.

Sir Martin greeted her apologetically and introduced his companion as Inspector Tremayle of the county police. Tremayle bowed clumsily over her hand, and Lucille invited them both to sit down.

'I'm sorry to disturb you, Lady Pickhurst,' Tremayle said, 'but when you hear the circumstances I am sure you'll understand. There has been another robbery. Some very valuable jewellery was stolen from Dunsby Court yesterday.'

'What?' Somehow this was the last thing she had expected. 'But I was there myself, at Miss Agatha Stoppen's party!'

'Yes, along with most of the county.' Sir Martin scowled. 'My wife and I would have attended, had my duties elsewhere not made it impossible. That's why I decided to involve myself personally in the investigation. We plan to speak to all the guests. Among so many we can only hope somebody will have noticed something out of the ordinary.'

Lucille's mind was racing, but she showed no outward sign of it, giving him a sympathetic smile. 'I wish I could help, but I can't think of anything. How awful. And poor Agatha, she must be terribly upset.'

'She is, although it was her mother who suffered the greatest loss. Mrs Stoppen is very distressed at the loss of her rubies.'

147

Lucille nodded. She had seen the two enormous rubies more than once. They were mounted in a tiara ringed with diamonds. She thought the thing vulgar, but there could be no doubt of its value. 'Had they given a more formal party she would have been wearing her jewels,' she said, with a certain satisfaction. 'I have never cared for garden parties.'

'Did you go inside the house?' Inspector Tremayle asked.

'I did, to the gallery. Reverend Stoppen was eager for my husband to see some new additions to his collection. I sat in a window seat and looked out over the garden. Sadly I saw nothing of interest to anyone except the local gossips.'

Sir Martin gave her a wintry smile as he rose to his feet, 'we've already heard of Miss Stoppen's many admirers; we shall be speaking to them all in due course. Thank you, Lady Pickhurst. Perhaps you'll be kind enough to mention our visit to his lordship, and ask him to contact me if he has any useful information. Oh, and there's this. With your permission I'll give a copy to your butler. I need it to be seen by all your staff, and as far as possible by tradesmen calling at the house.' He gestured to Tremayle who took a piece of paper from his pocket. It was a handbill, asking for information about a vagrant who was wanted for questioning in

148

connection with the robberies.

Lucille looked at it without interest. 'Whatever you wish. I'm sorry I couldn't help you further.'

Once the men had gone, Lucille rose to her feet and paced the floor for a few minutes, thinking hard. Biting on her lip, she rang the bell to summon the butler, and requested him to bring all the recent newspapers he could find.

Respite came for Beddowes only when he dropped to the ground through sheer exhaustion. Hours passed in a daze; he was transported to half-remembered marches through distant lands, unaware of any clear distinction between past and present. At times the sharp-spined gorse and rough heather flaying his legs became shifting sand, and at others it was deep clinging mud. His old sergeant major marched alongside him, and Beddowes was glad of the companionship, even though the man's orders made no sense, and he shimmered in a very disconcerting manner from time to time.

The day was coming to an end. He stumbled through yet another patch of bog, and as he dragged himself back to drier ground he thought he heard the sound of bells, brought to him on the breeze. Some part of his mind wondered if it might be Sunday. The idea pleased him for a second or two; it was the day of rest, he thought. Surely, even if he was no saint, he wouldn't die while the rest of the world was busy at their prayers. Suspecting there was something wrong with his logic, he soon forgot about it and slipped back into a daze.

When darkness fell Beddowes kept moving for a while, until he lost his footing, stumbling over a clump of heather and measuring his length on the ground. It seemed too much trouble to rise to his feet, so he allowed his eyes to drift shut. It would have been easy, he thought dreamily, to simply lie there and die. But that would mean he would never know who had been so intent on killing him. He felt an illogical need to discover the identity of the man whose body had been tipped into the makeshift grave before him. Had he been friend or foe? The thoughts spiralled until they vanished into darkness. For a long time he knew no more.

Chapter Eleven

Phoebe Drake splashed water on her aching eyes. Jonah was constantly on her mind and she'd hardly slept. Despite her best intentions she had gone to the window often during the night but this time she saw no stealthy prowlers, nor did she hear any quiet footsteps passing the nursery door.

Looking out into the cool morning light, she saw her cousin, his two assistants following behind, walking briskly towards the ruin to start their week's work. She thought the young mason looked as if he too had gone short of sleep; there were furrows on his forehead she'd never seen before.

Suddenly angry, Phoebe hurried back to her own room to dress; until Jonah came to his senses there was nothing she could do. She would spend all her energy on the two children under her care. Rodney in particular was unhappy and, although he didn't speak of the reason she could guess it; Lady Pickhurst did all she could to keep the children away from their uncle, and talked frequently about the benefits of their being sent away to school. Before their marriage, his lordship had indulged the boy, taking him around the estate. Sometimes Rodney had even been allowed to join his uncle at dinner, when there was no other company.

Once the children were having breakfast and safely in Annie's charge, Phoebe hurried downstairs to the dining room, where she guessed she would find Lord Pickhurst alone. Coper was on duty. His eyebrows lifted a little in surprise as she asked to be announced.

'Miss Drake.' His lordship put down his newspaper and beckoned her closer. 'I trust nothing is wrong?'

'No, your lordship, but I have a small request to ask of you. I was wondering if I might take Master Rodney on a little excursion. We are studying the history of Knytte, and have started with the monastery system. Would you give us permission to visit the ruins at Gretlyn this morning?'

'I don't see why not,' Lord Pickhurst said. 'The journey shouldn't take more than an hour if I order the bays, they've had little exercise lately, and they'll take you at a fair clip. You don't intend to take little Eliza?'

'I thought she would find the outing too tiring. Annie can look after her, just this once, unless you would prefer some other arrangement.' Phoebe felt suddenly light-hearted; she hadn't been away from Knytte since she took up the post of governess, and depending upon who was sent to drive, she might be allowed to take the reins of the two fine horses for part of the way.

'No, that will do.' Lord Pickhurst picked up the paper again, giving her a half-smile. 'Tell Rodney I shall try to find time to take him out myself sometime next week, Miss Drake, as I used to. I quite miss the boy's company.'

She almost ran to take this message back upstairs. Half an hour later she and the boy were seated behind Nunnings, with a stable-boy perched behind, and the matching bays pulling hard, as eager as she was to leave Knytte for a few hours.

A bright sun shone on his back and warmed him. It would have been easy, the sergeant thought hazily, never to make another move. He could simply lie there until death took him; he had a feeling it might not take too long. But then he'd never discover who had tried to kill him, or why. It would be annoying to leave such a mystery unsolved, and the offence unpunished.

It must have been halfway through the morning by the time Beddowes dragged himself to his feet once more. The spectre of his old sergeant stood grinning at him. 'One last day, lad,' the familiar voice was jovial. Beddowes tried to reply, but could make no sound. His lips were dry and cracked, his tongue felt too large for his mouth, and there was a nagging pain in his belly to add to the aches left by the beating he'd taken, but still he set himself into motion. He'd long since forgotten why he'd been heading west, but he saw no reason to change direction. His imaginary companion nodded approvingly and promptly vanished.

Beddowes had been following the track for some time before he noticed it. It had simply appeared under his feet. Looking back he saw his own footprints in a wet patch, but there were others, and the marks of shod hoofs, quite fresh. People came here.

Despite this discovery he couldn't pick up speed; he was close to the end of his strength. The track became wider. It led downhill, and stopped where it encountered a dusty lane. He halted for a long moment, unwilling to make a choice between left and right. He looked to the south. The sun felt too hot and bright on his face, so he turned north instead, and plodded on.

Barely conscious, he saw the gang of road menders before him as a group of moving trees. One of them, a lad of about eight, employed to gather stones while his older brothers dug out ditches, picked up a pebble and threw it at the tramp, jeering at the ragged scarecrow as he staggered by, and capering in delight when he scored a hit. This brought a laugh from some of the men, welcoming the brief diversion from their labours, and very soon they had all entered the game, scooping small stones from the road.

Shouts rang in Beddowes' ears, but his addled brain made no sense of them, and he slouched on, head down and shoulders hunched. Hits on his head and face were met with roars of delight, and an increasingly heavy barrage. Losing his balance, he fell to all fours. Shouting enthusiastically, the road gang crowded closer. Beddowes tried to regain his feet, but the world was slowly tilting and the sky above him darkened. Without making a sound, he dropped insensible to the ground.

The excursion to the ruins of Gretlyn monastery was a great success. Many of the walls still stood and they spread over a large area, making an exciting roofless maze to be explored. 'Take care, Master Rodney,' Phoebe warned, as the boy climbed the remains of a spiral staircase which vanished into the darkness of a narrow tower.

'It's quite safe,' came the reply, 'I'm holding onto the wall.' He went on climbing, his voice echoing as he went higher. 'I can see the top now. Why don't you come up?' A gleeful laugh drifted down to her. 'I'm on the roof, Miss Drake!'

With some trepidation she followed him, and found the climb easier than she expected. She was rewarded by a fine view over fields, villages and scattered farms, with a glimpse of the sea in the distance. 'How lovely! I would never have thought you could see so far.'

'I wish my uncle had come. He knows the name of every place from Hagstock to Clow Bay, he told me so.' The boy's face clouded. 'I never see him now.'

'He misses your company too,' Phoebe said. 'I believe he means to try to find some time for you. Maybe one day Lady Pickhurst will come to know you and your sister better, and be a little kinder.'

The child shook his head. 'I hate her, and she hates us. Knytte was supposed to be mine when my uncle dies, but now she's to have it.'

Phoebe bit her lip; she should reprimand the boy for saying such things, yet she suspected he was right about Lady Pickhurst. 'Surely that cannot be true. Everyone knows you're the heir.'

'I'll be Lord Pickhurst perhaps, if she doesn't have a boy, but I shan't have Knytte. My uncle told me, the first time she came here. I'm sure he was sorry, but she was smiling behind his back. She wants him to send me away to school.'

'Even if that happened, Knytte will be your home until you're grown up,' Phoebe said. 'And going to school might not be so bad. It might be quite an adventure. There would be lots of other boys, and you'd soon make friends.'

'Would I?' He looked doubtful.

'Of course. Anyway, let's forget that for now. We're here to work. Make the map first, with as many things labelled as you can manage. Once that's done we'll have some fun.' She looked at the view again. 'While you're busy I might bring my sketch book up here.'

'I'll fetch it, shall I?' Without waiting for a reply he was gone, coming back a few minutes later with Nunnings, who gave her a shy smile. 'I thought you'd like something to sit on, Miss Drake,' he said, putting one of the cushions from the dog cart on the stone ledge that ran around the inside of the wall. 'Don't worry about the young master, I'll keep an eye on him for you while he's poking about down below.'

'Thank you, that's very kind. Don't forget, Rodney, the map first, and see you make a good job of it.'

The two hours they had scheduled soon passed. Once his task was done Phoebe rewarded the boy with a game of hide and seek among the ruins. Flushed and laughing, they returned to the dogcart. Nunnings didn't object when Phoebe asked to take the reins for a while; she had often driven her father when he was visiting his parishioners although it was a challenge, managing a pair of blood horses rather than a staid pony. She was concentrating hard as they trotted briskly along the moorland road; Nunnings seemed happy to have her seated beside him, although he remained properly respectful, speaking only when it was necessary.

Phoebe was happier than she had been in months, lifting her face to feel the warmth of the sun and letting her eyes close, just for a moment. A startled sound from Nunnings jolted them open again. There was a swirl of dust ahead, and a strangely disturbing sound.

As they drew closer the dark moving mass turned into a knot of men and boys, intent on something that lay in their midst on the road. The sound of their shouts and laughter became more plainly audible above the rattle of the wheels, and Phoebe slowed the horses.

'Have they caught some poor animal? I believe they're throwing stones at it.' She hated to see senseless cruelty. Her father had been a compassionate man; in this situation she knew exactly what he would have done. She slowed the horses, fired with his crusading spirit.

Nunnings shrugged. 'Pull around them, Miss, it's none of our business.'

Ignoring him, she brought the bays to a smart halt. 'What do you think you're doing?' she called. 'What's going on here?'

The group opened up a little, and she saw to her horror that their target was not an animal but a man, who lay apparently senseless on the road.

One man, evidently in charge of the others, knuckled his forehead. ''Tis nothing to worrit you, missus,' he said cheerfully. ''Tis only a beggar. We'll see him out o' the road for ye.'

'Beggar or not, you've no business attacking the poor man. Get away from him at once. You should be ashamed of yourselves.'

'He's nobbut a stranger,' another of the road menders said sullenly. 'A man should keep to his own parish, not come beggin' from decent folk. Tain't no fault of ourn he got lost on the moor. We didn't do no harm, he were all but done-in anyways.'

'Then that's all the worse!' Phoebe leapt down before Nunnings could prevent her, pushed her way through the roadmen and went to stoop over the tramp. His clothes were in tatters, his hair and beard so long and matted that she could barely make out his face.

Phoebe had become used to dealing with charity cases from an early age, being only ten when her mother died. Her father had never shirked a local priest's less pleasant duties, and Phoebe had become his constant helpmate. Putting a hand to the man's filthy arm she felt his pulse. It was there, stronger

159

than she'd expected. However, his breathing was shallow, and his flesh felt hot and dry. She turned to the ganger. 'He's feverish. Bring him something to drink. At once!' she added fiercely, when he hesitated, 'don't you listen to your preacher? Have you never heard the story of the good Samaritan? Once the poor man has had a drink you can lift him into the dogcart.'

With the lad called from his perch to hold the horses, Nunnings came to her side, closely followed by young Rodney. 'I don't know that this is any business of ours, Miss Drake,' the coachman said. 'What will his lordship say if we bring home a toe-rag like that?'

'I don't know and I don't care, I'll not leave him here with these barbarians. Surely he can be spared a meal. I'll pay for it myself if necessary,' she added, taking the battered tin cup she was offered, and sniffing it. Strong cider; it would do. It was a relief to see the unconscious man's throat move as she tipped each tiny mouthful between his lips. 'Master Pengoar, get back in the carriage this minute, there's no call for you to be involved here.'

'But this could be the man Sir Martin Haylmer is after,' Rodney said, his eyes alight. He turned to Nunnings. 'There's a reward. Didn't you see the handbill?' The man looked mystified. 'It was in the stable-yard, pinned to one of the doors. I saw it there this morning.'

Nunnings shook his head. 'I saw it, but I didn't read it,' he mumbled, 'I'm not too good at my letters.'

'A tramp is wanted for questioning about the jewel robberies.' The boy was hopping up and down in his excitement. 'Maybe we've just caught the thief.'

'Hold on,' the road mender said. 'You say there's a reward? You reckon to tek him away, but who found the beggar, eh?'

'You found him, but you also half killed him,' Phoebe retorted. 'There'll be no reward for a dead man. Two of you lift him up and put him in the carriage. Handle him gently; you've done enough harm. Master Rodney, you will ride in front with Nunnings, and I'll do what I can to make this poor soul comfortable in the back. It's lucky we've room.'

The men obeyed, but the ganger wasn't prepared to let their captive go so easily. When Phoebe was settled with the unconscious man propped half on the floor and half on the seat, and Nunnings had taken up the reins, the road mender grabbed the off-side horse by the bit. 'I reckon we're owed summat,' he said obstinately.

'The poster said that they would pay anyone who could tell them where the tramp was,' Rodney said. 'You may go to Sir Martin at Clowmoor and tell him he's been taken to Knytte.'

'Yes, do that if you wish,' Phoebe nodded. 'If the Lord Lieutenant is looking for this man he should be told, but be sure I shall inform him of what happened here. Now step aside, if you please.'

The dogcart jolted into motion, but the unconscious man didn't stir. Phoebe looked down at what little she could see of his face, wondering how he'd come to such utter destitution; he looked as if he hadn't seen a square meal in years. However, the make-shift splint and bandage on his arm suggested that somebody had recently spent some care upon him, unless he'd managed it for himself.

They turned a corner and the tramp almost rolled from the seat, and Phoebe shifted away from him, startled by the movement. As she did so, she heard an echo of her father's voice in her head. 'We are all God's creatures, Phoebe, equal in his eyes.'

It wasn't easy, for he was heavy despite looking half-starved, but she managed to lift the man into a more comfortable position. Swallowing her revulsion, she set his filthy head upon her lap.

The vagrant stank, and his hair was matted with dirt and blood. Phoebe sighed; her dress would be difficult to clean. As if in sympathy, he too let out a deep sigh, a slight frown between his brows mirroring hers. She gave a rueful smile; they had more than their humanity in common. Her father, leaving her with his sense of duty, had bequeathed her little else; on his death she had been almost as destitute as the poor beggar who lay in her lap. That thought led to others, and the last vestiges of the holiday spirit left her; if Lord Pickhurst succumbed to his wife's wishes and sent the Pengoar children away, she would be looking for another post. The unpleasantness at Clowmoor Manor still haunted her. It had been such a relief to find a safe haven at Knytte, and even more reassuring with Jonah working nearby.

She sighed again. The accusation her cousin had made was untrue; she'd never considered marrying him as a way of escaping her poverty, nor would she, no matter how much she feared being cast out into the world again. She'd only ever seen him as a friend, but losing his friendship was hard to bear.

Phoebe stared unseeingly ahead, looking into a future that held no guarantees, no certainty of any kind. Like so many women who had to fend for themselves, if fate was unkind she could be no better off than this poor soul who lay injured and helpless in her care. Without conscious thought, she let a hand rest upon the filthy head, stroking it gently.

The ganger wasted no time. As soon as the dogcart drew away, he sent a boy to the nearest farm with a message and a sixpence, and within five minutes he returned with a borrowed pony, a shaggy half-tame colt off the moors. Giving his men orders to keep at their work, the roadman set out for Clow-moor. He feared the young woman's tongue; she might bring Sir Martin's wrath down upon him, but he thought if he acted quickly enough the reward would be his.

With the Lord Lieutenant's house within sight, he began to feel a little less sure of himself; he didn't think he could ride up to the front door of such a place, no matter what news he carried. He slowed the pony to a jog; he must go to the stable-yard and hope to meet somebody who could help him.

A tall black horse was being ridden fast from the opposite direction; seeing the diminutive pony the animal balked and veered across the road, almost unseating the gentleman upon its back. The rider soothed the black, and with some coaxing it came closer. Given a clear view of his face, the ganger recognized him at once. Mr Docket was well known all over Sir Martin's estate and beyond, and he was generally considered a decent man. The ganger waved a hand and shouted, kicking the pony on.

Docket frowned as the roadman told his tale. 'You'd better come with me,' he said. 'Sir Martin isn't at home, but this can't wait.'

Once they reached the stables, Docket gave the order for horses to be put to a carriage, urging the grooms to hurry. He sent a boy to Trembury, carrying a message for his master, while another was dispatched to summon the Lord Lieutenant's personal physician.

The roadman stood watching, open mouthed, amazed at so much fuss being made over a tramp.

'I shall go at once to Knytte,' Docket said, addressing the roadman as the carriage started down the drive. 'If this man you've found is the one we're looking for, then I'll see the reward is sent to you. In the meantime I suggest you get back to your work, and pray you've done him no serious damage.'

Chapter Twelve

Beddowes had been dreaming, rising gradually towards consciousness. There was an unfamiliar taste in his mouth. Swallowing, he remembered what it was. He'd never had a taste for cider, yet the pain in his head suggested a drinking bout lasting several days.

He floated nearer to the surface. There was movement. He could hear hoof beats, and the grate of metal tyres. Beyond the cider and the stench of his own filthy body, Beddowes noted a more pleasant scent, one that reminded him of summer meadows and the first cut of hay. A hand swept the tangled hair from his forehead, and the gentleness of the touch shocked him into opening his eyes.

Coming abruptly to full consciousness, Beddowes saw a young woman staring down at him. There was an expression of concern on her face; something about her seemed comforting, as if she was somebody he knew and trusted, yet he couldn't recall ever seeing her before.

'Look, he's awake.' The words were clear and shrill, and spoken by a child who belonged to a class far above his own. Beddowes tried to twist round so he could see

166

the speaker.

'Don't move,' the woman said; her voice as cultured as the boy's, and as gentle as her expression. 'You need to rest.' She turned her head a little, her tone changing to become almost severe, though somehow Beddowes doubted she could ever be anything but kind. 'Master Pengoar, pray mind your manners, it's rude to stare.'

With his senses unexpectedly keen, Beddowes understood at once; the young woman was a governess. A childish glee accompanied this feat of deduction; it reminded him that he gained great satisfaction from his work as a police detective. Pleasure was instantly replaced by something close to panic. His memory was patchy, incomplete; why was he here, in rags and apparently destitute? An event leading to dismissal would surely be hard to forget, but the recent past was a blank. One thing was plain; he was a long way from Scotland Yard.

The rhythm of the wheels changed as the vehicle turned between high gates. Here the dusty green leaves of late summer hung over them; he assumed they must be approaching the end of their journey.

'Don't worry, you'll be well cared for at Knytte,' the young woman said, as if his sudden fear had communicated itself to her. 'Lord Pickhurst is a humane man, he'll not send you away without a meal, and I shall make sure your hurts are tended.'

Talking was more difficult than he'd anticipated, but he forced the words from his throat, shocked to hear that they were little more than a croak. 'Thank you miss, you're very kind.'

He was rewarded by a smile. She really was pretty, he thought, his own cracked lips sketching an attempt to respond. Beddowes wondered briefly what her name was. At that instant he barely felt sure of his own; he hoped the rank which had been his for so long, both in the service of Her Majesty and in the police force, still belonged to him.

The news spread with exceptional speed. Within twenty-four hours it was common knowledge in every inn, stable-yard and kitchen between Hagstock and Trembury: a man had been captured and taken to Clowmoor House. The more knowledgeable among the gossip-mongers identified him as the tramp described on Mr Docket's handbills. Some said he had been arrested and charged with the theft of Mrs Stoppen's jewellery, while others scoffed at this idea, maintaining that he wasn't the thief, merely an accomplice. Very little was agreed upon, except that Sir Martin Haylmer would be handing out the maximum penalty when the man appeared before him in court.

As Monday afternoon turned to evening,

wilder rumours grew; it was said the militia were to be called out to escort the criminal to prison because he was known to have escaped before and might vanish into thin air if not watched for every second.

In contrast, a roadman assured his audience that the miscreant had been beaten to within an inch of his life by other members of a criminal gang, and was even now hovering between life and death. This particular rumour gained credence when it was confirmed that Dr Long had been summoned from Hagstock, and had remained at Clowmoor all afternoon.

Once the children were in bed and asleep, Phoebe sat at the window once more, staring into the darkness that enveloped the garden. The tramp was very much in her thoughts. She'd heard none of the gossip: belonging neither above stairs nor below. She'd stayed away from the servants' hall.

When he had taken charge of the fugitive the day before, Mr Docket had assured her the man would be properly cared for, but he had rushed him away in answer to Sir Martin's summons before she had a chance to fulfil her promise and see the poor soul fed and his hurts tended. Phoebe felt uneasy, for she hated to break her word.

Monday night was disturbed by dreams. She sat in a ruined tower. A man lay with his head on her lap, looking up at her. His eyes

169

were those of the penniless derelict, yet he was well-groomed, his beard and his hair trimmed and clean. As he smiled up at her he looked ten years younger, and when his hand reached for hers she took it eagerly. She awoke with a start, strangely perturbed.

Annie was already dashing noisily around doing her chores, seeming even more eager to finish than usual. Phoebe closed her ears to the girl's chatter. Once in the classroom she tried to concentrate on the children, but her thoughts kept returning to the tramp and her strange dream. She was still feeling distracted when there was a knock on the door, and a footman and maid entered.

'Excuse me, miss,' the footman said, 'Lord Pickhurst wants to see you in his study. Clara is to stay with the children while you're gone.' He held the door for her, curiosity in his eyes; obviously he had no idea what was behind this rare summons.

Phoebe ran her hands over her hair to check that it was suitably restrained. She hurried downstairs, her mind racing. Was she about to lose her post? Lady Pickhurst had been trying long enough to have the children sent to school, yet only yesterday his lordship had spoken of Rodney with such affection.

As Phoebe approached the door of his lordship's study a terrible thought struck her. Perhaps Jonah's foolish infatuation with Lady Pickhurst had been discovered; her poor cousin would lose both his job and his reputation. And if that was the cause of her summons then what of her own position? She would be tainted by her relationship to him.

Phoebe entered the study, and her heart plummeted; it seemed her worst fears were about to be realized. Jonah stood by Lord Pickhurst's desk, looking even larger than usual, and completely out of place in his dusty working clothes. He spared her no more than a glance before turning his head away; the breech that had been opened between them seemed wider than ever. Jonah was the last of her family, and she bit her lip to stem the flow of tears.

'Miss Drake, Sir Martin Haylmer, in his position as chief magistrate, sent a message this morning in which he asked me to speak to you. Since Jackman was already here to see me on business, and bearing in mind his connection to you, I trust you won't object to his remaining. Jackman, the plans are on the table by the window, you might occupy yourself with them for the moment.'

'Sir Martin?' The relief was so great that Phoebe felt suddenly faint, hardly hearing the rest of what her employer had said.

Lord Pickhurst looked at her with concern. 'Is something wrong?'

'No your lordship, I'm afraid I may have run downstairs a little too fast, but I'm quite well.'

'Good.' Lord Pickhurst gave her an uncertain smile. 'I have some news for you.'

Phoebe glanced at Jonah, but he had his back to them and showed no sign that he knew she was there. 'News?'

'About the man you brought off the moors yesterday,' Lord Pickhurst said. 'I gather you acted very sensibly. Sir Martin has asked me to express his gratitude for your help. Sadly the fellow was found too late. He died during the night.'

'Oh no!' Her hand flew to her mouth. It was the last thing she'd expected. 'I hadn't thought he was so ill,' she said, and suddenly the dream returned to her. It was disturbing to think that this stranger had entered her sleeping mind, alive and well, perhaps at the very moment of his death. She became aware that Lord Pickhurst was still watching her, and felt she must say something. 'I felt guilty about doing so little for him. Mr Docket promised that he would lack for nothing, but he hurried him away very quickly. Perhaps if he'd been allowed to stay here at Knytte the poor man might have survived.'

Lord Pickhurst shook his head. 'I fear not. I assure you he was well tended. It wasn't lack of attention that killed him. He'd suffered serious injuries which had been neglected for too long. However, he was conscious for a short time, and he asked that you should be thanked for your kindness.'

172

'I did very little. Tell me, do you know anything of his history?'

'It appears he was a dishonest rogue by the name of Cobb, and he wasn't nearly as poor as he appeared. He came from London to buy some of the jewellery stolen in the recent robberies.'

Phoebe stared at him. The dream had played her false; those eyes, that smile, hadn't looked like those of a sinful man.

'Yes, it's a bad business,' his lordship went on. 'I understand he was in some part repentant, but Sir Martin tells me he gave the police no useful information.' He looked up at her again. 'You may be aware that the reward for finding this man was claimed by a road mender, but Sir Martin feels that you played a significant part, and more to the point, he wishes you to be commended for your compassion. He has instructed me to give you this.' He handed over a small purse. 'Five guineas. I trust you feel no reluctance in accepting it.'

Her first instinct was to refuse, but Phoebe thought swiftly, and lifted her chin; thanks to Jonah her job was in jeopardy and she couldn't afford to have scruples. 'No. Thank you, your lordship. I am sorry the poor man died. I shall write to Sir Martin to express my gratitude.'

Phoebe returned to the nursery with the purse in her hand, and a tumble of thoughts running through her head. She felt some-how unclean, as if she shared some respon-sibility for the death of the tramp, although commonsense told her not to be a fool. Managed carefully, five guineas would keep her for quite a while if she lost her post.

'Mr Mortleigh, you've found time to return to us.' Lucille's heart was beating fast. She was eager to challenge her lover and con-firm her worst suspicions of him. Glancing at the clock, she could hardly believe it was only mid-afternoon. She daren't allow her gaze to linger on his face in case he read her thoughts.

Lord Pickhurst greeted their guest with more open enthusiasm, rising to usher him to a chair. 'You'll take a drink, Mortleigh? I was about to order tea, since my wife usually takes it about this time, but perhaps you would like something stronger after your journey from London?'

'Tea will be perfect, thank you.' Mortleigh smiled. He took the opportunity to mime a kiss to Lucille when her husband turned his back to reach for the bell-pull, but she ignored him.

They made small talk about the trains, and the inconvenience of having no station closer than Hagstock, until the servants withdrew and the three of them were alone again, seated around the small table.

'And how was London?' Lucille asked distantly, as she handed their visitor a cup.

'Too hot and very dusty,' their guest replied. 'I found myself longing for the time of my departure, so I could return to the delights of the country. And Knytte in particular,' he added, with a little bow towards his host.

'I trust you conveyed my good wishes to Mr Laidlaw,' Lord Pickhurst said. 'Did you leave him well?'

'He is much improved in every way, thank you. Indeed I have no more fears for him.' Mortleigh looked down into his teacup. 'I regret that his indisposition has soured our relationship, however. It is unlikely we shall ever see him back in this part of the country.'

'What a pity,' his lordship said. 'We had so little time to discuss my plans, and Laidlaw had a genuine interest in the alterations I'm making. He shared my enthusiasm for the remodelling of the ruins, it would be a shame if he never saw them completed.'

'I hope the work is making good progress,' Mortleigh said. 'I spent a full hour in your garden once, and I swear it was one of the most pleasurable times of my life. I trust I shall be able to spend a great deal longer exploring its delights. Unlike my friend, I find the country has many benefits.'

'Some people find it lonely,' Lord Pickhurst replied, glancing at his wife, who was bending, flush-cheeked, over the tea-pot. 'Evidently you are not one of them?'

Mortleigh shook his head. 'Hardly. I always find excellent company in the country.'

'I imagine that you are constantly in demand, particularly among young women,' Lucille said, having regained her composure; his reference to the delights of the garden had all too clearly referred to his clandestine visit that first night. 'There was a party at Dunsby Court on Saturday, and I'm sure you were sorely missed.'

'Yes, I had to refuse the invitation,' he replied, meeting her look squarely. 'Unlike the fairer sex, who have only to entertain themselves, men have business to attend to. With so many of your neighbours gathered together I don't doubt you had an enjoyable time.'

'I'm afraid not. Gardens are all very well, but I prefer to dance and dine within doors. We didn't stay more than two hours, which meant we missed all the excitement. I suppose you won't have heard the news. Mrs Stoppen was robbed. Her famed ruby tiara was stolen, that very afternoon, while the entire household were out in the grounds.'

'What, the jewel thief has struck again?' Mortleigh looked astounded.

Lord Pickhurst nodded gravely. 'The rogue gets more brazen. We are almost the last house of note to be left untouched, and

176

I fear he may make the attempt to break in here. I have taken the advice of the Lord Lieutenant, and deposited Lady Pickhurst's jewels in the bank. Since even he has been a victim I can't help but be uneasy.'

'I can hardly believe any stranger could enter Knytte undetected,' Mortleigh said.

'I prefer not to take the risk. Within the week I shall have a new safe installed.' He smiled at his wife. 'Perhaps you may keep at least some of your trinkets here again once it is done.'

'If you think it wise,' Lucille replied. 'Sir Martin is no nearer catching this villain. With all the fuss yesterday it seemed he was making progress, but it was a storm in a teacup.'

'Hardly that, my dear.' Lord Pickhurst turned to Mortleigh. 'Evidently a vagrant, a stranger who came here from London, was believed to have evidence that might lead to the arrest of this thief. After the robbery at Dunsby Court, Sir Martin had a handbill printed and circulated in a bid to find him. Imagine our shock when Miss Drake, who is governess to my sister's children, returned here yesterday morning with the very man. She and young Rodney had been on an excursion to Gretlyn, and they found this tramp upon the road, gravely wounded.'

Lucille studied Mortleigh's face. Anyone who didn't know him would notice nothing, but she saw a new tension in his jaw. 'The foolish girl brought him here,' she said, 'instead of taking him directly to Clowmoor Manor, but fortunately Sir Martin sent for him at once, and he was barely in the house five minutes. I feared we should have every-one below stairs infested with fleas and bedbugs and who knows what, had he stayed a minute longer, for you never saw such a miserable filthy sight.'

'So, Sir Martin has his man,' Mortleigh commented idly. 'But did I hear you right? You say the whole thing has led nowhere?'

Lucille met his look. There was a pulse drumming in his temple. She had been right, she was sure of it. The knowledge of the power he had unwittingly placed in her hands was like a draught of strong wine.

She smiled. 'The wretch died soon after he arrived at Clowmoor, before he could say a word.'

'I chose a bad time to be away,' Mortleigh said, his tone suddenly light-hearted, 'I seem to have missed a great deal. Never let it be said that life in the country is dull. The more I see and hear of it, the more I wish I could stay. Perhaps you have some small cottage in the grounds, my lord, where I could take a buxom milkmaid for a wife and rusticate to my heart's content.'

'The dower house is empty, but you might find it a trifle small,' Lord Pickhurst replied jovially. 'As to the milkmaid, if you come to the ball we are giving at Christmas I have no doubt Lucille will find you a dozen more eligible partners.'

'Are you serious about moving to the country, Mr Mortleigh?' Lucille asked, keeping her tone light, and looking down at the tea cups so neither man would see the thoughts her eyes might betray.

'I am considering it, if the right house becomes available. My business interests have prospered lately, so perhaps the opportunity will come sooner than I expected. If you hear of any suitable property to let, I beg you will let me know. This area would suit me well.'

'There are some fine properties quite near,' Lord Pickhurst said. 'I'm sure you will hear of something.' He rubbed a hand over his chin. 'I spoke of the Dower House without any serious thought,' he said, 'but if you don't mind a small establishment, with no more than half a dozen staff, it might suit you, for a short time at least. Of course you wouldn't be able to entertain on a large scale.'

'I doubt if that would trouble Mr Mortleigh, my dear,' Lucille said impishly, 'since you will constantly invite him to Knytte. Your plan is all very well, but the Dower House has been empty for several years.'

'I don't think there's much wrong with it,' Lord Pickhurst said. 'I tell you what, Mortleigh, if you have no other pressing plans, we'll take a look in the morning.'

'That's very kind of you.' Mortleigh looked at Lucille. 'If the Dower House proves suitable, I do hope you wouldn't object to having me as a close neighbour, Lady Pickhurst. I fear my presence hasn't always been as welcome to you as it is to his lordship.'

'I've no objection to anything or anyone that pleases my husband,' Lucille replied, with a laugh. 'But I warn you, if you stay in our neighbourhood then I shall do my best to provide you with a wife. Single gentlemen are so much more difficult to seat at the dinner table.'

Chapter Thirteen

The day was almost at an end, but Phoebe hadn't been aware of its passing. She'd rarely felt so unhappy. Even when she was at Clowmoor Manor, suffering the unwelcome attentions of young Roderick Haylmer and fearing the loss of both her reputation and her position through no fault of her own, she'd managed to remain cheerful.

On becoming a governess she'd schooled herself not to think of the happier life she left behind at the vicarage, the only home she'd ever known. Her mother was no more than a vague memory, along with the two small boys, Phoebe's brothers, each of whom lived less than two years. The harrowing months spent nursing her father before he died had left her rather withdrawn, but his belief, through all the suffering, that a better existence awaited him beyond the grave had remained with him. She'd always considered it would be a betrayal to allow herself to be despondent at his loss.

This total depression of the spirits, so unlike her normal character, refused to lift. Phoebe mourned the death of the tramp, without knowing why. A man she hadn't known shouldn't be so hard to dismiss from her mind, but she'd dreamt about him again, seeing him young and healthy, smiling at her. It made no sense, yet the feeling that the dream was significant refused to leave her.

Seeking another cause for her strange mood, Phoebe's thoughts fell upon Jonah. He was all the family she had since her father's death. Perhaps if she could mend her friendship with Jonah she'd get the unfortunate tramp out of her mind.

The daylight was fading and her cousin was tidying away his tools when she found him. He was alone, the other men having left already. The ruins were quiet and full of shadows and she shivered a little, recalling her night time excursion.

'Jonah?' She approached him warily.

He refused to acknowledge her presence, keeping his back turned.

'Jonah, please. I'm sorry I upset you.' There were tears pricking at her eyes. 'You're the only true friend I have. We both know how it feels to be alone in the world. Please, help me to mend this rift between us. I promise not to lecture you, if only you'll treat me as a sister again. I'm sorry. I was wrong to try to interfere.'

'It's a bit late to admit that, isn't it?' He turned to her then; there was no sign of brotherly love on his face. 'Why've you come?

182

If you really cared about me you wouldn't have come sneaking around the garden on Saturday night. Don't deny it. I saw you running back through the ruins. But spying on us wasn't enough, was it? You wanted Lucille's reputation ruined. Your nasty little plan might have worked, if I hadn't found another way into the house.'

'That wasn't my doing,' Phoebe cried. 'I turned out the lamp and moved it, that's all. I wanted to warn you; there could be others watching who'd betray you. And I didn't spy. I left and returned to the house as soon as I heard your voice.'

He still looked doubtful, but his expression had softened a little. Seeing it, Phoebe went on. 'I'm sorry, I shouldn't have followed Lady Pickhurst. I don't blame you for being angry with me. But it could have been anyone looking out of the window. You couldn't help falling in love, Jonah, but can't you see how dangerous it is, for both of you?'

'Do you expect me to believe you didn't make all that noise to rouse the whole house?' He shook his head in disbelief. 'You wanted us found.'

'No!' There were tears running freely down her face. 'It was an accident. The wind blew the door out of my hand and slammed it. Once all the fuss had calmed down Mr Henson locked and bolted the door, and ordered everyone back to bed. I would have gone back later, but I didn't have the key, even if I could have managed to draw the bolt.'

'Luckily Lucille had a key.'

She nodded. 'I'm glad, honestly I am.' She took a step towards him. 'Please Jonah, do you really think I'm lying to you?'

He stared at her for a moment, then slowly shook his head. 'Life's so hard for Lucille. She's got no friends here, only me. The servants complain behind her back. They make up stories, and say she's hard, but they don't know what she's really like. I know she's kind and gentle, but nobody else sees the best of her.' He gave Phoebe a challenging look and she nodded, if a little reluctantly.

Jonah ran a hand over his dusty hair. 'Her parents forced her into this marriage. Lord Pickhurst paid a lot of money for her, but he doesn't love her. He bought her to show off to his wealthy friends, just like any other piece of furniture in the big house. She's desperately unhappy, Phoebe.'

Jonah stared at the stone he'd been shaping, his thoughts obviously elsewhere. 'I tried to stop seeing her. It's so risky for her to meet the way we do, but what could I do? She begged me to come, and I was afraid she'd harm herself if I didn't.'

He looked earnestly into Phoebe's eyes, and this time he reminded her of the boy who'd been an older brother to her. 'I'd managed to stay away from her for nearly a month, but Lucille was so unhappy, I couldn't let her go to the summerhouse and find it empty. She says it's the one place at Knytte where she's known happiness.'

Phoebe set one of her hands upon his. 'But meeting in secret can only bring more misery for both of you in the end. You know that.' There was so much more she could have said. She could have told him of the vivid slap marks that stayed all day on a maid's cheeks after she dropped her lady-ship's glove, of Lady Pickhurst's attempt to be rid of the children, although her husband was fond of them, of the scratch of finger-nails on the door and the low laugh that tormented young Rodney Pengoar's sleep. It was pointless; love was blind, and Jonah wouldn't believe her.

'Phoebe, I should leave Knytte,' Jonah said. 'I know it's the only thing to do, though it'll be hard. There's work in Hagstock. Or I could go further away, where I'd never even hear her name. I swear I'll not go to her again. Listen Phoebe, it breaks my heart to leave her without a friend. If she had one person she could talk to, I'd go with an easier mind. You're a governess, and a lady, not really a servant at all, even if you do have a bumpkin like me for a cousin.'

She shook her head. 'I know what you're trying to say, Jonah, and I'm sorry but it's no

185

use. Lady Pickhurst has made my position very clear. We could never be friends.' She glanced back towards the house. It was almost dark now, and she should be with the children.

'I have to go. Dear Jonah, I'm glad you're talking to me again. I'll hate to see you leave, but I think it's the only way.' Phoebe stood on tiptoe so she could reach to pull his head down and give him a sisterly kiss on the cheek. 'Lady Pickhurst won't be the only one to lose a friend, but you must do what's best.'

Torn between relief and sadness, she ran round to the back entrance of the house. She passed the bevy of servants preparing for dinner with her cheeks flaming and the stain of tears still on her face, but she held her head high, not caring what they thought.

'Tell me, are Mrs Stoppens's rubies truly as beautiful as they say?'

Mortleigh jerked round, his hand still upon the cuff he was unfastening. 'What?' He stared at Lucille, then at the open door behind her. 'My man will be here—'

She shook her head and pushed the door shut. 'I sent him on an errand, we have ten minutes. You didn't answer my question.'

What would I know of Mrs Stoppens's jewellery?' He had command of himself again. 'You're likely to have seen more of it

186

than I.'

'Oh yes, on top of her horrid dyed hair.' She tossed her own, aware of its beauty and knowing he was watching her in the mirror. 'I never held those emeralds in my hand. Not like you.'

'Are you mad?' he turned his attention back to his cuffs. 'How would I come to handle the jewellery of an old and ugly woman? I don't have a clue what you're talking about.'

Her lips lifted in her cat-like smile. 'Are you telling me I'm wrong about the reason for your visit to Dunsby Court on Saturday? Perhaps my first suspicion was right, and you were courting sweet little Agatha. She's prettier than her mother, and they say she's worth a fortune, but I would have thought you might prefer a wife with half a brain.'

Mortleigh faced her. 'I was in London on Saturday.'

'So you say. And yet I saw you mount your horse in the little copse at the back of Dunsby Court and ride away. Rather strange, isn't it? If I'd chosen to tell my story to Sir Martin Haylmer instead of waiting to talk to you, perhaps he would have thought I was hallucinating. Or perhaps not.' She began to walk around the room. 'On the whole, I think I would prefer to know you for a common thief, rather than the kind of fool who'd marry Agatha Stoppen for her money, particularly as that would involve rejecting me. And Knytte, of course,' she added, as if it were an afterthought.

'I'd never thought of you as an inventor of fiction, Lady Pickhurst,' he said. 'This has been an interesting venture into fantasy, but I don't think your ladyship should be found dallying in a man's room at this hour. Perhaps you'd better go now.'

'You wouldn't believe how angry the idea of your rejection made me,' she went on, as if he hadn't spoken. 'I imagined you planning your strategies even as you visited my bed. I'll share no man's affections.' She came to a halt, standing close behind him, and lifted a hand to run a fingernail gently down the back of his neck. 'No, I much prefer to think of you as a daring renegade, risking his life by robbing the rich to help the poor, which in this case means yourself, of course.'

'You saw some man riding a horse that resembled mine, and concluded that I'm a thief?' His back was still turned to her; he sounded amused.

She grabbed his arm and pulled him to face her with extraordinary strength. 'I'm not a fool,' she said. 'I know you. I saw *you*. Poor Mortleigh, I've found you out. But you needn't worry, I've no intention of giving you away. In fact, you're exactly the man I need.'

'You say so. And yet you've been meeting

your rustic knight in the summer house again. You see, my dear Lucille, you're not the only one who knows how to discover secrets.' His hands captured her arms, holding them tight, his fingers digging into her flesh. 'It must be very convenient, having spyholes to watch and listen through. I have a somewhat less obvious system.' His lips were upon hers, hard, demanding, his tongue probing deep. Her back bent under his weight and he let go of one arm to grope beneath her skirts. 'You witch. Let it be you and me, then. A match made in heaven, or maybe in hell.'

With some difficulty she thrust him away. 'An hour,' she said huskily. 'Come to me in an hour.'

He cocked an enquiring eyebrow at her. 'In the garden, my sweet? Among the spiders, like your bucolic sweetheart?'

She scowled at him, then laughed, low and inviting. 'Not this time. Don't worry, his lordship will be sleeping sound, I'll see to that. He'll be waiting for me even now, all agog, for I've promised him a rare treat. He'll only have my body a little longer,' she added, seeing his look. 'My heart's already yours.'

'And what of your hulking Romeo?' His face was suddenly ugly and he tugged viciously at her hair. 'You want me to yourself, you're jealous of an empty-headed chit of a girl, but you expect me to share you with that ignorant peasant.'

'Come in an hour. I'll prove how little Jonah means to me.' She pulled him to her, and sank her teeth into his neck, biting hard. 'Don't be late.'

They lay curled together on her bed, sated at last. Beyond a locked door Lord Pickhurst was deep in a drugged sleep. Mortleigh stroked the soft flesh beneath his hand, and felt her instant response. He smiled, and desisted. 'I never knew a woman with such an appetite,' he whispered. 'Tell me, you can't have discovered my secret simply by seeing me at Dunsby Court? What else do you know?'

'Your exploits are notorious. I read the newspapers and checked on the dates. The night we first – shall I say, met?' She gave a languorous laugh. 'There are so many impolite ways of putting it. You left me, remember. At first I couldn't see how you came and went so freely from Knytte without detection, but of course there was your man, so quick and quiet on his feet.'

Mortleigh nodded. 'A good man, Tomms. Discreet and reliable.'

'Nobody thought it strange when he was sent to fetch your horses from the inn the next day. The newspaper report told me about the trap that was set at the Gallows crossroads. Two villains supposedly escaped unharmed, but that wasn't quite true, was it? Shots were fired, and one of them found a mark. How is poor Laidlaw?'

He curved a hand around her neck, his fingers soft and yet somehow threatening. 'What do you care? He only got in your way.'

Even as his fingers tightened she wouldn't be cowed; she knew her man, she was sure of him now. 'I don't care, I'm merely interested. You refused to fetch him a physician while he was at Knytte. What happened when you took him back to London?'

'He died,' Mortleigh said simply. 'So much the best solution, don't you think? As I told Lord Pickhurst, he's better in every way.'

She laughed. 'Well, he was a terrible bore.'

There was a brief silence before she spoke again. 'And when you came to Knytte, was it with the intention of robbing me? My husband likes to see me decked in his wealth. I have a string of pearls that would make your mouth water.'

'I had it in mind,' he said, relaxing his hold on her neck and beginning to caress her bare shoulder instead, 'but once I met you again there was nothing else at Knytte I wanted. Not that I wouldn't be tempted by the thought of owning some trinket that once lay against this white neck. Or better, perhaps a ring from this pretty hand.' He took her little finger into his mouth, sucking at it gently before nipping it with his teeth.

Lucille felt as if her flesh was melting. She moaned softly. 'Not yet. We have to talk. I'll not spend any longer than I must, married to that old goat.'

'You want him dead,' Mortleigh said baldly. 'Do you realize how difficult that will be? There must never be any cause for suspicion if you truly intend us to be together. I'm not averse to getting rid of a man if necessary, but I'll not swing from the gallows, even for you, my sweet.'

'I don't ask you to. I have a plan. My husband can be safely despatched. A week or two later, a month at most, we shall be together. What could be more natural than a grieving widow finding comfort in the company of her poor dead husband's friend?'

'You sound very sure of success, but accidents aren't easy to arrange.'

She draped herself sinuously on top of his body and lowered her lips to his ear. 'Let me tell you how it's to be done,' she whispered. 'I trust you don't find this too distracting.'

'I have a great ability to control myself,' he said smoothly. 'Unlike you.'

She laughed, and began to speak softly in his ear.

'We're no further forward.' Sir Martin Haylmer scowled across his desk at Docket. 'So much for the London detective. He did us no good at all.'

'To be fair, he got his hands on some of the stolen items,' Docket reminded him.

'Yes, and went and lost the damn things again. Tremayle has all but given up. One more robbery and I think he'll resign. I shall be a laughing stock. Please, tell me you have some small idea as to how we might proceed.'

'There's this,' Docket said, taking something small and glittering from his pocket.

'A ring from a dead man?' his lordship shook his head wearily. 'What do you think that might tell us?'

'I examined it through a glass. There are marks upon it, the sort a silversmith might be able to identify. Suppose we could find out where and when it was made?'

'The guilds keep their secrets to themselves,' Sir Martin was disparaging.

'Yes, but some men are less honest than others. With your permission I might take the thing to Hagstock and make some enquiries.'

'Very well, do what you can.' Sir Martin thrust himself suddenly up from his chair. 'I'm sick of the whole business, Docket. I need a change of air. If anyone asks I'm too busy to be disturbed. I'll be joining my son on Clow Top. He's gone off after rabbits, which sounds a lot more pleasant than chasing thoughts around my head. You'll see I'm left in peace for a couple of hours, if you value your skinny hide.'

Chapter Fourteen

There could be no denying the approach of autumn; the trees in Knytte's gardens and park were a riot of red and gold, although the colours were muted by the heavy morning mist that drifted from the lake. Phoebe stared out at the pearly brightness, seeing Jonah Jackman on his way to work. She felt for him; these days he wore his despondency like a huge weight on his wide shoulders. Her cousin had sworn to leave Knytte and she guessed it would be soon. As far as Phoebe could tell there had been no more night-time trysts at the summer house.

Unlike her cousin, Phoebe felt more settled now, for things had changed. There had been no more talk of finding schools for the Pengoar children. Lord and Lady Pickhurst occasionally summoned the youngsters to their presence; for half an hour Eliza would read to her ladyship, or play at cards with her, while his lordship talked to his nephew, their heads together over old maps and documents concerning the estate.

During her most benevolent moments, Phoebe thought perhaps she had misjudged her mistress, but the previous day, when she fetched the children from the salon, Phoebe caught an unguarded glance darted at Rodney from Lady Pickhurst's narrowed catlike eyes, and saw the hatred in them.

Shaking herself from her reverie, Phoebe opened the door that linked her room to the nursery; the children might already be awake.

A scream tore through the house, a sound of such horror that it seemed to stop her heart. It was not the cry of some hysterical young maid, but that of a man, full-throated and raw. As Phoebe stood frozen, Eliza came rushing from her bed, flushed of face and wide-eyed. She flung herself at the governess, sobbing wildly.

Rodney was only a pace behind the little girl. 'What's happened?' the boy demanded, as his sister hid her face in Phoebe's skirts. 'What was that noise?'

'I don't know. I can only imagine one of the pigs must have escaped from the home farm and got into the garden,' Phoebe said. 'It's amazing what an awful screech they can make.' She clasped her hands together to stop their shaking. 'Anyway, there's no call for you to be parading about in your night attire. Rodney, you are old enough to see to yourself, since Annie isn't here yet. I shall help your sister. Come along now, hurry.'

With her ears at full stretch Phoebe soothed the little girl and helped her dress;

she could make out the scurry of running feet, followed by the muttering of voices. The focus of activity was somewhere below the nursery, perhaps in the old library. It was strange, for none of those rooms were in use.

As she was brushing Eliza's hair she heard the sound of horses being ridden at speed down the drive. Glancing out of the window, Phoebe saw men mounted on two of Lord Pickhurst's fastest hunters, one taking the direct route across country that would take him to Trembury, while the other was heading for the main road.

Resisting the temptation to open the door and listen, or go seeking for information, Phoebe concentrated on the children. She would not add to whatever chaos reigned in the great house at that moment; if her help was needed it would be asked for. Annie had still not appeared, and Phoebe could imagine the servant's hall buzzing like a wasp's nest stirred by a stick.

Rodney went to open the door but she called him back. 'You are not to leave the nursery this morning without my express permission,' Phoebe said.

The boy looked mutinous, and she shook her head severely at him. 'You will behave as a gentleman should, Master Pengoar. Please remember who you are, and show your sister a good example. Ring the bell,' she added.

'No matter what has taken place, Annie should be here and tending to her duties.'

'But,' he began, tugging hard at the bell pull, 'suppose–'

'We shall suppose nothing,' Phoebe said firmly. 'I have heard no shout of "fire", and I know of no other reason for us to leave the nursery until you have performed your morning task and eaten your breakfast. We shall–'

The door burst open and Annie ran in, her hair escaping untidily from its cap, her apron askew and her cheeks flushed. 'Oh, Miss Drake, of all things! you'll never guess–'

'Hush!' Phoebe cut across the torrent of words, stepping past the girl to close the door. 'Look at the state of you. You should be ashamed to appear looking so unkempt, no matter what's happened. Straighten your cap, and calm down.'

'But it's his lordship.' Annie wasn't to be silenced, even as she pushed her hair out of sight. 'They just found him.'

'I asked you to be silent, you silly girl,' Phoebe said, taking the maid by the shoulder and giving her a little shake. 'Remember the children. Think before you speak.'

Her words fell on deaf ears. The maid was in a state of almost hysterical excitement.

'But we could all be murdered in our beds,' she shrieked. 'His lordship's dead!'

Two miles away, at the Dower House, the household was preparing to welcome its new master for the first time. Tomms stood looking from a window high in the roof. Given carte blanche by his indulgent employer, he had chosen the largest of the attics for himself; from here he could see across the park and make out the chimneys of Knytte in one direction, and the main road running north and south in the other.

Being apparently tired of waiting for the alterations to be completed, and claiming that he didn't wish to outstay his welcome at Knytte, his master was spending two days with an acquaintance near Hagstock. Mr Mortleigh was expected to arrive in time for luncheon. Tomms moved from one window to another, standing in silence and listening to the sounds of the household down below; he was satisfied that all was as it should be.

Two horses were being led from the stables for their morning exercise. In the garden an old man was raking fallen leaves from the lawns. Tomms lifted his gaze to the distance. Far off, glimpsed through the trees, he saw movement; a man was riding fast towards the Trembury Road. Moments later another horseman became visible, this time heading straight across the park to take the shortest route to Hagstock.

Tomms gave an abrupt nod, although his expression didn't change. Turning from the window, he dusted an imaginary speck of dirt from his immaculate sleeve. He started downstairs, the picture of the perfect man-servant, who, in his master's absence, had nothing on his mind but his breakfast.

Far across the moors, a slow procession was winding its way through the boggy wilderness. It had left a wayside inn at dawn with none to see but a yawning potboy. Two men led the way on foot, their clothes and demeanour marking them as miners. Behind came a blood horse ridden by a slender young man, alongside a cob bearing a larger man who rode one handed, his left arm held in a discreet black sling. A small wagon followed the riders, with a youth at the head of the rough-coated pony between the shafts. In the bed of the wagon lay a long narrow burden covered by a heap of sacking, topped with two spades and a short ladder.

Mist shifted around the feet of men and beasts, masking the faint path; sometimes it rose to above head-height to completely obscure their vision. The going was slow even when the mist cleared, for the track had barely been used since the mine at its end was abandoned some thirty years before. The cortege moved in silence. When the jagged top of a ruined chimney came into view the slender young man exclaimed and pointed, but his companion said nothing, merely nodding assent. Coming within fifty yards of their objective the wagon was halted; the pony at once dropped its head to graze on the rough greenery, while the two horses were handed into the care of the boy.

The tools were lifted from the wagon by the miners, and the four men trudged together down the slight dip beyond the ruined mine chimney. Still nobody spoke until they stood on the lip of a steep-sided pit.

'You gents will want to cover your noses,' one of the miners said, pushing a tentative heel into the edge of the hole.

'Aye, an' mebbe your eyes,' added the other, peering down. 'Tain't purty.'

'Just do your job,' the younger man ordered tautly. 'Should we not bring the box?'

'Not till we see 'ow to get the beggar out, Mr Docket.'

His partner gave a hoarse laugh. 'Could be him'll come by the shovelful, 'twouldn't be the first time. 'Member when Wheal Din-nock caved in, Dickon, thirty year gone, an' it took us six weeks to reach the last on 'em. Ye never saw such a sight.'

'That will do.' The older man had made no sound until now. He spoke quietly, but his order was instantly obeyed. Stationing himself at the rim of the pit, he watched as the miners manoeuvred the ladder into place and climbed down into its depths, gingerly avoiding the shapeless something that lay at the bottom. Docket, a scented handkerchief to his nose, stepped close enough to give the object a brief glance; he recoiled in horror and hurried away. Bending double behind a gorse bush, he retched noisily.

His companion returned to the wagon and lifted the covering off the plain coffin. He carried the sacking back to the pit and tossed it down to the miners without a word. Unflinching, he stood and watched as they went about their gristly business.

Nearly an hour passed before the little procession started back the way it had come, the pony leaning into its work now the coffin had an occupant. Docket's face was grey; he led the way, keeping up a pace the pony couldn't match, intent on distancing himself from the stench which dogged their footsteps.

'You really think this ghastly business was worthwhile?' he demanded irritably, when the man on the cob caught up with him. 'What can possibly be learnt when the body is in such a state? He might have been twenty years old or sixty, a dwarf or a giant, for all you could tell by looking at him.'

'I'm told this doctor in Hagstock is prepared to study the remains, no matter how badly decayed they are,' Sergeant Beddowes replied. 'There was a case in London not long ago when a murder victim was identified by the peculiar shape of his teeth.'

'But you claim you saw this man when he'd only been dead a day or two. You must already know more about him than we can learn by looking at that...' he broke off, his face blanching. 'If I had my way we'd have buried him where we found him.'

'Even villains like to have the proper words spoken over them by a parson,' Beddowes said mildly, 'and we have no idea whether this man was a saint or a sinner.'

Docket looked a little shame-faced. 'I suppose you think me weak.'

'I think you're lucky,' Beddowes said. 'As a soldier I grew accustomed to sights it's better not to see. As to what I saw last time I was here, that's partly why I'm so curious. His face was battered beyond all recognition. Either his attacker was driven by a terrible hatred, or he wanted to be sure the body couldn't be recognized.'

'But who would see it?' Docket objected. 'You were left for dead, and out here the body wasn't likely to be found.'

'Guilt can do strange things to a man's mind,' Beddowes observed. 'A murderer can never be sure that his crime won't come back to haunt him. I still have hopes that your enquiries of the silversmith may bring us a name to go with our faceless man.'

'At best he'll only suggest the name of a man who might be persuaded to help us,' Docket said. 'I see now why you're so well

203

thought of in your profession; you don't give up, do you?'

'Not when there's a worthwhile line of inquiry to be followed,' the sergeant replied, 'and it makes a difference when somebody tries to kill me. But you're right, I've never been good at admitting defeat.'

'Unlike Sir Martin,' Docket commented. 'He told me quite openly that as long as there are no more jewel robberies, he'd be happy to let the matter rest. Since there seems to be little hope of recovering the stolen items, even if the culprit is apprehended, the affair will always be remembered as a failure. He would prefer that the process of forgetting should begin as soon as possible.'

'He thinks like a politician,' Beddowes said. 'He might get his wish soon enough. I suspect he's written to my superiors and asked for me to be recalled, but until I receive a direct order I shan't be returning to London.'

'Somebody's in a hurry,' Docket commented as they turned onto the main road. A rider, leaning low over the sweating neck of his mount, was spurring hard in their direction. As he approached he slowed, and Docket brought his horse to a stand. 'It's Woodham. What's the matter, man?'

'I came to find you, Mr Docket,' Woodham said breathlessly. 'And the sergeant. Sir Martin asks that you go at once to Knytte.

Lord Pickhurst is dead. It looks as if the thief has struck again, only this time he did bloody murder.'

Knytte looked serenely indifferent to the drama unfolding within its ancient stone walls; the mist had cleared and the house glowed in the soft autumn sun. A groom came to take the horses, with only a slight delay, and the liveried footman who opened the door bowed to the two men with no show of emotion, though his face was flushed, and he seemed uncertain what to do with them once they were inside. A hysterical wail could be heard from somewhere above. Muted sobs from the direction of the kitchen were abruptly cut off by the noisy closing of a door.

'I am afraid Lady Pickhurst is indisposed,' the man said. He gulped. 'And I very much regret that his lordship–'

'We heard,' Docket said, 'that's why we're here, to give what assistance we can.'

The footman looked relieved. 'Inspector Tremayle arrived some time ago, sir. He was in the old library, which is where his lordship was found, but he stepped outside a few moments ago.'

'While we wait for his return it might be helpful if we have a look at the scene of the crime,' Beddowes suggested.

'I'm sorry, sir, but the inspector gave

205

orders that nobody should be allowed in that part of the house without his permission.'

Docket seemed prepared to argue, but Beddowes nodded. 'The case is under the inspector's jurisdiction, Mr Docket,' he pointed out.

'Then let him be told we're here,' Docket said.

The footman bowed. 'Very well, sir. If you gentlemen would care to wait in the morning room, I'll send somebody to tell him you've arrived.'

'We're wasting time,' Docket said impatiently.

Beddowes went to look out of the window. 'I've no right to become involved unless the local man requests help. Even if this crime is the work of our jewel thief, I should ask for Inspector Tremayle's agreement before taking part in the investigation.'

They weren't kept waiting long; Tremayle came to them, and was almost effusive in his welcome, his face positively beaming. 'I'm happy to say there's no need for you to exert yourself, Sergeant Beddowes. The murderer is caught. I have him locked up and under guard. In view of the serious nature of the crime, and the risk that the culprit might attempt to escape, I have sent to Hagstock for the secure carriage.'

'Congratulations,' Docket said. 'How did

you achieve such a speedy conclusion to the case? Did the villain confess?'

'No. In fact he insists he's innocent, but he's the only person who could possibly have committed the crime.' Tremayle smiled broadly, obviously very pleased with himself. 'Would you care to come and inspect the scene? Nothing has been moved, and I would be interested to hear your observations.' He led the way from the room, and for a few moments the frenzied screams became more audible.

'I'm afraid Lady Pickhurst is quite beside herself,' Tremayle remarked. 'Her maid and the housekeeper are with her, but they seem unable to comfort her. The doctor is expected soon.'

'I've found a large amount of cold water usually works well in cases of hysteria,' Beddowes said. 'And the sooner it's applied the quicker the cure.'

Docket looked shocked. 'Sergeant, you can't throw water over a member of the nobility!'

'Hmph,' Tremayle said non-committally. 'I'm afraid what you're about to see is rather gory, gentlemen.'

'Did Lady Pickhurst see the body?' Beddowes asked, thinking that might have caused the attack of hysteria.

'No. His lordship was found by Henson, the butler. The sight was too much for him.

207

Two footmen carried him to his room in a state of total collapse. He's not a young man, of course.'

Docket made a small sound, and Beddowes glanced at him in concern. His young companion managed a weak smile. 'At least my stomach can't betray me. I'm in no danger of losing my breakfast, since I rid myself of it some hours ago.'

The old library was dimly lit, only two of the shutters covering the windows that extended along one wall having been opened. A long table stood before the two men as they entered, with a broken chair lying on its side at the far end. Close to the chair, something dark lay sprawled in the shadows. The sergeant screwed up his eyes in an attempt to make out more detail, but he had to move closer to recognize it. Lord Pickhurst lay face down. From the side of his head ran a stain that shimmered in the uncertain light. Tremayle had gone to the windows, and as he opened another shutter, the splashes acquired colour, and became deep red, creamy white and grey. The contents of his lordship's skull, blood, bone and brains, were splattered across the dark pattern of the Persian carpet.

Behind him Beddowes heard a kind of sigh, then a slight thud, as Docket fainted.

Chapter Fifteen

Beddowes helped Docket to a sitting position, prudently keeping between the young man and the gory mess on the carpet. 'There's no need for you to stay. Go outside.'

Docket shook his head. 'No. I'm here as Sir Martin's representative. I'll do what I must.' He rose to his feet, visibly steeling himself before taking a step to the side so he could see what remained of Lord Pickhurst. 'What did that?' he asked, swallowing hard.

'We thought at first it must be a shotgun,' Tremayle replied, opening yet more shutters. 'But we were wrong. The murder weapon is over here.' With the morning light streaming in through six tall windows, the full horror of the scene was exposed.

Averting his gaze, Docket made his way around the long table to join the inspector, while Beddowes carefully traced the shorter route past the still damp patches which extended almost to the wall. He moved slowly, his eyes missing nothing.

The men met by the object which lay halfway between the windows and the upturned chair. It was the bust of a man, with a large strong-jawed head, and broad shoulders, modelled considerably larger than life-size. Beddowes stared at it with disbelief, it had the unmistakable look of solid marble, and he had never seen a less likely murder weapon. However, the evidence was plain enough; the side of the base and the right shoulder were horribly smeared with flesh, skin and blood.

'You see?' Tremayle was triumphant. He put his two hands around the neck of the bust, bent his knees in the classic strong-man's pose, and attempted to move the huge piece of marble from the floor. Exerting all his strength, the inspector could barely raise it an inch. Beddowes measured the man with his eye and frowned thoughtfully, flexing his injured arm; it wasn't sufficiently healed to risk the attempt, yet he was intrigued, want-ing to test the weight of the bust himself. He placed his one available hand beneath the bearded chin, where he could get a good grip. The burden was greater than he'd expected, and he felt his muscles protest; they'd been weakened by the enforced inactivity of convalescence, following his injuries, not to mention the spell of near-starvation.

Beddowes managed to lift the bust two inches from the floor. 'With two good hands I believe I could carry it,' he commented, 'but something like that isn't easy to use as a weapon.' He looked at the damage that had been done to Lord Pickhurst's skull and shook his head. 'He'd have to be a giant.'

'Exactly,' Tremayle said, rubbing his hands together, whether from glee or to remove the sting caused by his attempt at lifting the bust, Beddowes couldn't guess. 'Not a man in ten thousand could pick that thing up, let alone swing it over another man's head. It was immediately clear to me that this case was unconnected to the jewel robberies; I only had to ask if there was a particularly strong man known to be nearby, and the answer came. Jonah Jackman, a giant by comparison with the rest of us, has been employed at Knytte as a stonemason for nearly a year. I have a dozen witnesses who can swear they've seen him manhandling slabs of stone even larger than this during the course of his work.'

'But that's not the same,' Beddowes said. 'To lift is one thing, but to swing that great weight with enough power to do this—' he gestured at the body. 'It hardly seems possible.'

'Do you have any other suggestion as to how Lord Pickhurst met his death?' Tremayle asked. 'Perhaps three or four assailants joined together and threw the bust at him.' He pointed at the table, which was heavily scarred, his manner cheerfully sarcastic. 'Perhaps they jumped onto the table carrying the bust and dropped it, while he sat helpfully tilting his head to one side.'

Beddowes didn't answer. With the spread of blood and brain matter this last suggestion was plainly nonsense. He had seen that sort of damage done to a man's skull before, but only ever on the battlefield. Since joining the police force he'd encountered violent death many times; he recalled the case of a madwoman who battered a man to death with a sledge hammer. Slight in build, and apparently too weak to have committed the crime, she'd broken her victim's skull in a dozen places. However, she had rained down many blows upon her victim, and doctors at her trial had maintained that the insane were often possessed of exceptional strength.

The sergeant opened his mouth with the intention of making some comment, and then closed it again. Tremayle had made his position clear; this was nothing to do with the jewel robberies, and an outsider's opinion wasn't wanted.

'I wonder if we might go outside?' Docket suggested.

'By all means.' Tremayle took another complacent glance around the room. 'There is nothing more to learn here, and the wagon may have arrived. I must get my prisoner safely locked up. Once he has seen how the evidence speaks against him, he's bound to confess.'

'I hope the doctor has come,' Docket put in, his spirits clearly lifting once they'd left the scene of the crime, although the hysterical screams from the floor above had become clearly audible again. 'Poor Lady Pickhurst. I hate to hear a woman suffering so gravely. There were those who said the marriage was ill-matched, but I think the gossips got it wrong.'

'Since Inspector Tremayle has everything in hand, perhaps we should go,' Beddowes suggested.

Docket nodded. 'Sir Martin will want a report. I suspect he'll be happy that this matter has been so speedily resolved.' He gave Beddowes a sideways glance. 'I intend no slight, Sergeant. Sadly your own case has been dogged by bad luck.'

Outside, a one-horse phaeton stood in the drive. Wooden-faced, a footman informed them that Dr Pencoe had arrived, and was attending Lady Pickhurst; the sounds of distress from within had grown no less. The distant rattle of wheels could be heard; a Black Maria, with two constables on the box, turned the corner around the yew hedge and bowled up to the house.

'Excellent.' Tremayle beamed at Docket and Beddowes. 'Gentlemen, I'll confess my prisoner concerns me. He's a strong cove, Jackman. If he decided to attempt an escape we might have our hands full. I'd be obliged if you would remain while we move him to the wagon, just as a show of extra strength,

213

as it were.'

'Perhaps it would be wise for us to arm ourselves,' Docket suggested.

'I don't think that's necessary,' Tremayle said. 'My lads carry nightsticks, and we've got the manacles on him, but I'd be grateful if you'd stand by, just in case.'

Docket bit his lip, half turning to Beddowes. The sergeant said nothing, content to leave the decision to the Lord Lieutenant's secretary. He suspected Tremayle merely wanted an audience for his triumphal departure.

The man who was led from the stables attended by four constables was indeed a giant, several inches taller than Beddowes, who stood over six feet, and a great deal more powerfully built. The suspected murderer towered over his escort, but he walked slowly, looking straight ahead. It seemed he had no intention of attempting to escape.

Beddowes looked at the man's face, and felt a jolt of recognition. In battle Beddowes had seen both men and horses reach a point when they removed themselves from a reality that was too awful to be borne. They no longer wished to live, even though they'd suffered no acute physical harm, because life itself had become intolerable.

There was an obvious conclusion; Jackman must have committed the murder in a moment of madness, and now he was filled with horror at what he'd done. Perhaps he couldn't escape that terrible scene in the old library; it would haunt him, waking and sleeping, until he met his end on the gallows. Disliking his morbid thoughts and knowing the prisoner would need no further restraint, Beddowes turned towards the stable yard, eager to leave. A woman's voice stopped him, lifted in a heart-rending cry.

'No, oh no!'

Beddowes turned back. The captive was about to step into the Black Maria. A woman, small and slight and dressed in a plain grey gown, was running towards him.

'No!' she cried again. 'This is all wrong! Jonah, you can't let them take you. Tell them the truth.'

Inspector Tremayle stepped forward, the smile wiped momentarily from his face. He caught the woman by the shoulder before she could reach his prisoner. 'Come now, miss, this is police business. Step aside if you please.'

'But you're making a mistake!' She shook off his grip, but made no further move. 'Whoever killed Lord Pickhurst, it can't have been Jonah. He'd never hurt anyone, he's the gentlest person I know.' Jackman kept his gaze fixed on the ground as if he was unaware of her presence.

'Are you saying you know where this man was when Lord Pickhurst was killed?'

Tremayle had assured himself that this was a person of no position in the household and his tone was rough. 'Was he with you?' He shot the words at her like an accusation, making her recoil from him. 'This rogue's a single man, so I understand,' he went on relentlessly, 'but perhaps you were keeping him company last night.'

The woman stared at him in horror. 'I was in my room next to the nursery,' she said, finding her voice at last, 'as I am every night.' She faltered under the inspector's gaze. 'You don't understand. Jonah is my cousin. I've known him since we were children. He's not a violent man.'

'You're wasting my time,' Tremayle said. He brushed past her as the door at the back of the wagon was closed and locked. 'All right lads, take him.' With a nod to Docket he hurried to the carriage which had brought him to Knytte. There was the jingle of harness and the creak of springs, followed by the crunch and hush of wheels on gravel. The noise faded as the two vehicles went down the drive, until all that could be heard was the hysterical wailing floating from an open window above them.

Some instinct propelled Beddowes across the dozen yards that separated him from the young woman; he reached her just as she crumpled. She didn't weigh much; even with the use of only one arm, he was able to prevent her from falling. He half carried her to a stone seat, set beside the steps into the house.

'I'm quite well,' she was saying, as she sank onto the seat, 'a moment of weakness, that's all.' She turned her head, so that she could see who held her, and with a little gasp, she fainted.

Lucille flung out an arm, as if in a paroxysm of grief. She lay face down upon the bed, her pillow soaked with tears. For a while she'd relished the part of a widow driven mad by the loss of a beloved husband, but her hysterical shrieks had made her throat sore, and now she had a headache. Weary at last of her play-acting, she allowed her sobs to quieten, and heard her maid whisper to Dr Pencoe.

'Please sir, is there nothing you can do?'

'It's difficult while her ladyship refuses to allow me near her,' the man said testily. 'Physical force is a last resort in such cases, and since I understand Dr Long is expected, it may be best to await his arrival.'

'I believe her ladyship is close to exhausting herself,' the housekeeper put in. 'Should I order a fresh posset? We may be able to persuade her to take it now.'

'If you can persuade her to take anything it should be the medicament I have here, but since two doses have already been spilt

217

there seems little point wasting another.'

Biting at the bedclothes to keep from laughing, Lucille moaned and thrashed about again. This time she felt her hand connect with soft flesh, though which of the women she'd struck she couldn't tell. A hysterical laugh burst from her lips. She would continue the charade until Dr Long witnessed her prostration. He was both older and more widely respected than the local man, Pencoe; she wished to convince as many people as possible of the sincerity of her grief, for plenty of her neighbours would be sceptical.

'My Lady, please, try to be calm. I think I hear a carriage coming.' The maid ran to the window. 'Yes, at last! Will you not allow me to bathe your face and brush your hair before Dr Long comes upstairs?'

By way of answer Lucille gave another hysterical wail, flailing wildly. Stupid girl! What would be the point of working herself into this state if she was prinked and tidied before the old fool arrived? She lifted her head and immediately felt dizzy; that might be useful, for she felt a grand gesture was needed.

As the door opened a few minutes later Lucille rolled across the bed. 'My husband,' she sobbed, 'I must see my poor dear husband.' She rose to her feet before the two women could reach her and stood swaying;

exhausted as she was, this required no play acting. 'Help me, Doctor,' she wailed, 'please, if you have any compassion, let me hold my sweet love in my arms one last time!'

Phoebe pushed herself upright, forcing the man who held her to let go. 'I am quite well now,' she said, painfully embarrassed. She watched her rescuer as he withdrew, to stand a few feet away; he seemed almost as ill-at-ease as she was.

'Miss Drake,' Docket came to take the vacant space beside the governess; they had been acquainted when she worked at Clowmoor Manor, and he felt himself obliged to assist her. 'Should I send indoors for a maid? You've been badly shaken.'

'I need no help, thank you,' she replied, her chin lifting suddenly. She stared at the sergeant's back. 'Seeing a man alive and well, having been assured that he was dead, was a great shock, that's all.'

'It was a villain by the name of Fetch'n'carry Cobb who died.' The tall man turned again, and came to stand before her. 'I apologize for giving you such a shock.'

'Allow me to present Sergeant Beddowes, Miss Drake,' Docket said hastily. 'He's a detective from London.'

Phoebe rose to her feet. Her eyes were still a long way below those of the sergeant, but she met them fearlessly; this was the man of

219

her dream, but that was a secret she wouldn't disclose for the world. 'It was you,' she said. 'The tramp. And don't tell me I'm mistaken. I suppose there must have been a good reason for the deception, but I fail to see what it could be. Excuse me, I should return to my charges. They were fond of their uncle, and I'll not risk them seeing or hearing things that are best kept from them.'

'Of course,' Docket said, offering her his arm. Beddowes quelled him with a look.

'No, Docket, I believe this has to be set right. Miss Drake, I beg you will allow me to make a proper apology. I'm sure Mr Docket will carry any message you wish, regarding the care of the children.'

She had lowered her gaze and seemed not to want to look at him again. 'I left them with the nursery maid, Annie, but the girl has rather lost her head this morning. It would be better if I were there.'

Docket sketched a little bow in her direction. 'With your permission, I shall go to the nursery at once and speak to the children. I've met them before, I don't believe they'll be afraid of me. If they are, however, or if your presence is required, I shall return at once.' With a sidelong glance at Beddowes he sketched a bow, ran up the steps and into the house.

'Won't you sit down again?' Beddowes asked, gesturing at the seat. 'You've had two nasty shocks this morning.'

'No.' She shook out her skirt and turned her back on him. 'I prefer to walk around the lawn and clear my head. Mr Docket will find us easily enough if I'm needed.'

Beddowes hurried to follow her, a slight smile on his face. Miss Drake was not only pretty, she had a mind of her own.

'First,' he said, 'let me apologize for giving you such a shock. I'd been playing the part of this rogue called Cobb ever since I arrived in this county. We planned to lure the jewel thief into a trap, but it didn't work. In fact it went badly wrong. It was fortunate that a courageous young woman came to my rescue. I sent my thanks, but I'm afraid they weren't adequate. Please, let me repeat them in person.' He placed himself ahead of her, so she had to come to a halt.

Phoebe met his look with a slight flush on her cheeks. 'I assure you this isn't necessary.'

'On the contrary, it is. Miss Drake, thank you. I believe you saved my life. I really am sorry. I didn't expect anyone to recognize me.'

She didn't drop her gaze and for a long moment they stood motionless. He had been thinking what an attractive woman she was, but suddenly it was hard to frame any thought at all.

'It was your eyes,' she said simply. 'I

couldn't believe you were a villain, despite your outward appearance, and what I was told.'

'I think that's the kindest thing anyone has ever said to me.' He was the first to break the charged contact between them, turning away so they could resume their walk. They had almost reached the other side of the lawn before Beddowes spoke again.

'Miss Drake, I owe you a considerable debt. This business with your cousin; is there anything I can do to help?'

She shook her head. 'Not unless you believe poor Jonah is innocent, as I do. I suspect that being a policeman, you'll be inclined to see things the same way as Inspector Tremayle.'

'I understand his reasoning,' Beddowes conceded, 'but he may have been hasty.' He thought about his visit to the crime scene, and his uneasy feeling that all was not as it seemed. 'Why are you so sure Jackman didn't murder his lordship?'

'Because I know him. You called me kind, but I'm not as tender-hearted as my cousin. The trouble is, I can't prove he's innocent.' She made a helpless gesture. 'Things have been happening in this house. Please, would you speak to Jonah? I made promises to him, and I can't break them, but if you could persuade him to tell the truth, the whole thing might appear in a very different light.'

'I'm willing to try,' Beddowes said, intrigued. He said goodbye to Miss Drake without allowing himself to look her full in the face; he had enough to occupy his mind without getting entangled with a woman.

Fortunately Docket was silent as they returned to Clowmoor House, and Beddowes was left to his own thoughts; not all of them concerned the murder of Lord Pickhurst. Despite his best intentions, he was finding it hard to forget the soft voice declaring that he didn't have the look of a villain.

Lucille accepted the sleeping draught Dr Lock gave her. She had known he would deny her request to see her husband, but it had been a nice touch. Worn out by her play-acting, she awoke some hours later feeling refreshed. She stretched her arms languidly; it was late now, almost dark. Her maid knew better than to enter until she was sent for, but nevertheless Lucille checked the joyous laugh that had almost come unbidden to her lips. She put up a hand to touch them, enjoying the sensuous softness of her own body; never again would she have to submit to the press of that hateful dry skin against hers.

On silent feet she rose and went to the window, careful to remain a little way from the glass; let the world think her in deep mourning and still prostrate upon her bed. It would be tiresome keeping up the pretence. Once the old wretch was buried she would summon the steward and begin to learn everything about her estate. She smiled to herself, planning her strategy; she would be pale and fragile but determined, a woman left alone by fate, courageously taking the place of a man.

The Dower House was hidden by trees. She wondered if Mortleigh had returned there yet. The thought of him brought a warm tingle of pleasure. Throwing back her head, she imagined the touch of her lover's lips, hard and demanding upon her neck. As her body responded to the thought she smiled. She hadn't forgotten how he'd treated her that first time. His ruthless nature matched hers so well.

Lucille, Lady Pickhurst, sank down slowly upon her bed. She had promised to share Knytte with her lover. It was a great prize. She hadn't yet made up her mind whether she would honour that promise. Freedom was inexpressibly sweet.

Chapter Sixteen

Just two days after he was murdered, Lord Pickhurst was buried in the family crypt. His young widow, wearing a black veil which completely hid her face, leant heavily on her father's arm during the short walk to the chapel. The Honourable Mr Horace Gayne had arrived in a hired carriage. Sour-faced and breathless he told the assembled congregation that his wife was not well enough to travel, having collapsed when she heard about the death of her son-in-law.

Victor Mortleigh was among those to offer condolences, but said no more than a dozen formal words before withdrawing to the Dower House. Very soon after that Lucille returned home. Her father followed her into the salon. Those servants who hadn't re-treated behind the baize door were treated to the sound of a loud and vitriolic quarrel.

Lady Pickhurst rang the bell and ordered a carriage. Very soon after that Mr Gayne left, red faced and perspiring. It seemed he was no longer welcome at Knytte.

Left alone, Lucille looked idly through the letters and cards from solicitous neighbours. Mortleigh's was among them. The note was as formal and uninformative as the few words he'd spoken at the chapel. A frown creasing her forehead, she stepped towards the fire, intending to throw both card and envelope in. Just in time she noticed there were a few pencil lines on the inside of the envelope. At first glance Lucille thought they were random scribbles, but then she recognized the roughly outlined shape, and laughed aloud. Mortleigh had sent her a picture of the garden house, the location he had chosen for their first act of adultery.

Lucille kissed the drawing, then tossed it into the fire. Tomorrow she would find some excuse to call on her new neighbour. She decided she should pick a quarrel with him; let nobody say they had become friends too readily, or too soon after the death of her husband. As to meetings conducted at night, that was another matter.

Sir Martin Haylmer had requested his presence. Sergeant Beddowes was shown into a chilly parlour where he stood by the window looking out at the wide sweep of Clowmoor's park. The trees were bright with autumn colour and fat cattle grazed among the first of the fallen leaves. It was a beautiful scene, but he wasn't really seeing it; he had a great deal to think about.

His memory was improving; he'd recalled his encounter with the smugglers. After being tipped out of the rickety dogcart, he remembered deciding to take the road to the west and return to Clowmoor with the intention of speaking with Sir Martin. Beyond that it was still a blank, until he regained consciousness in the pit. Dr Long had warned him he might never remember those lost hours.

Immediately after Lord Pickhurst's funeral, Docket had taken the train to London, carrying the ring that Beddowes had taken from the naked corpse on the moor. Silversmiths were notoriously secretive, but thanks to his local informant, Docket hoped to prise some information from the marks contained within the little silver band. Beddowes was grateful for the young man's enthusiasm; but for that, he might have been forced to make an admission of defeat.

A footman came to summon him to Sir Martin's presence. The Lord Lieutenant looked more cheerful than he'd expected, and waved the sergeant to the chair opposite his own. 'Come in, Beddowes. I have some news for you. Good or bad, I'm not sure yet, but it's interesting at least.' He picked up a letter and handed it to the sergeant. 'What do you think of that?'

It was a report from the young doctor in Hagstock, the man with a taste for dead bodies, no matter how decayed they might be. Beddowes scanned the first few lines.

There was nothing new there; he already had a fair idea of the man's height, weight and age.

He reached the second paragraph and his eyes widened; he read on swiftly.

'I examined the cadaver's right arm with some care, as the decomposition seemed more advanced there. I found a bullet embedded between the radius and ulna. From the condition of the surrounding flesh I would guess the injury was sustained no more than two days before the man's death. The wound would have been painful but not necessarily fatal. A physician could have removed the bullet without too much difficulty. One must assume the wound had been left untreated.'

'Well?'

'One of the rogues was winged after all,' Beddowes said. 'I owe that man of yours an apology, and a pint of ale to go with it.'

Sir Martin nodded. 'One of the thieves died. His partner made sure he couldn't be recognized before disposing of the body.'

'I'm not so sure that's how it happened,' Beddowes said. Wrinkling his nose, he tried to remember his awakening next to the naked corpse. 'I don't think that man died of the gunshot wound. It might have killed him in time; his arm was swollen but it hadn't gone bad. I suspect his friend decided to get rid of him.'

Sir Martin scowled. 'That's pretty cold-blooded.'

'The man at the crossroads fits the bill. He gave the orders. When his pal showed his nerves and almost let something slip, he took a fist in the face for his carelessness. I'd say after nearly being caught, and with an injured man on his hands, our jewel thief decided he'd be better off alone. He certainly didn't trust Cobb, despite having dealt with him for several months. Obviously my attempts to convince him that I'd got nothing to do with the ambush at the crossroads didn't work, but maybe that close call scared him. He decided to cut loose from anyone who could identify him.'

'None of this helps us.' Sir Martin sounded despondent.

'Maybe not.'

The Lord Lieutenant was silent for a long moment. 'As chief magistrate I was responsible for asking Scotland Yard for help, Sergeant. When you arrived with a plan ready formed, thanks to Cobb's capture, I thought we'd soon be done with the affair, but here we are, weeks later and the rogue is still at large. I'm not saying it's all your fault, but we're no closer to finding him than we were a month ago.'

'I know what you're thinking, but there's a chance Docket may bring us some news. I'd be grateful if you'd allow me another week.'

Sir Martin hesitated, and before he could frame an answer Beddowes hurried on. 'I'd like to look into another matter while we're waiting. The jewel thief never attempted to rob Knytte, and now a much more serious crime has been committed in that house. Can it be a coincidence? After all, we know the thief's capable of murder.'

'I'm inclined to agree with Tremayle,' Sir Martin replied, 'the case looks quite straightforward. The trial's set for Monday, you know. I'm not expecting it to last long.'

'I agree the use of the marble bust as a murder weapon implicates Jonah Jackman,' Beddowes said, 'but what was his motive? Why would a respected stonemason suddenly decide to kill his employer? At least let me ask him.' He had Phoebe Drake very much in mind. He would hardly acknowledge it, even to himself, but his interest in the affair at Knytte had more to do with that young woman than a remote chance of connecting Lord Pickhurst's death with the jewel thief.

'I suppose that wouldn't hurt.' Sir Martin gave a decisive nod. 'You have your seven days, Beddowes, but no more. See Jackman. Tell Inspector Tremayle you're acting on my authority.'

Beddowes sat in the dismal little room in

Hagstock gaol. He had talked himself to a standstill, and had no idea what else he could do.

Jonah Jackman was refusing to speak. Perhaps after what he'd heard Miss Drake say he should have expected it. The stonemason had sat silent and unmoving for an hour, his large hands resting motionless on his knees. He showed no hint of nerves; he seemed unaware of the precariousness of his position. Even when Beddowes told him bluntly that his refusal to speak would be seen as an admission of guilt, Jackman wouldn't say a word.

'If you'll not speak up for your own sake, what about Miss Drake?' It was a low blow, but all he could think of. 'She cares for you and thinks nothing of herself, but how will things be for her, if you're hanged for murder? It would be disastrous for a governess to lose her post in such circumstances. Nobody would employ her. Would you die knowing you're responsible for leaving her destitute, or even that your refusal to tell the truth has seen her into her grave?'

Jackman looked up for the first time, as if this thought had never occurred to him.

'Did you kill Lord Pickhurst?' Beddowes stared into the man's face, and saw nothing there to reassure him; the eyes retained that dead haunted look he'd seen when Jackman walked to the Black Maria. 'Did you?' the

231

sergeant persisted.

Very slowly Jackman shook his head.

'But you know something of what happened that night,' Beddowes said. 'Miss Drake begged you to tell the truth. What did she mean by that?'

Jackman let his head droop again. Guilty or not, it seemed he was determined to hang. He looked as if he was wearied to death by some intolerable suffering. Had that shake of the head been a lie? Crushing Lord Pickhurst's skull might have been enough to unsettle his mind, but if so, why should he deny that it had been his work?

Riding the cob steadily along quiet lanes, Beddowes reviewed his attempt to interview Jackman. He could think of nothing else he might have tried. Still deep in thought he turned into the drive; ahead of him Knytte lay calm and unchanging amid the autumn colours, the afternoon sun lighting its walls and adding to its beauty. Handing the cob's reins to a groom, he found the man willing to talk, and he worked the conversation round to the subject of Jonah Jackman.

'Tain't my place to say,' the groom said, pulling the cob towards a stall. ''Tis only gossip, when all's said and done.'

'What do you mean? What gossip?'

The man shook his head, and refused to say another word. Beddowes cursed under his breath. There was something to learn here.

Despite questioning two footmen, the cook and several maids, he had no better success in the house. The butler, Henson, still looking pale and shaken, answered Beddowes's questions briefly, but gave nothing away.

'Was Jackman working alone?' Beddowes asked.

'No. He had two men with him. They'll be in the ruins now if you wish to speak to them. Since there's still a great deal to be done, I took it upon myself to keep them at their work, until Lady Pickhurst has recovered enough to be consulted.'

'And do you know when that will be?'

'She has sent a message to the estate steward. I believe she intends to see him tomorrow.'

Beddowes nodded. 'I'll see the masons today, at least.' If anybody here had known Jackman well, it should be these two. Henson summoned a footman to take him outside, by way of the tradesman's entrance.

The stonemasons were brothers, similar to Jackman in age, but not his match in height or build. They greeted the sergeant's questions with suspicion, the older brother taking it upon himself to give the answers. He said Jackman was a good man to work with, that they knew no reason why he should attack Lord Pickhurst. When Beddowes pressed him, the man said Jackman had never been overly talkative; if he had secrets they'd no way of knowing. Once or twice Beddowes noticed that the younger man looked ready to speak, but his habit of deference to his brother kept him silent.

'Jonah Jackman seems determined to go to the gallows,' Beddowes said, having grown tired of hearing nothing of any significance. 'His cousin, Miss Drake, swears he's innocent. If you're his friends, won't you at least say a word in his defence?'

'If he done murder, I'd say 'tweren't all his own fault.' These were the first words the younger man had uttered.

'What do you mean by that?' Beddowes asked sharply.

'Only that Jonah's not the violent type,' the elder man answered for him, shooting his brother a warning look. 'I s'pose he'd need a powerful good reason.'

'Whether it was Jackman or some other man, have you any idea how the murderer might have got into Knytte, once it was locked up for the night?'

The two men exchanged a glance; the elder brother shrugged. 'There's a door through the back here,' he said. 'Goes straight into the house. It were found unlocked once, a few weeks back, so we heard. Same thing must've happened again.' At Beddowes' request he led the way through the old refectory to the heavy oak door.

Looking around, Beddowes saw a piece of stone, similar in colour to the large blocks the brothers were working on. He bent to pick it up; it was wedge shaped, about two inches deep at its widest, and maybe five inches long. Its edges were sharp beneath his fingers. 'This looks as if it was cut recently,' he remarked.

'Reckon somebody brought it from back there,' the stonemason said, hitching a thumb towards the tower. 'It'll be a piece we split off, shaping blocks for the stairs. Jonah did some work inside, but that were months back.'

There was a deep mark on one of the longer sides of the stone, where the roughness had been worn off. 'What's caused this then?' Beddowes asked.

The man shrugged. 'Dunno. Nothing we've done. Can't see no point to it.'

Returning to the house, Beddowes asked Henson about the door. The butler looked distressed. 'It's usually kept locked but it was found wide open that morning,' he said. 'Inspector Tremayle saw that as more evidence against Jackman. When he was first employed here, nearly a year ago now, he repaired the fireplace in the old library. He used that door to come and go.'

'But whoever came in here the other night to attack Lord Pickhurst would have needed a key.'

'There was a key left in the lock while Jackman was working indoors,' Henson said, as he led the way down the corridor Beddowes had followed with Docket the day before. 'Perhaps he had a copy made.'

At Beddowes' request, Henson opened the heavy old door. 'As soon as I entered the corridor the other morning I felt the draught of air. It's dark along here, but I realized this must be open. When I came to investigate I glanced into the old library. That door was also standing wide open, and I saw his lordship's body.' Struggling to hold the door against the gusty wind, he picked up a piece of wood that lay on the floor nearby, and wedged it underneath.

Beddowes stepped through into the old refectory and recovered the scrap of stone he'd found before.

'That was used to wedge the door open the night his lordship was murdered,' Henson remarked, before Beddowes could ask the question.

'Why, though,' the sergeant pondered. 'Jackman would have known the wooden wedge was there. He must have used it when he was carrying stone or tools through.' He frowned, trying to make sense of it all. 'I'm told this door was found unlocked at night once before. Was it left wide open then?'

'No.' The butler shook his head decisively and told him how the household had been woken by a crash in the middle of the night, and how a search had shown no sign of any intruder.

Beddowes gave the door a powerful shove, to see if the wedge could be dislodged by a gust of wind. It shifted half an inch then stuck fast. 'If the wind had blown the door shut, the wedge could have been pushed inside.'

The butler shook his head. 'It hadn't been used. It was in its usual place. And there was nothing lying on the floor of the refectory either. I opened the door to look round before I locked up again.'

'Was everything in order the next morning?' Bedddowes asked.

'Yes. I took the precaution of bolting the door before leaving it.' Henson's face took on a haunted look. 'I should have made a point of bolting it every night. Who knows but it might have saved his lordship?'

Beddowes could offer him no comfort, but he had a hunch that Lord Pickhurst's death had been premeditated, the result of some careful planning. He didn't think a bolted door would have prevented it.

'I've finished here, Mr Henson, thank you. I'll take a look in the old library now. There's no need for you to come with me,' he added swiftly, seeing the butler's expression.

'It's Lady Pickhurst's intention to have the

room sealed,' Henson said. 'She has given orders that nobody is to enter.'

'I doubt if that would include an officer of the law in the pursuit of his duties,' Beddowes said confidently, as they walked along the corridor. 'Why do you think Lord Pickhurst was there that night?'

'I can think of no reason. The room had been kept locked since work on it was abandoned.'

'Abandoned? Of course, you said Jackman had been working on it. So, it was supposed to be part of the alterations.'

'His lordship planned to have it made into a ballroom, but Lady Pickhurst didn't consider it to be in the right position. She favoured adding a wing to the other side of the house.' Henson shook his head, looking distressed. 'Unless his lordship invited him in, Jackman would have needed a key to this door as well. Please, ring the bell if you require anything further.' The butler avoided looking into the room as he ushered the sergeant inside, and closed the door swiftly behind him.

Apart from the absence of Lord Pickhurst's body, little had changed. Nobody had closed the shutters since Tremayle opened them, and there was plenty of light. Beddowes went first to the marble bust, kneeling on the floor to have a closer look, turning it one way and another, until he'd studied every part. Next, standing beside the table, he took up the stance of the attacker, pretending to swing a heavy object at somebody sitting in the broken chair. He repeated the exercise from behind the chair, before making a minute examination of the table. Some library steps stood against the wall, and Beddowes gave them the same careful attention before returning to the table and taking careful note of some scratches on its surface. He then stood staring at the ceiling. Satisfied, he gave a nod.

When he had done, with everything returned to its proper place, Beddowes strode to the other end of the table, where he pulled out a chair and sat down. With the crucial half of the room before him, hc recreated the scene of the attack in his mind, the frown that had furrowed his brow gradually smoothing out. He rose and began to search the book shelves. It only took him ten minutes to find what he was looking for, and a satisfied smile lit his face. He knew exactly how Lord Pickhurst had been killed. Now all he had to do was discover why, and then he would know the identity of the murderer.

Chapter Seventeen

A thunderous roar jolted Docket awake, his eyes starting open to stare uncomprehendingly at the smoky atmosphere. Everything around him shook and rattled alarmingly, and he experienced a brief moment of panic until he recalled where he was. The shrill of a steam whistle as the passing train streaked by the window added to the ache that was tightening around his skull. He hadn't slept the previous night, his head was throbbing, and his bones ached.

Across the carriage the elderly woman began to snore again, and Docket felt irrationally angry; how could she sleep through such discomfort? He rubbed the condensation from the window. It was hard to see anything, for the rain was relentless.

He put two fingers into his fob pocket and felt the ring lying there. His mission had been successful in a small way; a guinea had bought him some heavy hints, and he was heading for Edinburgh, where it seemed the little keepsake had been made.

The train lurched. Docket sighed and closed his eyes, trying to find a comfortable position. Ever since he'd met Beddowes he'd felt strangely ashamed of his easy life; family connections had secured his position as Sir Martin's secretary, and his duties weren't onerous. He'd been content, until the former soldier had given him a scent of a wider and more adventurous world. That was bad enough, but now he feared he might be falling into another of the traps that life set for independent young men.

Miss Phoebe Drake was only a governess; when they'd both been employed by Sir Martin he'd hardly noticed her existence. The fact that his lordship's son had frequently pressed his unwanted attentions on her had been enough to keep Docket away. Now, however, she seemed to have become rather desirable. She had played rather an exciting part in the rescue of the injured Beddowes, and since her cousin's arrest she had become a damsel in distress. Her background was acceptable enough; she was the child of an impoverished clergyman and a woman who was considered to have married beneath her. That was of more importance than her poverty. Docket wasn't an ambitious man; he had a small private income, and enjoyed his status as the Lord Lieutenant's secretary.

Seeing Phoebe lying pale and vulnerable against the sergeant's shoulder as he carried her to the seat in Knytte's garden, Docket's heart had received its first serious wound.

The connection with Jackman was unfortunate, but that could hardly be held against her, even if the stonemason went to the gallows.

A slight smile curved itself onto Docket's mobile lips. It had been no hardship to spend a few minutes with the two Pengoar children; he'd found them interesting. He'd never thought seriously about acquiring a wife and family of his own, but suddenly the idea was rather appealing.

Several hundreds of miles from the train carrying the weary Docket to Scotland, Beddowes was also thinking about Miss Phoebe Drake. His visit to Knytte the previous day had convinced him of Jonah Jackman's innocence, but while everyone refused to talk he couldn't begin to identify the real murderer. His best hope was to force Miss Drake to break her promise.

There was something about Miss Drake that made him reluctant to confront her; they had only met twice, but both those encounters had been charged with rare emotions. He didn't think he could bear to see reproach in those bright and penetrating eyes.

The sergeant had never married, though while he was a soldier he'd shared his life with a woman for three years, and not complained when she'd claimed the title of wife.

She had sworn her love for him, during those brief spells when he was in England, and he'd offered to marry her when he returned home for the last time. However, before the ceremony could take place, he discovered that she'd promised herself to several other men. Each of them believed that he alone supported her, paying for the comfortable rooms she occupied in Colchester.

The deception had been easy enough to sustain. She'd been clever enough to choose men in different regiments, and all of them spent most of their time overseas. Beddowes had resisted the temptation to beat his unfaithful mistress, but having discovered the identity of three more of her victims, jealousy got the better of him. He informed these other 'husbands' of her deceit. Two weeks later her body was dragged from the Thames. He'd never stopped regretting his betrayal; if guilt had driven him to join the forces of law and order, he never spoke of it, but he'd never again become entangled with a woman.

The cob, finding its rider inattentive, drifted towards a tempting clump of cow parsley at the side of the road. As the animal tried to snatch the reins from his hand Beddowes was jolted back to awareness. They were almost at Knytte. He scolded the animal and shortened the reins before returning to his reverie. It was ridiculous to imagine himself in love. Miss Drake was a gentlewoman, and far beyond his reach. If she had been kind, that was just her nature, it meant nothing. Nevertheless, for the first time in many years, Beddowes found himself wondering if he really wanted to remain a bachelor for the rest of his life.

With her husband buried, Lady Pickhurst, pale of face but bravely putting her grief aside, was ready to take over her inheritance. She was disinclined to indulge the detective when he requested an audience with Miss Drake.

'I'm puzzled, Sergeant,' she said. The veil she wore today was lighter than the one she'd chosen for the funeral, but it still hid her expression. 'The villain has been arrested. I see no point in raking over the circumstances of my husband's death. I have to become accustomed to my lonely life, and this can only make my grief harder to bear.'

'I'm sorry, your ladyship, I quite understand. I apologize for troubling you, but I must be sure that your husband's murder wasn't the result of a bungled attempt at robbery. We have new evidence that suggests the jewel thief could be violent, even murderous.'

She looked at him directly for the first time, and he was sure he saw a flash of anger behind the concealing lace. His instinct, and rumour, had been right. Lord Pickhurst's widow wasn't grieving.

'Jonah Jackman may well be guilty,' Beddowes went on, 'but he has the right to a fair trial, and the case against him must be supported by evidence. I know this is a difficult time for you, but if you could answer one question for me, that would be a great help.'

'Very well.' She lifted the veil a little to hold a wisp of lace to her eyes.

'Do you know of any reason why Jackman should wish to kill your husband?'

She gave a faint sob, and took a few moments to compose herself. 'Yes.' The word was a whisper. 'My poor dear husband. If only I had told him, he would still be alive.'

Beddowes waited, knowing he was watching an actress of some skill. 'Told him what?' he prompted.

'The matter is indelicate. I'll speak bluntly, though I may sound immodest.' She lowered her head. 'It gives me no pleasure, the way men react to me, but I have grown used to it. I can't help the way I look. Jackman wasn't the first man to be infatuated with me. If he had been, perhaps I'd have realized the risks. In the past few months I couldn't venture into the grounds without his staring at me, following me, trying to speak to me if there was nobody else nearby. I should have had him sent away, but I never realized it would come to this. The man is clearly insane.'

'You think he killed your husband out of jealousy?' Beddowes would have liked a proper look at her eyes, for that was where the truth lay, but the veil was impenetrable.

Lady Pickhurst nodded. 'I suppose I should pity Jackman, that is what the Church tells us, isn't it? I tried to stay out of his way. I barely gave him a civil word. How could a man like that think I would even look at him?'

'You mustn't blame yourself, your ladyship,' Beddowes said. 'Thank you for being so frank with me. I shan't trouble you further. May I speak to Miss Drake? As Jackman's only close relative, I think it only right to prepare her for the worst.'

At that she consented graciously, and Beddowes was shown to a small parlour on the second floor, obviously adjoining a bedroom; he wondered idly why this place had been chosen for his meeting with the governess, but he supposed it must be because of its closeness to the nursery.

When she came to him some five minutes later Miss Drake looked pale, but she was composed, offering her hand and asking after his health before she consented to sit down. 'I hope you will take a seat, too, Sergeant,' she said, 'I'm used to speaking to men who loom over me, but I prefer not to crane my neck.'

Beddowes found himself smiling at her

directness as he sat down. Everything about this girl charmed him. Miss Drake had an inner beauty that added to the sweetness of her face, and her honest character shone from her eyes; after Lady Pickhurst she was like a breath of clean air.

'I've spoken to Lady Pickhurst,' he said, plunging in before he had time to change his mind. 'She tells me your cousin was infatuated with her. She suggests that because she gave him no encouragement he killed her husband in a fit of jealous rage.'

Phoebe made a helpless gesture with her hands. 'If I didn't know Jonah to be incapable of killing anybody, then even I might accept that as the truth,' she said despairingly. 'But of course she didn't tell you how she led him on, how they met in secret after midnight...' she blushed, lacing her fingers together in her lap.

'Why don't you tell me,' Beddowes prompted gently.

'I promised I wouldn't. But she's made it sound as if he's guilty—'

'Yes. So somebody should make sure Jonah's tale is heard. I've already tried speaking to him. He won't talk, not even to save his life. If you care for your cousin, if you want to save him from the gallows, then you must help me.'

She looked up then. 'You truly believe he didn't do this awful thing?' Her eyes were suddenly moist; tears were waiting to spill over onto her cheeks.

'I'm sure of it. Lord Pickhurst was the victim of a cold-blooded murder, and the culprit intended that your cousin should be blamed. Please Miss Drake, tell me what I need to know.'

Lucille's hands gripped the silk hangings that once more hid the spy hole, torn between fear and anger. She bit nervously at her lower lip. The wretched governess had said a great deal, and Sergeant Beddowes had listened attentively, apparently believing her every word.

The story of Jonah's declarations of love had done no harm, for she'd told the detective of his infatuation. Driven mad by his obsession he could have invented the rest, and Miss Drake's description of her own foray into the garden might be seen as an ill-conceived attempt to help his case. However, there was one thing that concerned her; the interfering chit had named a night when Jackman swore he'd remained in his bed. That had been the occasion of her first clandestine meeting with Mortleigh; she recalled how she'd run her fingers across the nursery door to disturb the brats within. She knew she'd prompted the boy to nightmares; she'd hoped it would help her persuade her husband that the child would be better sent away to school.

What would the sergeant do? As Lady Pickhurst, owner of Knytte and its mighty estate, she was a person of power and substance, but without a husband, any woman was weakened in the eyes of the world. Her position alone might not save her from further questioning, if the governess's story was believed.

She had to speak to Mortleigh. In answering his letter of condolence she must bring him to her, and urgently. While writing to a neighbour she hardly knew, what could be more natural than a mention of his first visit to Knytte as her husband's guest, and her hope that it would be repeated soon? Her lover knew her so well; she had no doubt he would come that very night.

'It won't do, Beddowes!' Sir Martin shook his head vehemently. 'You come to me with this story about Lady Pickhurst carrying on an affair with Jonah Jackman, but with no proof to back up such an outrageous accusation. And in the very next breath you tell me Jackman is innocent of murder! Have you lost your mind? If this is the best you can do, you'd better take the next train back to London.'

'But, Sir Martin, if you'd just come to Knytte with me and let me show you the evidence I found in the old library, you'd

249

understand. It was a most ingenious way of committing murder, and it didn't require a man with Jackman's strength. Even a woman might have done it, if she was ruthless and cold-blooded enough.'

'So you'd lay the blame entirely on Lady Pickhurst?' Sir Martin was red with anger.

'No, on the man who took Jackman's place as her lover once she tired of him. I don't know his identity yet. Please, come to Knytte and let me show you exactly how cleverly the murder was arranged. Lady Pickhurst told me Jackman was infatuated with her. She insisted she never gave him any encouragement, but I have a witness who can swear they met after midnight in the summer-house. I know that makes Jackman's guilt look more likely, but if her ladyship has lied about that, if she was already betraying her husband only months after their marriage, what else might she have done?'

'Who is this witness?'

'Miss Drake, the children's governess.'

Sir Martin snorted, dismissing this with an impatient gesture. 'As Jackman's cousin she can't be trusted to tell the truth.'

'I might agree with you, if her evidence didn't appear to prove his guilt. But there is more. She claims that Lady Pickhurst left the house late at night on another occasion, and that time, she didn't meet Jackman. Her ladyship had another paramour. I believe that if we can find that man we have our murderer.'

His lordship thrust himself back into his chair. Beddowes made to say something, but was stopped by a glare. He stood waiting in silence as Sir Martin scowled at the ceiling. A long minute passed.

'If it's true that the murder didn't require the strength of a giant, as Tremayle has so persistently pointed out, then I suppose you may have something,' Sir Martin conceded. 'There has been talk about Lady Pickhurst. Of course that's common enough when a young woman marries a man so much her senior, and I don't give much credence to common gossip. Facts, Beddowes, that's what we need. We'll call at Knytte in the morning and take a look at the scene of the murder. I shall send a note to Tremayle, asking him to join us.'

Rodney Pengoar's nightmares had returned since his uncle's death. Phoebe spent every night in the armchair by his bed, holding him until his screams subsided into sobs and he was able to sleep again. Her own fears troubled her, almost as nebulous as those which haunted the boy. Since that fateful night she'd hardly slept.

The meeting with Sergeant Beddowes had disturbed her; she was glad he didn't see the case against Jonah as hopeless, but she wished it hadn't been at such a cost. What must the detective think of her? She'd been forced to speak of such indelicate subjects; she flushed as she recalled how much she'd revealed to him; her promise to Jonah was not only broken but shattered.

The boy turned in his sleep, muttering restlessly, and Phoebe leant forward to lay a hand upon his damp forehead, murmuring soothing words until he settled into a deeper slumber. The uncomfortable position gave her pins and needles, and she rose to walk about the room. She peeped between the curtains; the sky was clear, and the garden lay still and serene under the light of the stars. There didn't appear to be a breath of wind.

Movement caught her eye. A man flitted across the path, close to the lake. He was only visible for a moment. Phoebe put a hand to her mouth; she had almost exclaimed aloud. Whoever that was, they had no wish to be seen, and she could be quite certain it wasn't Jonah. She crept to the door and stood with her ear pressed against it, hardly daring to breathe.

A creak of floorboards, the faintest hush of a foot on the carpet, told her all she needed to know. Phoebe looked back at Rodney. He was sleeping peacefully, one hand curled against his cheek. She moved the lamp onto a high shelf, safely beyond his reach. With luck he wouldn't wake, but if he did he wouldn't find himself alone in the dark.

She hurried to her own room, dressing swiftly in the black mourning clothes she had worn for the funeral. Remembering how she'd stumbled in the dark last time she ventured through the house so late at night, she paused to light a candle, then very quietly opened the door and crept out into the corridor.

The candle sent shadows spiralling wildly around the walls, in constant danger of being extinguished as Phoebe hurried down the stairs and along the lower corridor. She didn't allow herself to think of the risk she was taking, though she gave an involuntary shudder as she passed the door to the old library. Very soon she stood under the vaulted stone ceiling in the refectory. The sound of her footsteps produced an eerie echo as she crossed the room and stepped into the cloisters. There was no lamp left in the first carrel. Bending low in the corner, Phoebe allowed some drips of hot wax to puddle on the stone floor, and left the candle standing there instead. The flame flickered a little as she turned to leave, then steadied.

She crept towards the summerhouse, trying to make no sound. Her breathing became fast and shallow, and her heart pounded in her chest. Stopping in the depths of shadow beside a holly bush, she waited and listened.

Growing cold, her nerves taut and her muscles aching with the effort of keeping still for so long, Phoebe stood straining her eyes and ears. She heard a faint rustle from somewhere behind her and turned her head; a badger lumbered by, so close she could have touched it with her shoe. It went past the open door of the summerhouse, pausing for a second to sniff at the air, then moving on.

Phoebe heaved a sigh, and the terror that had kept her immobile for so long left her. The summerhouse was empty. Where else might Lady Pickhurst go? Lovers would seek a rendezvous that was secure from prying eyes. The dewy grass had soaked her shoes. Phoebe shivered, remembering what she'd seen from her window, and chose the path that led to the lake.

Chapter Eighteen

'Show me how much you've missed me,' Lucille demanded, as Mortleigh rose from the couch where he'd been waiting for her. 'I hardly saw you at the church.'

He opened her robe to kiss her breasts. 'If I'd stayed a moment longer I swear I'd have taken you there and then. Do you have to swathe yourself in this wretched black?' He finished undressing her then stood to look at her nakedness. 'Imagine those solemn fools at the graveside. They'd have been screaming blasphemy, wringing their pious hands, while every one of them was filled with envy.'

She made a strange sound, half laugh, half groan. 'I don't know how I've survived without you so long.'

'Perhaps murder improves the appetite.' Having rid himself of his clothes, Mortleigh grasped her wrists and forced her arms behind her, pushing her against the wall so hard that she gasped in pain. With his feet he forced her legs apart and Lucille bit his neck savagely, as eager and impatient as her lover. Their passion was swift and violent, and soon they collapsed onto the couch, to lie panting in each others' arms.

'I hear your rustic Romeo is safe in prison,' Mortleigh murmured a few moments later.

'Yes.' Lucille's voice was a contented purr. 'He'll be hanged within a week, as long as nobody listens to that interfering little chit of a governess.'

'Why, what do you mean? If anyone suspects...' He propped himself on an elbow to look into Lucille's face, his eyes bright with sudden fury. 'My God, if your plan's gone awry–'

'It's nothing. She won't be taken seriously. We're safe. Jackman's refusing to talk.'

He gripped her arm. 'Never mind Jackman. This is about the governess. What's she done?'

'I tell you it's nothing. She spoke to the detective sergeant, the London man. That little brat she looks after keeps her awake at night with his nightmares. With nothing better to do with her time she's taken to snooping. She knew about me and Jonah. It seems he swore he'd stayed home one night when she suspected he and I had been together; it was the time you first brought me here. But it doesn't matter what she says, nobody will take her seriously. There's no proof.'

Mortleigh's fingers digging deep into her flesh. 'Tell me the rest,' he demanded. 'What's a Scotland Yard detective doing here? Jackman was arrested exactly as you planned. The local police had no reason to call for help.'

'It all happened by accident. He was sent for because of the jewel robberies; he just happened to be at Knytte when Jackman was arrested. The murder's no business of his.'

'Are you mad?' he flung himself off her and rose to his feet. 'When he's looking for the self-same man, even if he doesn't know it? You stupid whore. Don't you realize what you've done? Suppose that nosy little governess watched you leave again tonight?'

Mortleigh dashed outside. Clutching her robe around her, Lucille rose from the couch and went to the door. She could see his naked body pale against the bushes as he ran, his bare feet silent on the grass. Before him a small dark figure fled towards the ruins. The gap between them was swiftly closing.

A slight smile on her face, Lucille watched the end of the uneven race; Mortleigh had the girl in his arms, a hand clamping swiftly over her mouth to cut off her cries. When she tried to struggle he hit her hard across the side of the head; she was still and silent as he carried her back across his shoulder. Just the way, Lucille thought, the pleasurable heat swelling through her body again, he had carried her on that first night, claiming her for his prize.

Mortleigh tossed the girl on the floor. She

flopped there in a lifeless huddle, and he stepped over her. The savage excitement of the chase and the capture had aroused him, and Lucille made half a step to greet her lover. Seeing his expression she faltered; it was the first time she had been truly frightened of him since he had unwrapped her on the night of the abduction.

His hands shot out to capture her. She made a futile attempt to break free, but he only gripped her more tightly until the pain made her gasp. He flung her to the floor beside the unconscious governess, his mouth upon hers. Again she struggled, finding strength in equal measures of rage and terror; she thought he was going to kill her. Unable to reach his eyes with her fingernails, she raked at his neck instead. Mortleigh grasped her by the hair and pulled it viciously, his other hand slapping her hard across the face. He took her, swiftly and brutally; despite herself, Lucille found her body responding to his, as it always did. They were a match, their pain and their pleasure in harmony.

When he eventually pushed her away Lucille's lower lip was torn, her mouth full of blood. Mortleigh spat a red gobbet on the floor. Trickles of his own blood ran from the marks she'd made on his neck and chest. 'Damn fool,' he snarled, rising to his feet. 'You could have sent the pair of us to the gallows. I told you, I'll swing for no woman. There's a ship sailing for France in the morning, I've half a mind to be on it.'

'You're the fool,' she shot back, exploring her abused face with her fingers. 'There's no need for either of us to run, as long as we keep our heads. But how am I to explain this?'

'Wear a veil, you're in mourning, aren't you? If you want something to worry over, tell me how we dispose of her.' He prodded Phoebe with his toe.

'Is she dead?'

'Not yet. But she'll have to vanish in some way that can be explained, we want no more bodies found. We'll make it look as if she's run off. With her cousin on his way to the gallows it won't seem so strange. Go back to the house and fetch her belongings.'

Lucille nodded, fastening her robe. As she went to the door he grabbed her arm and pulled her back. 'Bring paper, pen and ink. It'll look better if she leaves a note. And hurry, we have to get her out of here before the house starts stirring.'

The morning was bright, but the room where Lady Pickhurst sat was in semi-darkness. The shutters were closed and the solitary lamp was heavily draped. 'Am I never to be allowed to mourn my loss in peace?' she asked tremulously, as Sir Martin Haylmer bowed

259

over her hand. She was dressed in plain unrelieved black, and her head was covered by the thick veil she'd worn at the funeral.

'Believe me, I'm deeply saddened by the death of your husband,' the Lord Lieutenant said. 'I held Lord Pickhurst in great esteem, both as a man and a fellow magistrate. I regret disturbing you, but I was unable to come earlier, and as chief magistrate of the county there are certain duties I have to perform, no matter how unpleasant they may be. We need to see where he died.'

She gave a small sob, her fingers restless upon the black handkerchief she held. 'You don't realize, Sir Martin, how I blame myself for what happened. I knew that man was infatuated with me. My kindness has been my undoing. I should have had him sent away, but it seemed too harsh. Guilt and regret will haunt me for the rest of my life. I have given orders to seal that room. As far as I am concerned that terrible place will cease to exist.'

Beddowes took a step forward, but Sir Martin put up a hand to prevent his intervention. 'By all means let that be done, if that is what you wish. I need only to inspect the place where the crime was committed, and then I shan't trouble you about it again. If you would be kind enough to have us shown the way, the business will soon be done. I wish we hadn't found it necessary to intrude upon your grief.'

'There is one more thing, Lady Pickhurst,' Sergeant Beddowes put in. 'Please may we speak to Miss Drake?'

Lucille laughed, a high-pitched almost hysterical sound. 'Of course. If you can find her.'

'What do you mean?'

'She's gone. All because of that man. Despite the fact that they were cousins I was willing to allow her to stay at Knytte for the sake of the children, but she vanished, ran off in the middle of the night. It was so thoughtless. The poor boy started wailing for her before dawn.'

Beddowes began to protest but Sir Martin quelled him with a look. Turning to the woman he frowned. 'I always found Miss Drake to be a responsible person. Surely she wouldn't leave without some notice.'

'She left a note.' She gestured at a piece of paper on the table beside her. 'There. It's plain enough.'

Tremayle picked up the note and scanned it quickly. 'There doesn't seem to be any mistake. Miss Drake apologizes for causing such inconvenience, but says she's unable to face being here during Jackman's trial.'

'But she—'

Again Sir Martin silenced Beddowes. 'That can wait,' he said sternly. 'We have business elsewhere.'

The whole house was shuttered, and with few lamps lit the corridors were even gloomier than before. 'We'll need light,' Beddowes said, half his thoughts on Miss Drake. Why would she leave so suddenly? Either he'd misjudged her, or she'd not left of her own free will. If his suspicions of Lady Pickhurst were correct, she was already a murderess, and Miss Drake might have given a damning testimony against her.

'Nobody has been allowed in the old library to close the shutters,' Henson said, leading them along a passageway so dark he was only a shadow before them. 'Her ladyship has given orders for workmen from Trembury to be engaged to close the room up, and we're forbidden even to come along this passage without her permission.'

'A woman in mourning isn't always rational,' Inspector Tremayle murmured solemnly as they entered the library and suddenly there was light again. Beddowes shot him a scathing look; far from being irrational, he suspected Lady Pickhurst was a cold and calculating young woman.

Having opened the door for them, Henson scuttled away, averting his eyes from the inside of the room. Sir Martin looked with revulsion at the stain on the floor. 'Well, Beddowes?'

'Inspector Tremayle can tell you how he found things here,' the sergeant replied. With a sideways look, as if expecting some trickery, Tremayle complied, describing where Lord Pickhurst's body had been lying. 'It was obvious a blow from the bust had killed him. You can see why I immediately sought out a man of unusual strength.'

His lordship nodded. 'Indeed.' He looked enquiringly at Beddowes.

'I thought all along that the bust wasn't an ideal weapon,' Beddowes said. He turned to the fireplace and picked up the poker. 'This would have made a better one, and it was here, ready to hand. No matter how strong Jackman is, I couldn't see him picking up that great block of marble on an impulse. It couldn't be swung with great speed. Why would Lord Pickhurst sit at the table and ignore a man staggering towards him with that thing in his arms? On the other hand, if the person who committed the murder was standing here–' Beddowes walked to the other side of the table, '–to keep the victim's attention distracted from the bust as it swung down to hit him, perhaps he wouldn't have seen it coming.'

'So the attacker was in two places at once,' Tremayle said sarcastically, 'or are we looking for two murderers now?'

'Possibly.' Beddowes pointed to the ceiling. There was a large hook, once used to hold a chandelier, almost above their heads. 'The bust must have been hung from that.

These gouges in the edge of the table were probably made when the murderer was adjusting it to swing to exactly the right spot. It would have been tested earlier, probably the previous night.'

'What on earth are you talking about?' Tremayle burst out angrily.

Beddowes said nothing, but walked across to the nearest bookshelf. The volumes that filled it were tattered, dusty and unloved. Reaching behind them, the sergeant removed a great tangle of ropes, a piece of thinner cord, and two pulley blocks. 'I found these hidden here yesterday. Whoever thought up this scheme knew how to lift heavy weights. The library steps were placed on the table to reach the hook in the ceiling; if you look carefully you can see the marks of the feet are still there in the dust. This rope is splashed with blood; that end was tied round the neck of the bust. It's only a guess, but I imagine the thinner rope was used to anchor the bust, holding it just above the plinth. The hinge of that shutter has been pulled out of shape by the weight. I believe the rope was then passed beneath the table, and secured here with a suitable knot. Release that, and the axe, as you might say, would fall.'

'This doesn't prove Jackman's innocence, it only makes him a more likely murderer,' Tremayle said triumphantly. 'He'd know how to use this sort of tackle.'

'Yes, but any intelligent person could have learnt to do this by watching him. Over the last few months large pieces of stone were regularly brought in from the quarry. I agree Jackman is still a suspect, but this proves he isn't the only possible culprit. You arrested him because of his physical strength, but I think we should find out who had a reason to kill Lord Pickhurst.'

'We've established that.' Tremayle was impatient. 'Jackman was mad with jealousy.'

'If you say so,' Beddowes said. 'But why would his lordship meet him here in the middle of the night?'

'He must have been lured here,' Sir Martin said.

'Perhaps he was brought here by force,' Tremayle suggested.

Beddowes nodded. 'That's possible, but if the murderer was holding a gun to his head, why would he go to all this trouble? There's one more thing.' He returned to the book shelves, and brought back a large volume bound in crumbling leather. 'There were signs that this had been moved recently. It's the Pickhurst family bible, with records of births, marriages and deaths written inside.'

The other two men leant over the book as Beddowes opened it. A spattering of reddish brown stained the end paper where names and dates had been entered in a dozen different hands. 'It seems this was a silent witness to the crime.'

'There's an entry when Lord Pickhurst married his first wife,' Tremayle commented, 'and a note recording her death.'

'No mention of his second marriage.' Sir Martin commented. 'He made no secret that he was after an heir, but that pairing was no more successful than the first.'

'No doubt he'd have been happy to make an entry if he'd got what he wanted,' Beddowes said. 'Here, as you can see, somebody else has added Lucille Gayne, the third Lady Pickhurst. The ink looks fresh. I think she decided to make her own mark. And this little line here is interesting.' He pointed. From between the two names a straight vertical line had been drawn, with a tiny question mark in pencil, in the place where the name of a child would be entered. 'Perhaps his wife brought him down here to show him what she'd written. It would be a romantic way to give him news he wanted very much to hear.'

'You think Lady Pickhurst murdered her husband?' Sir Martin looked outraged.

'I didn't say that, but the stains are there, and this handwriting doesn't match this earlier entry made by Lord Pickhurst. It would be easy enough to find out if it belongs to her ladyship.'

'It's all very circumstantial,' Sir Martin

said. He shook his head. 'I don't know.'

'It could still be Jackman,' Tremayle reminded him.

Sir Martin agreed. 'All that's changed is the method by which the murder was committed. What do you say, Beddowes? You're very keen to prove Jackman innocent, but you've found no evidence in his defence.'

'No, because everything points to his guilt,' Beddowes said. 'It's all a little too convenient. I think he's meant to be the scapegoat. Suppose Lady Pickhurst returned his affections for a while but then grew tired of him? Another man caught her eye. She decided to rid herself of her husband and her discarded lover in one fell swoop.'

Sir Martin scowled at him. 'I've met Lady Pickhurst on a dozen occasions, and she always appeared to be a doting and dutiful wife.'

'Appearances can be deceptive,' Beddowes said, thinking again about Miss Drake. He hadn't thought she would run away. A flicker of fear coursed through him; perhaps she hadn't.

'Jackman remains the most likely suspect.' Sir Martin picked up the bible. 'However, I shall find out if her ladyship was responsible for the newest entry in this book, and when it was made.'

'But with her face covered by that veil, you won't be able to see how she reacts to your question,' Beddowes objected. 'Perhaps you might ask her to remove it.'

'We are dealing with a lady, Sergeant!' The Lord Lieutenant was scandalized. 'You aren't in your London stews now!'

'I've found men and women pretty much the same everywhere, Sir Martin,' Beddowes replied, unrepentant. 'Manners might vary between rich and poor, but not human nature.'

'It's Annie, isn't it?' Beddowes said. Ignoring Sir Martin's protests that he didn't have Lady Pickhurst's permission to roam freely about the house, he'd left the other two men downstairs, declaring his intention to seek out the nursery.

The maid looked warily at him. 'Yes sir,' she said. The sound of a child crying could be heard coming from somewhere close by.

'Perhaps you should go back to the children. It seems they're upset.'

'That's Master Rodney.' The girl's mouth turned down. 'It's no good me going to him, when 'tis Miss Drake he's wanting.'

'When did you last see Miss Drake, Annie?'

'Last night. The children were in their beds. I took down the tray from their supper.'

'Were you the one who discovered Miss Drake had gone?'

'No sir. That was her ladyship. Master

268

Rodney was screaming and carrying on so that she couldn't sleep. She rang the bell, and ordered her maid to see why Miss Drake wasn't tending to him.'

'And then you were sent for.' He didn't wait for an answer but wandered to the door at the far end of the nursery. 'Is this Miss Drake's bedroom?'

'Yes. But she didn't sleep in there much. Master Rodney was having so many nightmares she spent most nights in the chair beside his bed.' Annie pouted. 'Daft I call it, cosseting a boy that age.'

Beddowes opened the door onto a small sparsely furnished room. The bed was in disarray, the linen and bedcover half heaped on the bed and half on the floor. He swung round and stared at the girl, as if seeing her properly for the first time. 'Miss Drake wouldn't leave this sort of mess, would she Annie?' He stepped into the room, noticing that the drawer in the washstand had been left open. 'Do you think she left in a hurry?'

The girl flushed and stared at the floor. 'I wouldn't know, sir.'

Beddowes stayed where he was, looking sternly down at her and letting the silence stretch uncomfortably between them. Annie fidgeted, and he could see the flush of colour rising up her face.

'I think you have something to tell me, Annie,' the sergeant said. 'Were you the one

269

who searched this room? You'd better tell me the truth, or you'll be in serious trouble.'

She plucked nervously at her apron. 'The room were all upset when I come up,' she said. 'I only looked in the mattress, because I'd seen Miss Drake hiding something there, when she didn't know I was at the door.' She reached in her pocket and pulled out a purse, placing it reluctantly into Beddowes's outstretched hand.

Her voice dropped to a whisper. 'I thought if she hadn't taken it, then it weren't wanted.'

'Don't lie to me!' Beddowes voice was suddenly harsh, 'You're not a fool, Annie. If you don't want to find yourself in prison for theft you'd better tell me everything you know. I don't think Miss Drake packed her own belongings. What else is there that she wouldn't have left behind?'

'In here, sir.' The maid scurried out of the room and into the nursery. There was still no sign of the children, but the boy's crying had quieted to an occasional sob.

Annie took a small volume from a shelf among about a dozen books. 'Miss Drake always carried this when she went to church. She was proper attached to it.'

It was a prayer book, much used. Written inside the front cover was the name Bernard John Drake, and beneath that in a smaller hand, Phoebe had inscribed her own.

Chapter Nineteen

Beddowes took the book and went racing downstairs. Without even looking for a servant to announce him, he went barging into the room where Lady Pickhurst had received them, an accusation already forming on his lips as the door flew back. The words were never spoken for the room was empty. He spun back to the hall and found himself facing an outraged Henson.

'Can I be of assistance?' the butler asked stiffly.

'Where are Sir Martin and Inspector Tremayle?' Beddowes demanded, quite unrepentant.

'Sir Martin's secretary, Mr Docket, arrived a few minutes ago. I showed all three gentlemen into the morning room.' Henson took a step back and indicated a door across the hall. 'If you would come this way. I suggest if there is anything else you require, *sir,* you might ring the bell,' he said sternly, ushering him in.

A shutter had been opened here, and a shaft of sunlight fell on the three men seated round a small table. Docket looked up as Beddowes entered.

'I found it, Sergeant,' he said. The young secretary was obviously weary, his hair and clothes dishevelled, but his tone was triumphant. 'I have a name for the dead man. That ring was sold to a Mr Laidlaw, nearly forty years ago, on the occasion of his marriage. I was able to ascertain that the couple were no longer living, but they were survived by a son who moved to London about three years ago.'

'And that son is almost certainly our corpse,' Sir Martin said. 'We have our answers at last. A Mr Laidlaw from London was a guest at Hagstock Hall the night the first robbery took place, along with a friend by the name of Mortleigh. In appearance they match what little we know of the men you encountered at the crossroads.'

'There was no reason to suspect them,' Tremayle said defensively. 'They'd returned to the Castle Inn before the robbery took place. Since they weren't well known in the area I took a little trouble when questioning the two gentlemen. They appeared to have a very good alibi.'

'The details of how they carried out the robbery hardly matter at the moment,' Beddowes cut in. 'Where's Mortleigh now?'

'He's here. At Knytte,' Sir Martin said. 'I think we can be sure we have our villain. He certainly has plenty of nerve; it appears he intended to settle down amongst the victims

272

of his crimes. He took up the tenancy of the Dower House a few days ago.'

Beddowes felt as if somebody had just struck a killing blow over his heart. The purse and the prayer book were still in his hand. He flung them down on the table 'I'm afraid we may have another crime to investigate, maybe even another murder, though God forbid. Whoever packed Miss Drake's things made a big mistake. They left these behind. The poor girl didn't leave Knytte of her own free will. I'm afraid we may be too late to help her.'

'What are you talking about?' Inspector Tremayle took a sheet of paper from his pocket. 'We have her letter here. She makes her reasons for leaving quite plain. Perhaps she was in a hurry–'

'She would hardly leave behind five guineas.' Beddowes said. 'Nor this. It belonged to her father. The maid was sure she wouldn't willingly have abandoned it.' He opened the prayer book, displaying the young woman's name, before taking the paper from the inspector. 'The handwriting's different. This note wasn't written by Phoebe Drake. Don't you see? She told me Lady Pickhurst was leaving the house at night to meet her lover, but on at least one occasion she knew it couldn't have been Jackman who was waiting for her in the grounds. Somebody else took his place. It has to be Mortleigh.'

'We certainly have cause enough to question the man,' Tremayle said.

'Question him?' Beddowes rounded on him furiously. 'Miss Drake has gone missing. For some reason they suspected that she knew too much; her ladyship knew Miss Drake had spoken to me. All this may well be my fault. God willing we may still find her alive, but we must be quick.'

'Come, Beddowes, you surely can't think Mortleigh has killed the girl?' Sir Martin was brusque.

'He killed his friend,' Docket broke in, too exhausted to show proper deference to his employer. 'Sergeant? You really believe Miss Drake was taken by force?'

Beddowes nodded. 'I'm sure of it.'

'What are we waiting for?' Docket leapt to his feet. 'We have to go to the Dower House.'

'It would be unwise to rush to arrest Mortleigh without proper precautions,' Tremayle said, pushing back his chair. 'Assuming Beddowes is right the man is dangerous. I'll send to Hagstock for help.'

'That would take too long,' Beddowes protested.

'You think we can tackle him on our own?' Tremayle looked around at his companions, the portly and ageing Lord Lieutenant, Docket, painfully young and eager, and Beddowes, who still had one arm in a sling.

'Ring the bell, Tremayle,' Sir Martin said,

suddenly decisive. 'We'll need to arm ourselves.'

'What about Lady Pickhurst?' Beddowes blocked the inspector's way to the bell rope. 'You can't doubt her part in all this. Why would Mortleigh kill Lord Pickhurst, and in such a way that Jackman was blamed, unless there was some benefit for him? Her ladyship must be involved. If she gets to know that we're after her lover she may run away.'

'For the moment that's neither here nor there,' Sir Martin said. 'A woman alone wouldn't get far. We need to deal with Mortleigh. If word gets to him that he's under suspicion he'll be gone.'

Henson was summoned. With some reluctance he surrendered the key to the gunroom. 'Lady Pickhurst must be informed before any of the guns are removed,' he said. 'If you'd remain here, please, gentlemen, I shan't keep you a moment.'

'It might be wise to have fresh horses saddled,' Beddowes suggested, as Henson left them. 'If we have a chase on our hands I don't want to be riding that cob.'

Sir Martin nodded, sending Docket to the stables. 'Four horses,' he said. 'Tell them it's by order of the Lord Lieutenant, and we want the best.'

'What about Lady Pickhurst?' Beddowes asked again, once Docket had gone.

Sir Martin frowned. 'She'll be safe enough

here. We–'

He was interrupted by Henson, returning pink-faced and slightly breathless. 'Her ladyship has left the house. I gather she went directly to the stables and ordered her horse, as soon as she was alone.'

'She'll have gone to the Dower House,' Tremayle said, rising swiftly to his feet. 'Dammit Beddowes, you were right! Let's go and hurry those horses.'

'Not until we've armed ourselves,' Sir Martin snapped. 'The gunroom first.'

They halted their mounts and peered at the Dower House from the cover of a narrow belt of woodland. Beddowes eased his arm from the sling and adjusted the rifle more comfortably across his shoulder.

'We don't want a shooting match,' Tremayle said, seeing him.

Sir Martin snorted. 'I doubt if the man will walk tamely to the gallows, Tremayle. For my part, I heartily wish we'd had time to turn out the militia.' He rubbed a hand across his chin. 'Still, we want him alive, Beddowes, if it can be managed.'

'I'll do my best,' Beddowes said, edging his horse forward. 'If you want to approach the front door as if nothing's wrong, I'll ride round to the back of the house. They could have gone already; we can't afford to waste time.' He clapped his heels to the horse's flanks, bending low over the pommel. The beast shot from among the trees at a flat gallop, leaping over an ornamental flower bed and turning sharply towards the stables.

The yard was a hive of activity. Two horses were being led out, saddled and bridled, while a team of matched greys were being coaxed between the shafts of a closed carriage. Men shouted in surprise and horses spun in alarm as Beddowes, still spurring hard, galloped into their midst. A torrent of abuse followed him; one of the men by the carriage tried to intercept him, and narrowly missed his grasp at the sergeant's boot.

It had been unwise to ride in without being sure of an exit. There was an archway in the opposite wall, too narrow for comfort and barred by a gate, but with the grooms gathering to block the way behind him it was his only option. He was aware of his mount's reluctance, but urged it on. Ducking low, Beddowes felt the sharp scrape of brick on his back, but they were safely through. Wheeling his mount, he took stock of his situation. He was in an orchard, overlooked by a dozen windows in the side of the house. The trees were too small and well trimmed to offer him decent cover. It would be unwise to linger.

He'd hoped to find Mortleigh in the yard, but none of those he'd scattered had been dressed as a gentleman. It would be good to see his enemy, to recognize him. As he'd slowly recovered parts of his memory, he'd wondered if a meeting, face to face, with the man who'd tried so hard to kill him, would bring back the last bits that were missing.

The blast of a shot rattled the windows; a draught skimmed past Beddowes's cheek. Not stopping to check where the bullet had come from, he flung his horse back the way they had come.

Things had changed. Raising his head after ducking to get through the archway, Beddowes saw that the last of the horses was being hurried back into the stables. The carriage stood abandoned.

A slight figure clad in black from head to toe was suddenly right before him. With a shift of his weight the sergeant made the horse veer left, its shoulder missing the woman by an inch. She hardly seemed to notice. On an impulse, Beddowes leant from the saddle as he passed to twitch the veil from her head.

Slowing a fraction to look back, Beddowes saw the damaged face; Lady Pickhurst's mouth was torn, the bottom lip swollen and black with congealed blood. Her cheek and chin were disfigured by darkening bruises.

Distracted, the sergeant slowed the horse to a trot; had he been wrong about this woman? His mount shied violently as another figure appeared, running from the doorway to the stables. Darkly handsome and dressed in a gentleman's travelling clothes, Beddowes knew him at once. It was as if a light had been kindled within his mind, illuminating the gaps in his memory. He could see the road, Mortleigh and his servant advancing, intent on killing him, while the doomed Laidlaw sat watching from the carriage.

There was nowhere to go, no time to turn and attempt the archway again. Mortleigh had a shotgun in his hands, and a slight smile on his face as he lifted it towards his shoulder. He had a second, maybe less. Taking the reins in his left hand Beddowes twisted savagely at the horse's mouth, feeling sinews and muscles in his half-healed arm protesting, while his right dragged the rifle off his shoulder. Throwing his weight back, he felt a twinge of guilt; the horse had done all that had been asked of it. Like so many on the battlefield, the reward for its obedience would be death. As the animal reared, obedient to his command, Beddowes threw himself from the saddle.

The expected blast of shot didn't come, only the crack of a pistol, quickly followed by another. As the sergeant landed and rolled, the rifle held tightly against his body, Beddowes realized that help had come just in time; the shots fired by his allies had sent Mortleigh running back into the stables.

Sir Martin and Inspector Tremayle were hidden behind the carriage, while Docket stood a few yards further back, making no attempt to seek cover, his face blank with shock. Beddowes lay still. He was out in the open and an easy target. His only hope lay in playing dead. Mortleigh might well believe he was out of the fight, for he'd landed badly. The crack his skull received as it hit the cobbles had left his head ringing.

As if awakening from a trance, Lady Pickhurst started uncertainly towards Sir Martin.

'Thank the heavens you're here,' she cried, stumbling across the cobbles. 'I've been so scared.' She waved a hand vaguely towards the stable doorway. 'He's the jewel thief. I saw him. At Dunsby Court, where he stole Mrs Stoppens's rubies.'

'But you said nothing of it,' Sir Martin said sternly. 'If you'd told us then, he'd be behind bars by now.'

The woman faltered, looking almost as if she might faint. 'I dared not. I already knew him to have no morals, to be a vicious evil sort of man. When he came to stay at Knytte as my husband's guest, he took every chance to be alone with me, to press his unwelcome attentions on me.' She put her hands up to her ravaged face. 'Must I tell you of the shame, the humiliation he brought me? Mortleigh swore he'd kill me if I told anyone of his true character. We'd known each other slightly in London you see, long before I was married. It was his idea to murder my poor husband. He meant to marry me and take Knytte for himself. Please, help me, I–'

Evidently Sir Martin was touched by her defencelessness. He took a few steps to meet her, but he was stopped by Mortleigh's voice, which echoed from the stable.

'Women are such liars! Is this how you keep your word, Lucille? Those wayward eyes seduced me the first time we met; they promised so much. And yet you're no better than a cheap whore. You witch, you'd send me to the gallows without a thought, just like that other poor fool who fell under your spell. But I warned you, Lucille, I'll hang for no woman. You'll lead no more men astray. There'll be no more lies from those pretty lips.'

A shot rang out, not the deep-throated blast of a shotgun, but the crack of a pistol. Lady Pickhurst gave a faint cry and began to fall. Even before she hit the ground, a horse came racing from the stable.

Mortleigh lay flat along the animal's neck. Inspector Tremayle fired a shot, but neither Docket nor Sir Martin reacted quickly enough. The inspector's shot missed by a foot, and by the time Beddowes had risen to his feet Mortleigh was already a hundred yards away.

Grimly recalling his old sergeant major,

Beddowes lifted the rifle and took in a deep steadying breath as he lined up the sights. The range was lengthening by the second, but he'd picked the prize among Lord Pickhurst's guns; the butt kicked hard into his right shoulder, and he thought he felt bone grate in his left arm before the flare of pain hit.

The horse was still galloping away from him. Gritting his teeth Beddowes took aim for a second time, but then he saw the animal turn a little. The rider slipped sideways and as the scent of blood reached its nostrils the horse's measured pace became a wild careering flight. Mortleigh's body hung out behind the panicking animal for a few strides, then his foot pulled free of the stirrup and he dropped bonelessly to the ground.

'I'd rather have seen him hang,' Sir Martin said testily, glaring at Beddowes. The sergeant had caught his own horse and raced across the field, concerned that Mortleigh might yet offer some resistance. He arrived to find the man dead, and returned more slowly, passing Tremayle and four grooms carrying a hurdle.

Beddowes winced as he dismounted, and placed his arm back into the sling. 'I'm sorry, Sir Martin. At that range I might have missed altogether if I'd aimed to wing him. How is Lady Pickhurst?'

'Still breathing, but not for long I suspect. Docket's with her, and a doctor's been sent for. Listen, Sergeant, it seems Mortleigh's valet was very much in his confidence. I gather his name is Tomms. He needs to be found. There's a chance some of the jewels may yet be recovered.'

Beddowes nodded. 'Seeing Mortleigh set my memory straight. I owe Tomms a knock or two. I'll find him, don't you worry, but not until we ask her ladyship about Miss Drake.'

Sir Martin harrumphed and led the way into the house.

A footman stood by the door, and Beddowes paused to speak to him. 'Mortleigh's valet, Tomms,' he said quietly, 'is he still here?'

'He ran off towards the big house a few minutes ago,' the man replied.

Beddowes nodded his thanks. He could spare a minute or two, no more. Tomms was probably intending to steal himself a mount and vanish; he mustn't be given the chance to get too much of a lead.

Lady Pickhurst lay on a couch, a growing pool of blood spreading beneath her slim body, while an elderly maid fluttered helplessly over her. Docket was on his knees at the woman's side. 'Please,' he was saying. 'Tell me what happened to Miss Drake. If you believe in redemption, help yourself by having some mercy now. Is she still alive? Did Mortleigh kill her?'

'No time,' Lucille murmured, through lips that were drained of all colour, making the dark scabs and bruises look all the more vivid. 'Should have done it then. Might have done, but the brat was wailing.'

'Miss Drake was crying?'

'No. The boy. I thought he'd wake the whole house.' Her face twisted in sudden pain. 'Mortleigh?'

Docket looked up at Sir Martin who shook his head.

'Dead, Lady Pickhurst,' Sir Martin said. 'Mortleigh is dead. If you hope for God's forgiveness, please tell us where we can find Miss Drake.'

'Mortleigh. Such a man. We might have...' She sighed. 'Interfering chit.' Her mouth curved, as if she was smiling. 'She'll be cold by now. But she was always cold. No fire in her blood. So unfair...'

Lucille's eyes drifted shut, and a minute later she died, without uttering another word.

Docket got swiftly to his feet, looking wildly at Beddowes. 'Cold – she said she's cold. Have they killed her?'

'I don't know.' Beddowes closed his eyes, thinking about the woman's exact words. *No time. Should have done it then.* That had seemed to be her answer, before her spite had prompted her to give them a more enigmatic reply. 'Maybe not.'

If they were to have any chance of recovering even a little of the stolen jewellery, and with it his reputation, then he had to go after Tomms. But where was Phoebe Drake? He recalled the look in her eyes, the trusting innocence; she had been so grateful when he promised to help her cousin. He had questioned her, persuaded her to tell Jonah Jackman's secret, and given no thought to her own safety. It was his fault she'd fallen foul of Lady Pickhurst and her murderous lover. If she was dead then the blame lay squarely at his door, and it would haunt him for the rest of his life.

'But where would she be cold?' Docket was saying. 'The ruins? The tower's always cold, but even though Jackman's not there, the other men will still be at work.'

'A cellar?' Beddowes hazarded, looking at Sir Martin.

'Not the one at Knytte, it's in constant use. Here. I don't know.' The Lord Lieutenant looked enquiringly at the footman.

'There's not one here, sir. The wine is stored next to the buttery.'

'Where else then?' Beddowes began to stride the room, his right fist clenching. 'Somewhere close. They were short of time.'

'There's an ice house,' the elderly maid

said. She had covered Lady Pickhurst's face, and knelt to say a prayer over her, now she rose to her feet, all brisk normality. 'It's not been in use since his lordship's father died. There's nothing to see but a mound at the edge of the wood.'

'That grassy mound. I saw it as we passed,' Docket cried, dashing to the door.

As Beddowes made to follow, Sir Martin caught at his arm. 'Sergeant, we need Tomms. He can't be allowed to escape.'

The sergeant nodded, torn between his duty and his feelings for Phoebe Drake. He adjusted the rifle on his shoulder again, giving himself a moment to think. 'I'll go now. But I'd be obliged if you'd send some men after Docket, Sir Martin, and maybe go yourself. If Miss Drake's in the ice house they may need to break the door down.'

Beddowes took the shortest route back to the gardens. His mount hesitated for only a second when asked to jump up the ha-ha, a feat it accomplished with apparent ease, before galloping on across the lawns. It seemed Lord Pickhurst was a good judge of horses, as well as guns.

Chapter Twenty

There were half a dozen men in the stable-yard, clustered together around something lying on the cobbles. As Beddowes drew closer he saw it was a boy, and that his tow-coloured hair was streaked with red.

'What's happened?' Beddowes demanded.

'It was Tomms,' one of the grooms replied, 'Him what works for Mr Mortleigh. He come running up and snatched her lady-ship's Arabian mare. Simeon were walkin' her, takin' her to the paddock. Tomms jumped on her, bare-ridged an' all. Sim tried to stop him and got kicked in the head for his pains.'

'Is Simeon alive?'

'Reckon so. Breathin' any rate.'

'Send somebody to the Dower House to tell Sir Martin. There's a doctor on the way but he won't be needed now. He might as well be of use here. Which way did Tomms go?'

'North, sir.' The groom pointed.

'Aye,' another man said. 'Looks to be headin' for Hagstock. What's he done?'

The question went unanswered. With a nod of thanks Beddowes turned the horse.

He rode across in front of the house, and with a pang he remembered how he'd caught Phoebe Drake in his arms on that very spot. Suppose their guess was wrong and she wasn't in the ice house? Wasn't even alive? He put the thought aside; he had a man to catch.

He gave the horse a kick that was more urging than it needed; with a great leap the animal flung itself down across the ha-ha again, landing far out on the pasture. They were in open country and free to gallop. No more than half a mile ahead was a man on a grey horse.

The mare was no match for the hunter Beddowes rode, and Tomms was riding bare-back; the gap between them closed quickly.

'Pull up, Tomms,' Beddowes roared, when he was no more than ten yards behind.

In response the fugitive drummed the mare's sides with frantic kicks of his heels. He was fumbling at the pocket of his coat as he rode, in evident danger of sliding from his precarious seat with every stride. The gap shrunk to eight yards, to seven and then six.

Tomms half turned; he had a pistol in his right hand, the left was tangled with the reins and the mare's mane as he struggled to hold himself steady.

Beddowes took his horse swinging out to

the other side; his quarry must either swivel even further, not easy to do without a saddle, or turn back to aim across his body. Either way he would be too late, for the gap had closed to a mere three feet. Mindful of the damage he'd already done to his injured arm, Beddowes took the reins between his teeth, swept the rifle from his shoulder and swung it, butt first, at the other man's head.

Beddowes horse reared away as Tomms fell under its hoofs, but he kept his seat. The mare was spent, and once rid of her rider she dropped instantly to a jogtrot. With the rifle cocked and ready, Beddowes dismounted where the valet lay still, face down. The pistol was nowhere to be seen. Warily the sergeant prodded Tomms in the ribs with the toe of his boot. The man rolled, moving fast, but not fast enough, intending to fire the gun he'd held concealed beneath his body. Using the rifle barrel as a club this time, though with a guilty awareness that it was no way to treat such a splendid weapon, Beddowes cracked the man's elbow a hefty blow. The pistol dropped from a now useless hand, and the sergeant put his foot on it.

'Get up,' Beddowes ordered, 'and catch that mare. Sir Martin Haylmer wants to see you. And you'd better have the answers he wants, or your neck will be in a noose, since your master's gone to hell the quicker way.'

They had to follow a circuitous route back

to the house. Beddowes rode towards the stableyard, his captive before him, subdued and silent on the mare. A procession could be seen coming up the garden from the ice house, led by Docket. Slightly built as he was, it was plain that Docket found Miss Drake no easy burden, but he strode on manfully. The governess lay unmoving in her young rescuer's arms. Beddowes brought his mount to a halt. His heart was pounding; for all he could tell she might be dead. Docket's face told him nothing; the young secretary was tight-lipped, barely glancing at her pale face as he carried her up the steps; behind him Sir Martin was already barking orders. They vanished into the house.

Cursing Tomms, letting loose with words he'd not used in a dozen years, Beddowes pulled Mortleigh's servant off the grey mare. The man landed awkwardly and half fell against the sergeant's sore arm, and in response Beddowes kicked him hard on the shin. Duty demanded that he stayed with his prisoner until Inspector Tremayle's constables arrived, and meantime he had no way of knowing if Phoebe Drake still lived.

London was every bit as loud, ill-mannered and dirty as Sergeant Beddowes recalled; only the smell was worse than he remembered. At odd moments in the three days since he'd returned he found himself missing the sweeter scents of the country. The fresh perfume of soap and ripe hayfields, coupled with the murmur of a gentle voice, haunted his dreams. He was glad to be busy, to be too distracted to dwell on the past; this was his life, among the smog and noise of the great city. Phoebe Drake was a distant memory, last seen in Docket's arms as she was carried into Knytte's great entrance hall. He'd learnt to accept that he'd never see her again.

Here in the office of his superior, the smell of stale tobacco smoke and mouldy leather, mingled with the odour of wet wool rising from his damp coat, was enough to drive all other scents from his head. He stood rigidly to attention, his eyes focused on the religious tract which hung incongruously next to a rack of pipes upon the wall.

'You were careless,' Inspector Laker said. He scowled at the discreet black sling worn by the detective who stood silent and attentive before his desk. 'I told you masquerading as that villain Cobb was a scatter-brained scheme. Not your proudest hour, Sergeant.'

Sighing, Laker leant back in his chair. 'You're expected to give evidence against this man Tomms; unfortunately Sir Martin Haylmer tells me the job can't be done without you, and I can hardly refuse a request from Her Majesty's Lord Lieutenant. You'll catch the one seventeen this afternoon.' The

291

line between his brows deepened a little. 'As you can see, we're busy, which means I've nobody else to send with you, to take care of these baubles.'

The inspector opened a drawer and took out three packages wrapped in brown paper, handing them to Beddowes. 'Names and addresses are written on each one. Make sure you bring back signed receipts, and don't lose the damned things, that's all I ask.'

Laker watched as the parcels were secreted beneath the sergeant's coat, before glancing at the printed calendar on his desk. 'I want that arm mended, so keep out of trouble, understood?' He reached into the drawer again. 'Train tickets. You report here for duty on the ninth. Be as much as a minute late and you'll be back in a constable's uniform, that's if I don't decide to be rid of you altogether.' Beddowes hesitated. The date on the return ticket was the eighth. Allowing for two days to be taken up with the trial and the restoration of stolen property to its owners, he would still have five days to fill, and he didn't want them. He wondered if it was worth trying to explain.

'Dismissed,' Inspector Laker barked.

'Sir.' With a parade ground salute, the sergeant marched from the room. Once he'd left Scotland Yard his pace slowed. He made his way back to his lodgings; he had plenty of time to pick up his bag and have a bite to eat before he caught his train.

As he walked his mood was black. Laker's words had cut deeply, though the end of the affair had gone quite smoothly. Tomms had proved to be a mine of information, having spied most effectively on Mortleigh whenever he felt his master hadn't taken him sufficiently into his confidence.

Once Beddowes had sent a telegram giving his superior a full report, he'd travelled to London on the overnight train and arrived in time to help arrest the fence Mortleigh had found to replace Fetch'n'carry Cobb. Luckily the jewels Beddowes had held in his possession so briefly, during what Laker called his masquerade, had been among the recovered loot; another few hours and they'd have been across the channel, and out of reach. In that event, the sergeant thought gloomily, as he climbed the three long staircases up to his room, he would probably have been thrown out of the force. As it was, Laker had made the precariousness of his position quite clear.

Propped uncomfortably into the corner of the railway carriage, Beddowes slept, and dreamt of a girl, slender yet shapely, who lay snugly in his arms. She felt as if she belonged there. The familiar scent of soap and freshly mown hay was sweet, as he smiled down at her. Lifting her hand to his lips he kissed it, but at that moment the innocent

293

young face underwent a terrible change. The sensuous mouth of Lady Pickhurst, disfigured by bloody bruises, curved in a cat-like travesty of a smile. Her face lifted to his, while her brilliant eyes flashed a blatant invitation.

He woke with a cry of horror on his lips, to find the compartment's other passengers viewing him with distaste. For the rest of the journey he stayed awake, his thoughts becoming progressively darker as the miles unwound beneath the wheels. He made up his mind to discharge his duty quickly, and return to London as soon as he could, even if he had to pay his own train fare.

'Welcome back, Sergeant.' Docket shook his hand. Beddowes summoned up some suitable words as they walked into the yard where Sir Martin's carriage stood waiting. He thought the young man seemed subdued, as if his mind was elsewhere.

Docket motioned him to step in first. 'You'll have heard the trial is set for the day after tomorrow?'

'Yes. I take it Jonah Jackman has been released?' Beddowes asked, settling himself into the seat with a sigh; he would have liked a little longer to stretch his legs after the long hours in the train.

'He has,' Docket said, joining him. 'Sir Martin sent me to Hagstock gaol yesterday with the papers. He's to appear as a witness, and of course the whole county knows the story by now, or some version of it; it'll take a long time for the talk to die down. He'll not find it easy to get work.'

'I suppose not.' Beddowes stared out of the window, not seeing the houses and streets gradually give way to countryside. A thought occurred to him and he patted the breast of his coat. 'I'll be off back to London as soon as possible once the trial's over. I've some bits and pieces in my pocket, one of them is to be delivered to a house not far from here. Do you think Sir Martin would mind if I get that out of the way at once?'

Sleep had eluded Jonah Jackman while he was in prison, but he had expected better once he was back at home. He lay in the familiar room and stared into the darkness for long hours, helplessly trying to make sense of his life. Lucille's betrayal had left him so bewildered, so deeply hurt, that he almost wished the crime had never been solved. He would have been dead by now, hanged as a murderer. Through the endless nights that seemed not so bad a fate.

His release had restored him to life, but brought little comfort. He would be forever branded as a lecher; no decent man who had a wife or a daughter would employ him. He might travel a hundred miles and more to look for work, but he knew his past would go with him, a shadow always at his back.

Unable to bear being within four walls any longer, Jonah walked out into the light of dawn, taking long strides away from the place that had been his home since childhood. His thoughts were not of life, but of death.

Some hours later, exhausted by his mad dash across a dozen miles of wild country, he looked down onto the surging water from the top of the rocky cliffs. Did it take more courage to live, or to die? Lifting his eyes to the horizon he noticed that it was a fine day. He was suddenly filled with a calm certainty. Shuddering he turned away from the coast, to stride back across the moors. His mind and his heart felt numb, but he knew what he had to do.

He kept to the open country and little-used tracks, avoiding people as best he could, and reaching Knytte as the light began to fade. As he followed the long drive, keeping in cover, Jonah saw a small figure, standing alone by the lake, staring into the water.

Phoebe looked like a lost child; the sight wrung his heart. He began to run but then his steps faltered; he'd spurned her attempts to help him, and because of that she'd almost died. His certainty deserted him. She wouldn't want to see the man who'd caused her such an ordeal. He began to back away, but some instinct must have told her he was there, and she turned.

Her face lit up at the sight of him. 'Jonah!' She ran into his arms.

For more than a minute they clung to each other in silence.

'I'm sorry,' Jonah said eventually, easing away from her. 'I was such a fool. If only I'd listened to you. I'll never forgive myself. Because of my stupidity, Mortleigh might have killed you.'

'That's nonsense,' Phoebe said, taking hold of one of his large hands in both of her own. 'I'll take my share of blame, if you don't mind. What I did, following Lady Pickhurst out into the garden, when I knew what she was – that was every bit as foolish. Anyway, it's all over, and I intend to forget it.' She lifted a hand to his forehead as if to wipe away the new lines that scored it. 'I'm afraid things won't be so easy for you.'

He shook his head. 'It's no more than I deserve. How can I look my neighbours in the face after what happened? Lord Pickhurst was a decent man, not the monster she made him out to be. I think I always knew it, but...'

'She was an accomplished actress,' Phoebe said gently, 'and very beautiful.'

'Only on the surface.' He offered her a rueful smile. 'Not like you. Sweet Phoebe. You have all the qualities she lacked.' He pulled her back into a brotherly embrace.

Her head against his chest, she looked up so she could see his face. 'What will you do?'

'I'm leaving. There's a steamboat to America that leaves in six days. Will you come with me? We could be brother and sister again.'

She was silent for a long time. 'No. I'm sorry. I'll always be your sister, and I'll be sorry to see you leave, but I can't go with you.'

He nodded in understanding. 'You're right not to trust me, after what happened.'

'It's not that. It's the children. Rodney has hardly slept since that awful night, and Eliza isn't much better. Dr Pencoe has given them something to make them sleep the clock round. That's why I'm free to come out here. Annie's sitting with them until dinner time, and for once I think she's glad to do as she's told. The whole house is in turmoil, although Mr Henson does his best to carry on as normal, as if the family had merely gone away for a few weeks. I know he's worried about what the future will bring to Knytte. I gather there are no close relatives, except some very distant cousins in Scotland.'

'You could find yourself alone and friendless, and quite soon,' Jonah said, his frown deepening.

She smiled suddenly. 'There's another option.'

He brightened. 'Would you come and join

me later?'

The smile vanished. 'No, I'm sorry, Jonah, I don't think I'll ever leave this country.' Her cheeks flushed a little. 'Mr Docket has asked me to marry him.'

'Mr Docket?' He looked astonished, and it took him a moment to find his voice again. 'I hardly know what to say, except to congratulate you, of course.'

'That wouldn't be appropriate,' she said, and the smile reappeared. 'I turned him down, though I'm afraid he may repeat the offer. He's so terribly young.'

'But he must be as old as you.'

'Exactly.' She half turned, to look at the lake again. 'The trouble is, Jonah, there's another man, one I'd have answered differently.' She was silent but only for a moment. When she looked back at her cousin Phoebe was completely in control of herself. 'I'll say no more. It was only a silly dream. I'm a governess, and for the moment Master Rodney Pengoar and his sister are in need of me. That will suffice.'

Jonah hugged her. 'Dear Phoebe, I'll only say that I hope the future is kind, whatever it brings. You'll keep in touch with me? I could leave you a little money, enough to pay your fare in case you change your mind.'

'No. Thank you, I've a little money put by. I promise I'll write, as long as you let me know where to address my letters.'

The inquests into the deaths of Lord and Lady Pickhurst and Victor Mortleigh were over. An avid public devoured lurid newspaper accounts of the affair, and the court was crowded when Tomms appeared, although their most bloodthirsty appetites were not to be satisfied. Thanks to his eagerness to cooperate with the police, Tomms wasn't being charged with the most serious offences. He was cleared of being involved in murder; Beddowes had made light of the valet's part in the attack on the road, in exchange for the information that had led to the recovery of so much of Mortleigh's loot. Nevertheless, Sir Martin's judgement was considered lenient, when Tomms was sentenced to five years hard labour.

Docket met Beddowes outside the court and ushered him through the crowd to where the carriage waited. 'Sir Martin will be engaged for several hours yet,' the secretary said. 'I'm to take you wherever you wish.'

Beddowes gave the young man a searching look; he had been quiet on their last meeting but now he looked positively downcast. 'My bag's at Clowmoor,' Beddowes said. 'If I'd brought it with me I could have caught a train back to town this afternoon.'

Docket seemed to be wrestling with some deep thought, his face going through a plethora of emotions. 'I rather expected you

300

might want to call at Knytte.'

'Knytte?'

'To see Miss Drake.' Docket stared out of the window as he spoke, and his voice was almost sepulchral in tone. 'If I didn't have such respect for you, I should take it very hard,' the young man went on.

'I don't understand,' Beddowes said, though he found his heart was suddenly beating faster.

'Then I'll be plain. I asked Miss Drake to do me the honour of becoming my wife,' Docket said. 'Being an honest and plain speaking young woman, she gave me a direct answer. She turned me down.'

'What does that have to do with me?' Beddowes asked. Breathing seemed to have become a little difficult.

'I'm not a fool,' Docket said, 'though it took me a day or two to realize the truth. Miss Drake was hoping to be borne in another pair of arms when she was carried out of the ice house. I should have realized sooner. She hung on every word Sir Martin said when he spoke of you. Her thoughts were all of you, and whether you'd returned safely after your encounter with Tomms. She seemed shocked when she heard of your speedy departure for London.'

Sergeant Beddowes stared at the young man for several seconds. 'I'm sorry for your disappointment, Mr Docket, I truly am,' he

301

said, but he couldn't suppress a smile. 'You've acted in a very gentlemanly fashion, and I'm grateful.' He put his head out of the window and bellowed at the coachman. 'Take us to Knytte.'

The publishers hope that this book has given you enjoyable reading. Large Print Books are especially designed to be as easy to see and hold as possible. If you wish a complete list of our books please ask at your local library or write directly to:

Magna Large Print Books
Magna House, Long Preston,
Skipton, North Yorkshire.
BD23 4ND

This Large Print Book, for people
who cannot read normal print,
is published under the auspices of

THE ULVERSCROFT FOUNDATION